$\mathcal{V}$OICES OF THE $\mathcal{S}$OUTH

The Widows of Thornton

Peter Taylor

THE WIDOWS OF THORNTON

Louisiana State University Press
Baton Rouge and London

Of the stories in this collection, the following appeared originally in
somewhat different form in the *New Yorker:* "Porte-Cochere," "A Wife
of Nashville," "Their Losses," "What You Hear from 'Em?" "Two Ladies
in Retirement," "Bad Dreams," and "Cookie" (originally published
under the title "Middle Age"). "The Death of a Kinsman" appeared in
the *Sewanee Review* and "The Dark Walk" in *Harper's Bazaar.*

The paper in this book meets the guidelines for permanence and dura-
bility of the Committee on Production Guidelines for Book Longevity
of the Council on Library Resources ⊗

TO ALLEN AND CAROLINE

Contents

The Widows of Thornton

THEIR LOSSES

At Grand Junction, the train slowed down for its last stop before getting into the outskirts of Memphis. Just when it had jerked to a standstill, Miss Patty Bean came out of the drawing room. She had not slept there but had hurried into the drawing room the minute she'd waked up to see how her aunt, who was gravely ill and who occupied the room with a trained nurse, had borne the last hours of the trip. Miss Patty had been in there with her aunt for nearly an hour. As she came out the nurse was whispering to her, but Miss Patty pulled the door closed with apparent indifference to what the nurse might be saying. The train had jerked to a standstill. For a moment Miss Patty, clad in a dark dressing gown and with her graying auburn hair contained in a sort of mesh cap, faced the other passengers in the Pullman car with an expression of alarm.

The other passengers, several of whom, already dressed, were standing in the aisle while the porter made up their berths, glanced at Miss Patty, then returned their attention immediately to their luggage

3

or to their morning papers, which had been brought aboard at Corinth. They were mostly businessmen, and the scattering of women appeared to be business-women. In the silence and stillness of the train stop, not even those who were traveling together spoke to each other. At least half the berths had already been converted into seats, but the passengers did not look out the windows. They were fifty miles from Memphis, and they knew that nothing outside the windows would interest them until the train slowed down again, for the suburban stop of Buntyn.

After a moment Miss Patty's expression faded from one of absolute alarm to one of suspicion. Then, as though finally gathering her wits, she leaned over abruptly and peered out a window of the first section on her left. What she saw was only a deserted-looking cotton shed and, far beyond it, past winter fields of cotton stalks and dead grass, a two-story clapboard house with a sagging double gallery. The depot and the town were on the other side of the train, but Miss Patty knew this scene and she gave a sigh of relief. "Oh, uh-huh," she muttered to herself. "Grand Junction."

"Yes, sweet old Grand Junction," came a soft whisper.

For an instant Miss Patty could not locate the speaker. Then she became aware of a very tiny lady, dressed in black, seated right beside where she stood; indeed, she was leaning almost directly across the lady's lap. Miss Patty brought herself up straight, throwing her shoulders back and her heavy, square chin into the air, and said, "I was not aware that this section was occupied."

"Why, now, of course you weren't—of course you weren't, my dear," said the tiny lady. She was such an inconspicuous little soul that her presence could not alter the impression that there were only Memphis business-people in the car.

"I didn't know you were there," Miss Patty explained again.

"Why, of course you didn't."

"It was very rude of me," Miss Patty said solemnly, blinking her eyes.

"Oh, no," the tiny lady protested gently.

"Oh, but indeed it was," Miss Patty assured her.

"Why, it was all right."

"I didn't see you there. I beg your pardon."

The tiny lady was smiling up at Miss Patty with eyes that seemed as green as the Pullman upholstery. "I came aboard at Sweetwater during the night," she said. She nodded toward the curtains of Miss Patty's berth, across the aisle. "I guess you were as snug as a bug in a rug when I got on."

Miss Patty lowered her chin and scowled.

"You're traveling with your sick aunt, aren't you?" the lady went on. "I saw you go in there awhile ago, and I inquired of the porter." The smile faded from her eyes but remained on her lips. "You see, I haven't been to bed. I'm bringing my mother to Brownsville for burial." She nodded in the direction of the baggage car ahead.

"I see," Miss Patty replied. She had now fixed this

5

diminutive person with a stare of appraisal. She was someone from her own world. If she heard the name, she would undoubtedly know the family. Without the name, she already *knew* the life history of the lady, and she could almost have guessed the name, or made up one that would have done as well. Her impulse was to turn away, but the green eyes of Miss Ellen Watkins prevented her. They were too full of unmistakable sweetness and charity. Miss Patty remained a moment, observing the telltale paraphernalia: the black gloves and purse on the seat beside Miss Ellen; the unobtrusive hat, with its wisp of a veil turned back; the fresh powder on the wrinkled neck.

"I'm Ellen Louise Watkins," the tiny lady said. "I believe you're Miss Bean, from Thornton."

Miss Patty gave a formal little bow—a Watkins from Brownsville, a daughter of the late Judge Davy Watkins. They were kin to the Crocketts. Davy Crockett's blood had come to this end: a whispering old maid in a Pullman car.

"How *is* your aunt this morning?" Miss Ellen whispered, leaning forward.

But Miss Patty had turned her back. She put her head and shoulders inside the curtains of her berth, and as Miss Ellen waited for an answer, all to be seen of Miss Patty was the dark watered silk of her dressing gown, drawn tightly about her narrow hips and falling straight to a hemline just above her very white and very thin and bony ankles.

When Miss Patty pushed herself into the aisle again and faced Miss Ellen, she held, thrown over her arms,

6

a navy-blue dress, various white and pink particulars of underwear, and a pair of extremely long and rumpled silk stockings, and in her hands she had bunched together her black pumps, an ivory comb and brush, and other articles she would need in the dressing room. The train began to move as she spoke. "I believe," she said, as though she were taking an oath, "that there has been no change in my aunt's condition during the night."

Miss Ellen nodded. The display of clothing over Miss Patty's arms brought a smile to her lips, and she was plainly making an effort to keep her eyes off the clothing and on Miss Patty's face. This uninhibited and even unladylike display reminded her of what she had always heard about the Bean family at Thornton. They were eccentric people, and bigoted. But quickly she reproached herself for retaining such gossip in her mind. Some of the Beans used to be in politics, and unfair things are always said about people in public life. Further, Miss Ellen reminded herself, the first instant she had set eyes on Miss Patty, she had known the sort of person she was. Even if the porter had not been able to tell her the name, she could almost have guessed it. She knew how Miss Patty would look when she had got into those garments—as though she had dressed in the dark and were proud of it. And there would be a hat—a sort of brown fedora—that she would pull on at the last minute before she got off the train. She had known many a Miss Patty Bean in her time, and their gruffness and their mannish ways didn't frighten her. Indeed, she felt sorry for such women.

7

"Are you going to have breakfast in the diner?" she asked.

"I am," Miss Patty replied.

"Then I'll save you a seat. I'll go ahead and get a table. There's not too much time, Miss Bean."

"As you will, Miss Watkins." Miss Patty turned toward the narrow passage that led to the ladies' dressing room. Suddenly she stopped and backed into Miss Ellen's section. She was making way for the conductor and a passenger who had evidently come aboard at Grand Junction. A porter followed, carrying a large piece of airplane luggage. The Pullman conductor came first, and the passenger, a lady, was addressing him over his shoulder. "But why could not they stop the *Pullman* at the platform, instead of the *coaches?*" It was a remarkably loud voice, and it paused after every word, obviously trying for a humorous effect.

The conductor was smiling grimly. "Here you are, ma'am," he said. "You can sit here till I find space for you—if this lady don't mind. She has the whole section." He indicated Miss Ellen's section and continued down the aisle, followed by the porter, without once looking back.

"But suppose she *does* mind?" the new passenger called after him, and she laughed heartily. Some of the other passengers looked up briefly and smiled. The lady turned to Miss Patty, who was still there holding her possessions. "*Do* you mind?" And then, "Why, Patty Bean! How very nice!"

"It is not my section." Miss Patty thrust herself into the aisle. "It is not my section, Cornelia."

8

"Then it must be— Why, will wonders never cease? Ellen Louise Watkins!"

Miss Ellen and Miss Patty exchanged surprised glances. Why, of course you shall sit here with me," Miss Ellen said. "How good to see you, Cornelia!"

Cornelia Weatherby Werner had already seated herself, facing Miss Ellen. She was a large woman in all her dimensions, but a good-looking woman still. She wore a smart three-cornered hat, which drew attention to her handsome profile, and a cloth coat trimmed with Persian lamb. "I declare it's like old times," she said breathlessly. "Riding the Southern from Grand Junction to Memphis and seeing everybody you know! Nowadays it's mostly *that* sort you see on the Southern." She gestured openly toward the other passengers. "I'll bet you two have been gadding off to Washington. Are you traveling together?"

Miss Ellen and Miss Patty shook their heads.

"Ellen and I are old schoolmates, too, Patty," Cornelia continued. "We were at Ward's together after I was dismissed from Belmont. By the way," she said, smiling roguishly and digging into her purse for cigarettes, "I still have that infernal habit. It's old-fashioned now, but I still call them my coffin nails. Which reminds me—" She hesitated, a package of cigarettes in one hand, a silver lighter in the other. "Oh, do either of you smoke? Well, not before breakfast anyhow. And not on a Pullman, even when the conductor isn't looking, I'll bet. I was saying it reminds me I have just been to Grand Junction to put my old

9

mother to her last rest." As she lit her cigarette, she watched their faces, eager for the signs of shock.

Miss Ellen gave a sympathetic "Oh." Miss Patty stared.

"You mustn't look so lugubrious," Cornelia went on. "The old dear hadn't spoken to me in thirty-one years—not since I got married and went to Memphis. I married a Jew, you know. You've both met Jake? He's a bank examiner and a good husband. Let's see, Patty, when was it I came down to Thornton with Jake? During the Depression sometime—but we saw Ellen only last May."

Miss Ellen leaned forward and stopped her, resting a tiny hand on her knee. "Cornelia, dear," she whispered, "we're all making sad trips these days. I'm taking Mother to Brownsville for burial. She died while we were visiting her invalid cousin at Sweetwater."

Cornelia said nothing. Presently she raised her eyes questioningly to Miss Patty.

"My aged aunt," Miss Patty said. "She is not dead. She is in the drawing room with an Irish nurse. I'm bringing her from Washington to spend her last days at Thornton, where she is greatly loved."

Miss Ellen looked up at Miss Patty and said, "I'm sure she is."

"She is," Miss Patty affirmed. There was a civility in her tone that had not been there when she had last addressed Miss Ellen, and the two exchanged a rather long glance.

Cornelia gazed out the window at the passing fields. Her features in repose looked tired. It was with obvious effort that she faced her two friends again. Miss Patty was still standing there, with her lips slightly parted, and Miss Ellen still rested a hand on Cornelia's knee. Cornelia shuddered visibly. She blushed and said, "A rabbit ran over my grave, I guess." Then she blushed again, but now she had regained her spirit. "Oh, just listen to me." She smiled. "I've never said the right thing once in my life. Is there a diner? Can we get any breakfast? You used to get the *best* breakfast on the Southern."

At the word "breakfast," Miss Patty did an about-face and disappeared down the passage to the ladies' room. Miss Ellen seized her purse and gloves. "Of course, my dear," she said. "Come along. We'll all have breakfast together."

There were no other passengers in the diner when Cornelia and Miss Ellen went in. The steward was eating at a small table at the rear of the car. Two Negro waiters were standing by the table talking to him, but he jumped to his feet and came toward the ladies. He stopped at the third table on the right, as though all the others might be reserved, and after wiping his mouth with a large white napkin, he asked if there would be anyone else in their party.

"Why, yes, as a matter of fact," Miss Ellen answered politely, "there will be one other."

"Do you think you can squeeze one more in?" Cornelia asked, narrowing her eyes and laughing. The steward did not reply. He helped them into chairs opposite each other and by the broad window, and darted away to get menus from his desk at the front of the car. A smiling Negro waiter set three goblets upright, filled them with water, and removed a fourth goblet and a setting of silver. "Sometime during the past thirty years," Cornelia remarked when the waiter had gone, "conductors and stewards lost their sense of humor. It makes you thank God for porters and waiters, doesn't it? Next thing you know— Why, merciful heavens, here's Patty already!"

Miss Ellen glanced over her shoulder. There was Miss Patty, looking as though she had dressed in the dark and were proud of it. She was hatless, her hair pulled into a loose knot on the back of her neck but apparently without benefit of the ivory comb and brush. The steward was leading her toward their table. Without smiling, Cornelia said, "He didn't have to ask her if she were the other member of this party." Miss Ellen raised her eyebrows slightly. "Most passengers don't eat in the diner any more," Cornelia clarified. "They feel they're too near to Memphis to bother." When Miss Patty sat down beside Miss Ellen, Cornelia said, "Gosh a'might, Patty, we left you only two seconds ago and here you are dressed and in your right mind. How do you do it?"

They received their menus, and when they had ordered, Miss Patty smiled airily. "I'm always in my right mind, Cornelia, and I don't reckon I've ever been 'dressed' in my life." As she said "dressed," her eyes traveled from the three-cornered hat to the brocaded bosom of Cornelia's rust-colored dress.

Cornelia looked out the window, silently vowing not

to speak again during the meal, or, since speaking was for her the most irresistible of all life's temptations, at least not to let herself speak sharply to either of these crotchety old maids. She sat looking out the window, thanking her stars for the great good luck of being Mrs. Jake Werner, of Memphis, instead of an embittered old maid from Grand Junction.

Miss Ellen was also looking out the window. "Doesn't it look bleak?" she said, referring to the brown-and-gray fields under an overcast sky.

"Oh, doesn't it!" Cornelia agreed at once, revealing that Miss Ellen had guessed her very thoughts.

"It *is* bleak," Miss Patty said. "See how it's washed. This land along here didn't use to look like that." The two others nodded agreement, each remembering how it had used to look. "This used to be fine land," she continued, "but it seems to me that all West Tennessee is washing away. Look at those gullies! And not a piece of brush piled in them." Miss Ellen and Cornelia shook their heads vaguely; they were not really certain why there should be brush in the gullies. Cornelia discovered that a glass of tomato juice had been set before her and she began pouring salt into it. Miss Ellen was eating her oatmeal. Miss Patty took a sip from her first cup of coffee. She had specified that it be brought in a cup instead of a pot. It was black and a little cool, the way she liked it. She peered out the window again and pursued her discourse warmly. "And the towns! Look! We're going through Moscow. It's a shambles. Why, half the square's been torn away, and the rest ought to be. Mind you, we went through

La Grange without even noticing it. They used to be good towns, fine towns."

"Lovely towns!" responded Miss Ellen. The thought of the vanishing towns touched her.

"There was something about them," Cornelia said, groping. "An atmosphere, I think."

Miss Patty cleared her throat and defined it: "The atmosphere of a prosperous and civilized existence."

Miss Ellen looked bewildered, and Cornelia frowned thoughtfully and pursed her lips. Presently Cornelia said profoundly, "All the business has gone to Memphis."

"Yes," Miss Patty said. "Indeed it has!"

They were being served their main course now. Cornelia looked at her trout and said to the waiter, "It looks delicious. Did you cook this, boy?"

"No, ma'am," the waiter said cheerfully.

"Well, it looks delicious. The same old Southern Railway cooking."

Miss Patty and Miss Ellen had scrambled eggs and ham. Miss Patty eyed hers critically. "The Southern Railway didn't use to cook eggs this way," she said. "And it's no improvement."

Miss Ellen leaned forward and bent her neck in order to look directly up into Miss Patty's face. "Why, now, you probably like them country style, with some white showing," she said. "*These* are what my niece calls Toddle House style. They cook them with milk, of course. They're a little like an omelet." The subject held great interest for her, and she was happy to be able to inform Miss Patty. "And you don't break them

14

into such a hot pan. You don't really break them in the pan, that is." Miss Patty was reaching across Miss Ellen's plate for the pepper. Miss Ellen said no more about the eggs. She busied herself with a small silver box of saccharin, prying the lid open with her fingernail. She saw Cornelia looking at the box and said, "It was my grandmother's snuffbox. For years it was just a keepsake, but now I carry my tablets in it."

The old box, which Miss Patty was now examining admiringly, somehow made Cornelia return to the subject they had left off. "In my grandmother's day, there was a lot of life in this section—entertainment and social life. My own mother used to say, 'In Mama's day, there were people in the country; in my day, there were people in town; now there's nobody.' "

Miss Patty gazed at Cornelia with astonishment. "Your mother was a very wise woman, Cornelia," she said.

"That's a moot question," Cornelia answered. Now they were on a subject that she was sure she knew something about, and she threw caution to the wind. She spoke excitedly and seemed to begin every sentence without knowing how it would end. "My mother is dead now, and I don't mean to ever say another word against her, but just because she is dead, I don't intend to start deceiving myself. The fact remains that she was opinionated and narrow and mentally cruel to her children and her husband and was tied to things that were over and done with before she was born. She's dead now, but I shall make no pretense of mourn-

15

ing someone I did not love. We don't mourn people
we don't love. It's not honest."

"No, we don't, do we?" Miss Ellen said sympathetically.

"I beg to differ with you," Miss Patty said with the
merest suggestion of a smile. She, too, felt on firm
ground. She had already mourned the deaths of all
her immediate family and of most of her near kin.
She addressed her remarks to Miss Ellen. "Mourning
is an obligation. We only mourn those with whom we
have some real connection, people who have represented something important and fundamental in our
lives."

Miss Ellen was determined to find agreement. "Of
course, of course—you are speaking of wearing black."

"I am not speaking of the symbol. I am speaking of
the mourning itself. I shall mourn the loss of my aunt
when she goes, because she is my aunt, because she is
the last of my aunts, and particularly because she is
an aunt who has maintained a worthwhile position in
the world."

Miss Ellen gasped. "Oh, no, Miss Bean! Not because
of her position in the world!"

"Don't mistake me, Miss Watkins."

"I beg you to reconsider. Why, why—" She fumbled,
and Miss Patty waited. "Now that Mother's gone, I've
lost nearly everybody, and it has always been my part
and my privilege to look after the sick in our family.
My two older brothers never married; they were quiet,
simple, home-loving men, who made little stir in the
world, content to live there in the house with Mother

16

and Nora and me after Father was gone. And Nora, my only sister, developed melancholia. One morning, she could just not finish lacing her high shoes, and after that she seldom left the house or saw anybody. What I want to say is that we also had a younger brother, who was a distinguished professor at Knoxville, with four beautiful children. You see, I've lost them all, one by one, and it's been no different whether they were distinguished or not. I can't conceive—" She stopped suddenly, in real confusion.

"Don't mistake me," Miss Patty said calmly. "I am speaking of my aunt's moral position in the world."

"Why, of course you are," said Miss Ellen, still out of breath.

"My aunt has been an indomitable character," Miss Patty continued. "Her husband died during his first term in Congress, forty years ago, and she has felt it her duty to remain in Washington ever since. With very slight means, she has maintained herself there in the right manner through all the years, returning to Thornton every summer, enduring the heat and the inconvenience, with no definite place of abode, visiting the kin, subjecting herself to the role of the indigent relation, so that she could afford to return to Washington in the fall. Her passing will be a loss to us all, for through her wit and charm she was an influence on Capitol Hill. In a sense, she represented our district in Washington as none of our elected officials has done since the days of"—bowing her head deferentially toward Miss Ellen—"of David Crockett."

"What a marvelous woman!" exclaimed Miss Ellen.

17

Cornelia looked at Miss Ellen to see whether she meant Miss Patty's aunt or Miss Patty. She had been marveling privately at Miss Patty's flow of speech, and reflected that she could already see it in print in the county paper's obituary column. "If my mother had been a person of such wit and charm," she said, "I would mourn her, too."

"I never knew your mother," Miss Patty replied, "but from what you say I can easily guess the sort of woman she was. I would mourn her passing if I were in your shoes, Cornelia. She wanted to retain the standards of a past era, a better era for all of *us*. A person can't do that and be a pleasant, charming personality and the darling of a family."

"All I know," said Cornelia, taking the last bite of her trout, "is that my young-ladyhood was a misery under that woman's roof and in that town." She glanced dreamily out the window. The train was speeding through the same sort of country as before, perhaps a little more hilly, a little more eroded. It sped through small towns and past solitary stations where only the tiresome afternoon local stopped—Rossville, Collierville, Bailey, Forest Hill. Cornelia saw a two-story farmhouse that was painted up only to the level of the second story. "That house has been that way as long as I can remember," she said, and smiled. "Why do you suppose they don't make them a ladder, or lean out the upstairs windows?" Then, still looking out at the dismal landscape—the uncultivated land growing up in sweet gum and old field pine, with a gutted mud road crossing and recrossing the railroad track every half mile or so—Cornelia said, "I only got away by the skin of my teeth! I came back from Ward's with a scrapbook full of names, but they were nothing but 'cute Vanderbilt boys.' I would have been stuck in Grand Junction for life, nursing Mama and all the hypochondriac kin, if I hadn't met Jake. I met him in Memphis doing Christmas shopping. He was a bank teller at Union Planters." She laughed heartily for the first time since she had come into the diner. "It was an out-and-out pickup. Jake still tells everybody it was an out-and-out pickup."

"I don't like Memphis," said Miss Patty. "I never have."

"I've never felt that Memphis liked me," said Miss Ellen.

"It's a wretched place!" Cornelia said suddenly. And now she saw that she had unwittingly shocked her two friends. The train had passed through Germantown; big suburban estates and scattered subdivisions began to appear in the countryside. There was even a bull-dozer at work on the horizon, grading the land for new suburban sites. "It's the most completely snobbish place in the world," she went on. "They can't forgive you for being from the country—they hate the country so, and they can't forgive your being a Jew. They dare not. If you're either one of those, it's rough going. If you're both, you're just out! I mean *socially,* of course. Oh, Jake's done *well,* and we have our friends. But as Mama would have said—and, God knows, probably did say about us many a time—*we're* nobody." Then, for

19

no reason at all, she added, "And we don't have any children."

"What a shame," Miss Ellen said, hastening to explain, "that you have no children, I mean. I've always thought that if—"

"Oh, no, Ellen. They might have liked me about the way I liked Mama. I'm glad that when I die, there'll be no question of to mourn or not to mourn."

"In truly happy families, Cornelia, there is no question," Miss Ellen said softly. She stole a glance at Miss Patty. "I'm just certain that Miss Bean had a very congenial and happy family, and that she loved them all dearly, in addition to being naturally proud of the things they stood for."

Miss Patty had produced a wallet from somewhere on her person and was examining her check. She slammed the wallet on the table, turned her head, and glared at the diminutive Miss Ellen. "How I regarded the members of my family as individuals is neither here nor there, Miss Watkins."

But Miss Ellen raised her rather receding chin and gazed directly up at Miss Patty. "To me, it seems of the greatest consequence." Her voice trembled, yet there was a firmness in it. "I am mourning my mother today. I spent last night remembering every endearing trait she had. Some of them were faults and some were virtues, but they were nonetheless endearing. And so I feel strongly about what you say, Miss Bean. We must love people as people, not for what they are, or were, in the world."

"My people happened to be very much *of* the world,

Miss Watkins," said Miss Patty. "Not of *this* world but of *a* world that we have seen disappear. In mourning my family, I mourn that world's disappearance. How could I know whether or not I really loved them, or whether or not we were really happy? There wasn't ever time for asking that. We were all like Aunt Lottie, in yonder, and there was surely never any love or happiness in the end of it. When I went to Washington last week to fetch Aunt Lottie home, I found her living in a hateful little hole at the Stoneleigh Court. All the furniture from larger apartments she had once had was jammed together in two rooms. The tables were covered with framed photographs of the wives of Presidents, Vice-Presidents, Senators, inscribed to Lottie Hathcock. But there was not a friend in sight. During the five days I was there, not one person called." Miss Patty stood up and waved her check and two one-dollar bills at the waiter.

Miss Ellen sat watching the check and the two bills with a stunned expression. But Cornelia twisted about in her chair excitedly. "Your aunt was Mrs. Hathcock!" she fairly screamed. "Oh, Patty, of course! She was *famous* in her day. And don't you remember? I met her once with you at the Maxwell House, when we were at Belmont. You took me along, and after supper my true love from Vandy turned up in the lobby. You were so furious, and Mrs. Hathcock was so cute about it. She was the cleverest talker I've ever listened to, Patty. She was interested in spiritualism and offered to take us to a séance at Mr. Ben Allen's house."

Miss Patty looked at Cornelia absent-mindedly. Her

21

antagonism toward the two women seemed suddenly to have left her, and she spoke without any restraint at all. "Aunt Lottie has long since become a Roman Catholic. Her will leaves her little pittance of money and her furniture to the Catholic Church, and her religious oil paintings to me. The nurse we brought along has turned out to be an Irish Catholic." She glanced in the direction of their Pullman car and said, "The nurse has conceived the notion that Aunt Lottie is worse this morning, and she wanted to wire ahead for a Memphis priest to meet us at the Union Station. She knows there won't be any priests at Thornton."

Cornelia, carried away by incorrigible gregariousness, began, "Ah, Patty, might I see her? It would be such fun to see her again, just for old times' sake. It might even cheer her a little."

Miss Patty stared at Cornelia in silence. Finally she said, "My aunt is a mental patient. She doesn't even remember me, Cornelia." She snatched a piece of change from the waiter's tray and hurried past the steward and out of the car.

Miss Ellen was almost staggering as she rose from the table. She fumbled in her purse, trying to find the correct change for the waiter. She was shaking her head from side to side, and opening and closing her eyes with the same rhythm.

Cornelia made no move toward rising. "Depend upon *me*," she said. "Did you *know?*"

Miss Ellen only increased the speed of her head-shaking. When she saw Cornelia still sitting there, casually lighting a cigarette, she said, "We're approaching Buntyn. I imagine you're getting off there."

"No, that's the country-club stop. I don't get off at the country-club stop."

"There's not much time," Miss Ellen said.

Presently Cornelia pulled a bill from her purse and summoned the waiter. "Well, Ellen," she said, still not getting up, "I guess there's no way I could be of help to you at the station, is there?"

"No, there's nothing, dear."

In her lethargy Cornelia seemed unable to rise and even unable to tell Miss Ellen to go ahead without her. " I suppose you'll be met by a hearse," she said, "and Patty will be met by an ambulance, and—and I'll be met by Jake." For a moment, she sat behind a cloud of cigarette smoke. There was a puzzled expression in her eyes, and she was laughing quietly at what she had said. It was one of those sentences that Cornelia began without knowing how it would end.

WHAT YOU HEAR
FROM 'EM?

Sometimes people misunderstood Aunt Munsie's question, but she wouldn't bother to clarify it. She might repeat it two or three times, in order to drown out some fool answer she was getting from some fool white woman, or man, either. "What you hear from 'em?" she would ask. And, then, louder and louder: "What you hear from 'em? *What you hear from 'em?*" She was so deaf that anyone whom she thoroughly drowned out only laughed and said Aunt Munsie had got so deaf she couldn't hear it thunder.

It was, of course, only the most utterly fool answers that ever received Aunt Munsie's drowning-out treatment. She was, for a number of years at least, willing to listen to those who mistook her "'em" to mean any and all of the Dr. Tolliver children. And for more years than that she was willing to listen to those who thought she wanted just *any* news of her two favorites among the Tolliver children—Thad and Will. But later on she stopped putting the question to all insensitive and frivolous souls who didn't understand that what she was interested in hearing—and *all* she was

24

interested in hearing—was when Mr. Thad Tolliver and Mr. Will Tolliver were going to pack up their families and come back to Thornton for good.

They had always promised her to come back—to come back sure enough, once and for all. On separate occasions, both Thad and Will had actually given her their word. She had not seen them together for ten years, but each of them had made visits to Thornton now and then with his own family. She would see a big car stopping in front of her house on a Sunday afternoon and see either Will or Thad with his wife and children piling out into the dusty street—it was nearly always summer when they came—and then see them filing across the street, jumping the ditch, and unlatching the gate to her yard. She always met them in that pen of a yard, but long before they had jumped the ditch she was clapping her hands and calling out, "Hai-ee! Hai-ee, now! Look-a-here! Whee! Whee! Look-a-here!" She had got so blind that she was never sure whether it was Mr. Thad or Mr. Will until she had her arms around his waist. They had always looked a good deal alike, and their city clothes made them look even more alike nowadays. Aunt Munsie's eyes were so bad, besides being so full of moisture on those occasions, that she really recognized them by their girth. Will had grown a regular wash pot of a stomach and Thad was still thin as a rail. They would sit on her porch for twenty or thirty minutes—whichever one it was and his family—and then they would be gone again.

Aunt Munsie would never try to detain them—not

seriously. Those short little old visits didn't mean a thing to her. He—Thad or Will—would lean against the banister rail and tell her how well his children were doing in school or college, and she would make each child in turn come and sit beside her on the swing for a minute and receive a hug around the waist or shoulders. They were timid with her, not seeing her any more than they did, but she could tell from their big Tolliver smiles that they liked her to hug them and make over them. Usually, she would lead them all out to her back yard and show them her pigs and dogs and chickens. (She always had at least one frizzly chicken to show the children.) They would traipse through her house to the back yard and then traipse through again to the front porch. It would be time for them to go when they came back, and Aunt Munsie would look up at *him*—Mr. Thad or Mr. Will (she had begun calling them "Mr." the day they married)—and say, "Now, look-a-here. When you comin' back?"

Both Thad and Will knew what she meant, of course, and whichever it was would tell her he was making definite plans to wind up his business and that he was going to buy a certain piece of property, "a mile north of town" or "on the old River Road," and build a jim-dandy house there. He would say, too, how good Aunt Munsie's own house was looking, and his wife would say how grand the zinnias and cannas looked in the yard. (The yard was all flowers—not a blade of grass, and the ground packed hard in little paths between the flower beds.) The visit was almost over then. There remained only the exchange of presents. One of the children would hand Aunt Munsie a paper bag containing a pint of whisky or a carton of cigarettes. Aunt Munsie would go to her back porch or to the pit in the yard and get a fern or a wandering Jew, potted in a rusty lard bucket, and make Mrs. Thad or Mrs. Will take it along. Then the visit was over, and they would leave. From the porch Aunt Munsie would wave good-by with one hand and lay the other hand, trembling slightly, on the banister rail. And sometimes her departing guests, looking back from the yard, would observe that the banisters themselves were trembling under her hand—so insecurely were those knobby banisters attached to the knobby porch pillars. Often as not Thad or Will, observing this, would remind his wife that Aunt Munsie's porch banisters and pillars had come off a porch of the house where he had grown up. (Their father, Dr. Tolliver, had been one of the first to widen his porches and remove the gingerbread from his house.) The children and their mother would wave to Aunt Munsie from the street. Their father would close the gate, resting his hand a moment on its familiar wrought-iron frame, and wave to her before he jumped the ditch. If the children had not gone too far ahead, he might even draw their attention to the iron fence which, with its iron gate, had been around the yard at the Tolliver place till Dr. Tolliver took it down and set out a hedge, just a few weeks before he died.

✦

But such paltry little visits meant nothing to Aunt Munsie. No more did the letters that came with "her things" at Christmas. She was supposed to get her daughter, Lucrecie, who lived next door, to read the letters, but in late years she had taken to putting them away unopened, and some of the presents, too. All she wanted to hear from *them* was when they were coming back for good, and she had learned that the Christmas letters never told her that. On her daily route with her slop wagon through the Square, up Jackson Street, and down Jefferson, there were only four or five houses left where she asked her question. These were houses where the amount of pig slop was not worth stopping for, houses where one old maid, or maybe two, lived, or a widow with one old bachelor son who had never amounted to anything and ate no more than a woman. And so—in the summertime, anyway—she took to calling out at the top of her lungs, when she approached the house of one of the elect, "What you hear from 'em?" Sometimes a Miss Patty or a Miss Lucille or a Mr. Ralph would get up out of a porch chair and come down the brick walk to converse with Aunt Munsie. Or sometimes one of them would just lean out over the shrubbery planted around the porch and call, "Not a thing, Munsie. Not a thing lately."

She would shake her head and call back, "Naw. Naw. Not a thing. Nobody don't hear from 'em. Too busy, they be."

Aunt Munsie's skin was the color of a faded tow sack. She was hardly four feet tall. She was generally believed to be totally bald, and on her head she always wore a white dust cap with an elastic band. She wore an apron, too, while making her rounds with her slop wagon. Even when the weather got bad and she tied a wool scarf about her head and wore an overcoat, she put on an apron over the coat. Her hands and feet were delicately small, which made the old-timers sure she was of Guinea stock that had come to Tennessee out of South Carolina. What most touched the hearts of old ladies on Jackson and Jefferson Streets were her little feet. The sight of her feet "took them back to the old days," they said, because Aunt Munsie still wore flat-heeled, high button shoes. Where ever did Munsie find such shoes any more?

She walked down the street, down the very center of the street, with a spry step, and she was continually turning her head from side to side, as though looking at the old houses and trees for the first time. If her sight was as bad as she sometimes let on it was, she probably recognized the houses only by their roof lines against the Thornton sky. Since this was nearly thirty years ago, most of the big Victorian and ante-bellum houses were still standing, though with their lovely gingerbread work beginning to go. (It went first from houses where there was someone, like Dr. Tolliver, with a special eye for style and for keeping up with the times.) The streets hadn't yet been broadened—or only Nashville Street had—and the maples and elms met above the streets. In the autumn, their leaves covered the high banks and filled the deep ditches on either side. The dark macadam surfacing itself was barely wide enough for two automobiles to pass. Aunt

29

Munsie, pulling her slop wagon, which was a long, low, four-wheeled vehicle about the size and shape of a coffin, paraded down the center of the street without any regard for, if with any awareness of, the traffic problems she sometimes made. Seizing the wagon's heavy, sawed-off-looking tongue, she hauled it after her with a series of impatient jerks, just as though that tongue were the arm of some very stubborn, over-grown white child she had to nurse in her old age. Strangers in town or trifling high-school boys would blow their horns at her, but she was never known to so much as glance over her shoulder at the sound of a horn. Now and then a pedestrian on the sidewalk would call out to the driver of an automobile, "She's so deaf she can't hear it thunder."

It wouldn't have occurred to anyone in Thornton—not in those days—that something ought to be done about Aunt Munsie and her wagon for the sake of the public good. In those days, everyone had equal rights on the streets of Thornton. A vehicle was a vehicle, and a person was a person, each with the right to move as slowly as he pleased and to stop where and as often as he pleased. In the Thornton mind, there was no imaginary line down the middle of the street, and, indeed, no one there at that time had heard of drawing a real line on *any* street. It was merely out of politeness that you made room for others to pass. No-body would have blown a horn at an old colored woman with her slop wagon—nobody but some Yankee stranger or a trifling high-school boy or maybe old Mr. Ralph Hadley in a special fit of temper. When citizens of Thornton were in a particular hurry and got caught behind Aunt Munsie, they leaned out their car windows and shouted: "Aunt Munsie, can you make a little room?" And Aunt Munsie didn't fail to hear *them*. She would holler, "Hai-ee, now! Whee! Look-a-here!" and jerk her wagon to one side. As they passed her, she would wave her little hand and grin a toothless, pink-gummed grin.

Yet, without any concern for the public good, Aunt Munsie's friends and connections among the white women began to worry more and more about the danger of her being run down by an automobile. They talked among themselves and they talked to her about it. They wanted her to give up collecting slop, now she had got so blind and deaf. "Pshaw," said Aunt Munsie, closing her eyes contemptuously. "Not me." She meant by that that no one would dare run into her or her wagon. Sometimes when she crossed the Square on a busy Saturday morning or on a first Monday, she would hold up one hand with the palm turned outward and stop all traffic until she was safely across and in the alley beside the hotel.

Thornton wasn't even then what it had been before the Great World War. In every other house there was a stranger or a mill hand who had moved up from Factory Town. Some of the biggest old places stood empty, the way Dr. Tolliver's had until it burned. They stood empty not because nobody wanted to rent them or buy them but because the heirs who had gone off somewhere making money could never be got to

part with "the home place." The story was that Thad
Tolliver nearly went crazy when he heard their old
house had burned, and wanted to sue the town, and
even said he was going to help get the Republicans
into office. Yet Thad had hardly put foot in the house
since the day his daddy died. It was said the Tolliver
house had caught fire from the Major Pettigru house,
which had burned two nights before. And no doubt
it had. Sparks could have smoldered in that roof of
rotten shingles for a long time before bursting into
flame. Some even said the Pettigru house might have
caught from the Johnston house, which had burned
earlier that same fall. But Thad knew and Will knew
and everybody knew the town wasn't to blame, and
knew there was no firebug. Why, those old houses
stood there empty year after year, and in the fall the
leaves fell from the trees and settled around the
porches and stoops, and who was there to rake the
leaves? Maybe it was a good thing those houses burned,
and maybe it would have been as well if some of the
houses that still had people in them burned, too.
There were houses in Thornton the heirs had never
left that looked far worse than the Tolliver or the
Pettigru or the Johnston house ever had. The people
who lived in them were the ones who gave Aunt
Munsie the biggest fool answers to her question, the
people whom she soon quit asking her question of or
even passing the time of day with, except when she
couldn't help it, out of politeness. For, truly, to Aunt
Munsie there were things under the sun worse than
going off and getting rich in Nashville or in Memphis

or even in Washington, D.C. It was a subject she and her daughter Lucrecie sometimes mouthed at each other about across their back fence. Lucrecie was shiftless, and she liked shiftless white people like the ones who didn't have the ambition to leave Thornton. She thought their shiftlessness showed they were *quality*. "Quality?" Aunt Munsie would echo, her voice full of sarcasm. "Whee! Hai-ee! You talk like *you* was *my* mammy, Crecie. Well, if there be quality, there be quality *and* quality. There's quality and there's *has-been* quality, Crecie." There was no end to that argument Aunt Munsie had with Crecie, and it wasn't at all important to Aunt Munsie. The people who still lived in those houses—the ones she called has-been quality—meant little more to her than the mill hands, or the strangers from up North who ran the Piggly Wiggly, the five-and-ten-cent store, and the roller-skating rink.

There was this to be said, though, for the has-been quality: They knew *who* Aunt Munsie was, and in a limited, literal way they understood what she said. But those *others*—why, they thought Aunt Munsie a beggar, and she knew they did. They spoke of her as Old What You Have for Mom, because that's what they thought she was saying when she called out, "What you hear from 'em?" Their ears were not attuned to that soft "r" she put in "from" or the elision that made "from 'em" sound to them like "for Mom." Many's the time Aunt Munsie had seen or sensed the presence of one of those *other* people, watching from next door, when Miss Leonora Lovell, say, came down

33

her front walk and handed her a little parcel of scraps across the ditch. Aunt Munsie knew what they thought of her—how they laughed at her and felt sorry for her and despised her all at once. But, like the has-been quality, they didn't matter, never had, never would. Not ever.

Oh, they mattered in a way to Lucrecie. Lucrecie thought about them and talked about them a lot. She called them "white trash" and even "radical Republicans." It made Aunt Munsie grin to hear Crecie go on, because she knew Crecie got all her notions from her own has-been-quality people. And so it didn't matter, except that Aunt Munsie knew that Crecie truly had all sorts of good sense and had only been carried away and spoiled by such folks as she had worked for, such folks as had really raised Crecie from the time she was big enough to run errands for them, fifty years back. In her heart, Aunt Munsie knew that even Lucrecie didn't matter to her the way a daughter might. It was because while Aunt Munsie had been raising a family of white children, a different sort of white people from hers had been raising her own child, Crecie. Sometimes, if Aunt Munsie was in her chicken yard or out in her little patch of cotton when Mr. Thad or Mr. Will arrived, Crecie would come out to the fence and say, "Mama, some of your chillun's out front."

Miss Leonora Lovell and Miss Patty Bean, and especially Miss Lucille Satterfield, were all the time after Aunt Munsie to give up collecting slop. "You're going to get run over by one of those crazy drivers, Munsie," they said. Miss Lucille was the widow of old Judge Satterfield. "If the Judge were alive, Munsie," she said, "I'd make him find a way to stop you. But the men down at the courthouse don't listen to the women in this town any more. Not since we got the vote. And I think they'd be most too scared of you to do what I want them to do." Aunt Munsie wouldn't listen to any of that. She knew that if Miss Lucille had come out there to her gate, she must have *something* she was going to say about Mr. Thad or Mr. Will. Miss Lucille had two brothers and a son of her own who were lawyers in Memphis, and who lived in style down there and kept Miss Lucille in style here in Thornton. Memphis was where Thad Tolliver had his Ford and Lincoln agency, and so Miss Lucille always had news about Thad, and indirectly about Will, too.

"Is they doin' any good? What you hear from 'em?" Aunt Munsie asked Miss Lucille one afternoon in early spring. She had come along just when Miss Lucille was out picking some of the jonquils that grew in profusion on the steep bank between the sidewalk and the ditch in front of her house.

"Mr. Thad and his folks will be up one day in April, Munsie," Miss Lucille said in her pleasantly hoarse voice. "I understand Mr. Will and his crowd may come for Easter Sunday."

"One day, and gone again!" said Aunt Munsie.

"We always try to get them to stay at least one night, but they're busy folks, Munsie."

35

"When they comin' back sure enough, Miss Lucille?"

"Goodness knows, Munsie. Goodness knows. Goodness knows when any of them are coming back to stay." Miss Lucille took three quick little steps down the bank and hopped lightly across the ditch. "They're prospering so, Munsie," she said, throwing her chin up and smiling proudly. This fragile lady, this daughter, wife, sister, mother of lawyers (and, of course, the darling of all their hearts), stood there in the street with her pretty little feet and shapely ankles close together, and holding a handful of jonquils before her as if it were her bridal bouquet. "They're *all* prospering so, Munsie. Mine *and* yours. You ought to go down to Memphis to see them now and then, the way I do. Or go up to Nashville to see Mr. Will. I understand he's got an even finer establishment than Thad. They've done well, Munsie—yours *and* mine—and we can be proud of them. You owe it to yourself to go and see how well they're fixed. They're rich men by our standards in Thornton, and they're going farther—*all* of them."

Aunt Munsie dropped the tongue of her wagon noisily on the pavement. "What I want to go see 'em for?" she said angrily and with a lowering brow. Then she stooped and, picking up the wagon tongue again, she wheeled her vehicle toward the middle of the street, to get by Miss Lucille, and started off toward the Square. As she turned out into the street, the brakes of a car, as so often, screeched behind her. Presently everyone in the neighborhood could hear

Mr. Ralph Hadley tooting the insignificant little horn on his mama's coupé and shouting at Aunt Munsie in his own tooty voice, above the sound of the horn. Aunt Munsie pulled over, making just enough room to let poor old Mr. Ralph get by but without once looking back at him. Then, before Mr. Ralph could get his car started again, Miss Lucille was running along beside Aunt Munsie, saying, "Munsie, you be careful! You're going to meet your death on the streets of Thornton, Tennessee!"

"Let 'em," said Aunt Munsie.

Miss Lucille didn't know whether Munsie meant "Let 'em run over me; I don't care" or meant "Let 'em just dare!" Miss Lucille soon turned back, without Aunt Munsie's ever looking at her. And when Mr. Ralph Hadley did get his motor started, and sailed past in his mama's coupé, Aunt Munsie didn't give him a look, either. Nor did Mr. Ralph bother to turn his face to look at Aunt Munsie. He was on his way to the drugstore, to pick up his mama's prescriptions, and he was too entirely put out, peeved, and upset to endure even the briefest exchange with that ugly, uppity old Munsie of the Tollivers.

Aunt Munsie continued to tug her slop wagon on toward the Square. There was a more animated expression on her face than usual, and every so often her lips would move rapidly and emphatically over a phrase or sentence. Why should she go to Memphis and Nashville and see how rich they were? No matter how rich they were, what difference did it make; they didn't own any land, did they? Or at least none in

Cameron County. She had heard the old Doctor tell them—tell his boys and tell his girls, and tell the old lady, too, in her day—that nobody was rich who didn't own land, and nobody stayed rich who didn't see after his land firsthand. But of course Aunt Munsie had herself mocked the old Doctor to his face for going on about land so much. She knew it was only something he had heard his own daddy go on about. She would say right to his face that she hadn't ever seen *him* behind a plow. And was there ever anybody more scared of a mule than Dr. Tolliver was? Mules or horses, either? Aunt Munsie had heard him say that the happiest day of his life was the day he first learned that the horseless carriage was a reality.

No, it was not really to own land that Thad and Will ought to come back to Thornton. It was more that if they were going to be rich, they ought to come home, where their granddaddy had owned land and where their money counted for something. How could they ever be rich anywhere else? They could have a lot of money in the bank and a fine house, that was all—like that mill manager from Chi. The mill manager could have a yard full of big cars and a stucco house as big as you like, but who would ever take him for rich? Aunt Munsie would sometimes say all these things to Crecie, or something as nearly like them as she could find words for. Crecie might nod her head in agreement or she might be in a mood to say being rich wasn't any good for anybody and didn't matter, and that you could live on just being quality better than on being rich in Thornton. "Quality's better than land or better than money in the bank here," Crecie would say.

Aunt Munsie would sneer at her and say, "It never were."

Lucrecie could talk all she wanted about the old times! Aunt Munsie knew too much about what they were like, for both the richest white folks and the blackest field hands. Nothing about the old times was as good as these days, and there were going to be better times yet when Mr. Thad and Mr. Will Tolliver came back. Everybody lived easier now than they used to, and were better off. She could never be got to reminisce about her childhood in slavery, or her life with her husband, or even about those halcyon days after the old Mizziz had died and Aunt Munsie's word had become law in the Tolliver household. Without being able to book-read or even to make numbers, she had finished raising the whole pack of towheaded Tollivers just as the Mizziz would have wanted it done. The Doctor told her she *had* to—he didn't ever once think about getting another wife, or taking in some cousin, not after his "Molly darling"—and Aunt Munsie *did*. But, as Crecie said, when a time was past in her mama's life, it seemed to be gone and done with in her head, too.

Lucrecie would say frankly she thought her mama was "hard about people and things in the world." She talked about her mama not only to the Blalocks, for whom she had worked all her life, but to anybody else who gave her an opening. It wasn't just about her

39

mama, though, that she would talk to anybody. She liked to talk, and she talked about Aunt Munsie not in any ugly, resentful way but as she would about when the sheep-rains would begin or where the fire was last night. (Crecie was twice the size of her mama, and black the way her old daddy had been, and loud and good-natured the way he was—or at least the way Aunt Munsie wasn't. You wouldn't have known they were mother and daughter, and not many of the young people in town did realize it. Only by accident did they live next door to each other; Mr. Thad and Mr. Will had bought Munsie her house, and Crecie had heired hers from her second husband.) *That* was how she talked about her mama—as she would have about any lonely, eccentric, harmless neighbor. "I may be dead wrong, but I think Mama's kind of hardhearted," she would say. "Mama's a good old soul, I reckon, but when something's past, it's gone and done with for Mama. She don't think about day before yestiddy—yestiddy, either. I don't know, maybe that's the way to be. Maybe that's why the old soul's gonna outlive us all." Then, obviously thinking about what a picture of health she herself was at sixty, Crecie would toss her head about and laugh so loud you might hear her all the way out to the fair grounds.

Crecie, however, knew her mama was not honest-to-God mean and hadn't ever been mean to the Tolliver children, the way the Blalocks liked to make out she had. All the Tolliver children but Mr. Thad and Mr. Will had quarreled with her for good by the time they were grown, but they had quarreled with the old

Doctor, too (and as if they were the only ones who shook off their old folks this day and time). When Crecie talked about her mama, she didn't spare her anything, but she was fair to her, too. And it was in no hateful or disloyal spirit that she took part in the conspiracy that finally got Aunt Munsie and her slop wagon off the streets of Thornton. Crecie would have done the same for any neighbor. She had small part enough, actually, in that conspiracy. Her part was merely to break the news to Aunt Munsie that there was now a law against keeping pigs within the city limits. It was a small part but one that no one else quite dared to take.

"They ain't no such law!" Aunt Munsie roared back at Crecie. She was slopping her pigs when Crecie came to the fence and told her about the law. It had seemed the most appropriate time to Lucrecie. "They ain't never been such a law, Crecie," Aunt Munsie said. "Every house on Jackson and Jefferson used to keep pigs."

"It's a brand-new law, Mama."

Aunt Munsie finished bailing out the last of the slop from her wagon. It was just before twilight. The last, weak rays of the sun colored the clouds behind the mock orange tree in Crecie's yard. When Aunt Munsie turned around from the sty, she pretended that that little bit of light in the clouds hurt her eyes, and turned away her head. And when Lucrecie said that everybody had until the first of the year to get rid of their pigs, Aunt Munsie was in a spell of deafness. She headed out toward the crib to get some corn for

41

the chickens. She was trying to think whether anybody else inside the town still kept pigs. Herb Mallory did— two doors beyond Crecie. Then Aunt Munsie remembered Herb didn't pay town taxes. The town line ran between him and Shad Willis.

That was sometime in June, and before July came, Aunt Munsie knew all there was worth knowing about the conspiracy. Mr. Thad and Mr. Will had each been in town for a day during the spring. They and their families had been to her house and sat on the porch; the children had gone back to look at her half-grown collie dog and the two hounds, at the old sow and her farrow of new pigs, and at the frizzliest frizzly chicken Aunt Munsie had ever had. And on those visits to Thornton, Mr. Thad and Mr. Will had also made their usual round among their distant kin and close friends. Everywhere they went, they had heard of the near-accidents Aunt Munsie was causing with her slop wagon and the real danger there was of her being run over. Miss Lucille Satterfield and Miss Patty Bean had both been to the mayor's office and also to see Judge Lawrence to try to get Aunt Munsie "ruled" off the streets, but the men in the courthouse and in the mayor's office didn't listen to the women in Thornton any more. And so either Mr. Thad or Mr. Will—how would which one of them it was matter to Munsie?— had been prevailed upon to stop by Mayor Lunt's office, and in a few seconds' time had set the wheels of conspiracy in motion. Soon a general inquiry had been made in the town as to how many citizens still kept pigs. Only two property owners besides Aunt Munsie had been found to have pigs on their premises, and they, being men, had been docile and reasonable enough to sell what they had on hand to Mr. Will or Mr. Thad Tolliver. Immediately afterward—within a matter of weeks, that is—a town ordinance had been passed forbidding the possession of swine within the corporate limits of Thornton. Aunt Munsie had got the story bit by bit from Miss Leonora and Miss Patty and Miss Lucille and others, including the constable himself, whom she did not hesitate to stop right in the middle of the Square on a Saturday noon. Whether it was Mr. Thad or Mr. Will who had been prevailed upon by the ladies she never ferreted out, but that was only because she did not wish to do so.

The constable's word was the last word for her. The constable said yes, it was the law, and he admitted yes, he had sold his own pigs—for the constable was one of those two reasonable souls—to Mr. Thad or Mr. Will. He didn't say which of them it was, or if he did, Aunt Munsie didn't bother to remember it. And after her interview with the constable, Aunt Munsie never again exchanged words with any human being about the ordinance against pigs. That afternoon, she took a fishing pole from under her house and drove the old sow and the nine shoats down to Herb Mallory's, on the outside of town. They were his, she said, if he wanted them, and he could pay her at killing time.

It was literally true that Aunt Munsie never again exchanged words with anyone about the ordinance against pigs or about the conspiracy she had discov-

43

ered against herself. But her daughter Lucrecie had a tale to tell about what Aunt Munsie did that afternoon after she had seen the constable and before she drove the pigs over to Herb Mallory's. It was mostly a tale of what Aunt Munsie said to her pigs and to her dogs and her chickens.

Crecie was in her own back yard washing her hair when her mama came down the rickety porch steps and into the yard next door. Crecie had her head in the pot of suds, and so she couldn't look up, but she knew by the way Mama flew down the steps that there was trouble. "She come down them steps like she was wasp-nest bit, or like some youngon who's got hisself wasp-nest bit—and her all of eighty, I reckon!" Then, as Crecie told it, her mama scurried around in the yard for a minute or so like she thought Judgment was about to catch up with her, and pretty soon she commenced slamming at something. Crecie wrapped a towel about her soapy head, squatted low, and edged over toward the plank fence. She peered between the planks and saw what her mama was up to. Since there never had been a gate to the fence around the pigsty, Mama had taken the wood ax and was knocking a hole in it. But directly, just after Crecie had taken her place by the plank fence, her mama had left off her slamming at the sty and turned about so quickly and so exactly toward Crecie that Crecie thought the poor, blind old soul had managed to spy her squatting there. Right away, though, Crecie realized it was not *her* that Mama was staring at. She saw that all Aunt Munsie's chickens

44

and those three dogs of hers had come up behind her, and were all clucking and whining to know why she didn't stop that infernal racket and put out some feed for them.

Crecie's mama set one hand on her hip and rested the ax on the ground. "Just look at yuh!" she said, and then she let the chickens and the dogs—and the pigs, too—have it. She told them what a miserable bunch of creatures they were, and asked them what right they had to always be looking for handouts from her. She sounded like the boss-man who's caught all his pickers laying off before sundown, and she sounded, too, like the preacher giving his sinners Hail Columbia at camp meeting. Finally, shouting at the top of her voice and swinging the ax wide and broad above their heads, she sent the dogs howling under the house and the chickens scattering in every direction. "Now, g'wine! G'wine widja!" she shouted after them. Only the collie pup, of the three dogs, didn't scamper to the farthest corner underneath the house. He stopped under the porch steps, and not two seconds later he was poking his long head out again and showing the whites of his doleful brown eyes. Crecie's mama took a step toward him and then she halted. "You want to know what's the commotion about? I reckoned you would," she said with profound contempt, as though the collie were a more reasonable soul than the other animals, and as though there were nothing she held in such thorough disrespect as reason. "I tell you what the commotion's about," she said. "They *ain't* comin' back. They ain't never comin' back. They ain't never had no notion of

45

comin' back." She turned her head to one side, and the only explanation Crecie could find for her mama's next words was that that collie pup did look so much like Miss Lucille Satterfield.

"Why don't I go down to Memphis or up to Nashville and see 'em sometime, like *you* does?" Aunt Munsie asked the collie. "I tell you why. Becaze I ain't nothin' to 'em in Memphis, and they ain't nothin' to me in Nashville. *You* can go!" she said, advancing and shaking the big ax at the dog. "A collie dog's a collie dog anywhar. But Aunt Munsie, she's just their Aunt Munsie here in Thornton. I got mind enough to see *that.*" The collie slowly pulled his head back under the steps, and Aunt Munsie watched for a minute to see if he would show himself again. When he didn't, she went and jerked the fishing pole out from under the house and headed toward the pigsty. Crecie remained squatting beside the fence until her mama and the pigs were out in the street and on their way to Herb Mallory's.

That was the end of Aunt Munsie's keeping pigs and the end of her daily rounds with her slop wagon, but it was not the end of Aunt Munsie. She lived on for nearly twenty years after that, till long after Lucrecie had been put away, in fine style, by the Blalocks. Ever afterward, though, Aunt Munsie seemed different to people. They said she softened, and everybody said it was a change for the better. She would take paper money from under her carpet, or out of the chinks in her walls, and buy things for up at the church, or

46

buy her own whisky when she got sick, instead of making somebody bring her a nip. On the Square she would laugh and holler with the white folks the way they liked her to and the way Crecie and all the other old-timers did, and she even took to tying a bandanna about her head—took to talking old-nigger foolishness, too, about the Bell Witch, and claiming she remembered the day General N. B. Forrest rode into town and saved all the cotton from the Yankees at the depot. When Mr. Will and Mr. Thad came to see her with their families, she got so she would reminisce with them about their daddy and tease them about all the silly little things they had done when they were growing up: "Mr. Thad—him still in kilts, too—he says, 'Aunt Munsie, reach down in yo' stockin' and git me a copper cent. I want some store candy.' " She told them about how Miss Yola Ewing, the sewing woman, heard her threatening to bust Will's back wide open when he broke the lamp chimney, and how Miss Yola went to the Doctor and told him he ought to run Aunt Munsie off. Then Aunt Munsie and the Doctor had had a big laugh about it out in the kitchen, and Miss Yola must have eavesdropped on them, because she left without finishing the girls' Easter dresses.

Indeed, these visits from Mr. Thad and Mr. Will continued as long as Aunt Munsie lived, but she never asked them any more about when they were sure enough coming back. And the children, though she hugged them more than ever—and, toward the last, there were the children's children to be hugged—never again set foot in her back yard. Aunt Munsie lived on for nearly twenty years, and when they finally buried her, they put on her tombstone that she was aged one hundred years, though nobody knew how old she was. There was no record of when she was born. All anyone knew was that in her last years she had said she was a girl helping about the big house when freedom came. That would have made her probably about twelve years old in 1865, according to her statements and depictions. But all agreed that in her extreme old age Aunt Munsie, like other old darkies, was not very reliable about dates and such things. Her spirit softened, even her voice lost some of the rasping quality that it had always had, and in general she became not very reliable about facts.

PORTE-COCHERE

Clifford and Ben Junior always came for Old Ben's birthday. Clifford came all the way from Dallas. Ben Junior came only from Cincinnati. They usually stayed in Nashville through the following week end, or came the week end before and stayed through the birthday. Old Ben, who was seventy-six and nearly blind—the cataracts had been removed twice since he was seventy—could hear them now on the side porch, their voices louder than the others', Clifford's the loudest and strongest of all. "Clifford's the real man amongst them," he said to himself, hating to say it but needing to say it. There was no knowing what went on in the heads of the other children, but there were certain things Clifford did know and understand. Clifford, being a lawyer, knew something about history—about Tennessee history he knew, for instance, the difference between Chucky Jack Sevier and Judge John Overton and could debate with you the question of whether or not Andy Jackson had played the part of the coward when he and Chucky Jack met in the wilderness that time. Old Ben kept listening for Cliff's voice above the

49

others. All of his grown-up children were down on the octagonal side porch, which was beyond the porte-cochere and which, under its red tile roof, looked like a pagoda stuck out there on the side lawn. Old Ben was in his study.

His study was directly above the porte-cochere, or what his wife, in her day, had called the porte-cochere —he called it the drive-under and the children used to call it the portcullis—but the study was not a part of the second floor; it opened off the landing halfway up the stairs. Under his south window was the red roof of the porch. He sat by the open window, wearing his dark glasses, his watery old eyes focused vaguely on the peak of the roof. He had napped a little since dinner but had not removed his suit coat or even unbuttoned his linen vest. During most of the afternoon, he had been awake and had heard his five children talking down there on the porch—Cliff and Ben Junior had arrived only that morning—talking on and on in such loud voices that his good right ear could catch individual words and sometimes whole sentences.

Midday dinner had been a considerable ordeal for Old Ben. Laura Nell's interminable chatter had been particularly taxing and obnoxious. Afterward, he had hurried to his study for his prescribed nap and had spent a good part of the afternoon dreading the expedition to the country club for supper that had been planned for that evening. Now it was almost time to begin getting ready for that expedition, and simultaneously with the thought of it and with the movement of his hand toward his watch pocket he became aware that Clifford was taking his leave of the group on the side porch. Ah, yes, at dinner time Clifford had said he had a letter to write before supper—to his wife. Yet here it was six and he had dawdled away the afternoon palavering with the others down there on the porch. Old Ben could recognize Cliff's leave-taking and the teasing voices of the others, and then he heard Cliff's footsteps on the cement driveway, below the study—a hurried step. He heard Cliff in the side hall and then his footsteps at the bottom of the stairs. In a moment he would go sailing by Old Ben's door, without a thought for anyone but himself. Old Ben's lower lip trembled. Wasn't there some business matter he could take up with Cliff? Or some personal matter? And now Cliff's footsteps on the stairs—heavy footsteps,• like his own. Suddenly, though, the footsteps halted, and Clifford went downstairs again. His father heard him go across the hall and into the living room, where the carpet silenced his footsteps; he was getting writing paper from the desk there. Old Ben hastily pulled the cord that closed the draperies across the south window, leaving only the vague light from the east window in the room. No, sir, he would not advertise his presence when Cliff passed on the landing.

With the draperies drawn, the light in the room had a strange quality—strange because Old Ben seldom drew the draperies before night. For one moment, he felt that his eyes or his glasses were playing him some new trick. Then he dropped his head on the chair back, for the strange quality now seemed strangely familiar, and now no longer strange—only familiar. It

51

was like the light in that cellar where, long ago, he used to go to fetch Mason jars for his great-aunt Nell Partee. Aunt Nell would send for him all the way across town to come fetch her Mason jars, and even when he was ten or twelve, she made him whistle the whole time he was down in the cellar, to make certain he didn't drink her wine. Aunt Nell, dead and gone. Was this something for Clifford's attention? Where Aunt Nell's shackly house had been, the Trust Company now stood—a near-skyscraper. Her cellar, he supposed, had been in the space now occupied by the basement barbershop—not quite so deep or so large as the shop, its area without boundaries now, suspended in the center of the barber shop, where the ceiling fan revolved. Would this be of interest to Cliff, who would soon ascend the stairs with his own train of thoughts and would pass the open door to the study without a word or a glance? And whatever Cliff was thinking about—his law, his golf, or his wife and children—would be of no real interest to Old Ben. But did not Clifford know that merely the sound of his voice gave his father hope, that his attention gave him comfort? What would old age be without children? Desolation, desolation. But what would old age be with children who chose to ignore the small demands that he would make upon them, that he had ever made upon them? A nameless torment! And with his thoughts Old Ben Brantley's white head rocked on his shoulders and his smoked glasses went so crooked on his nose that he had to frown them back into position.

But now Clifford was hurrying up the stairs again.

He was on the landing outside the open study door. It was almost despite himself that the old man cleared his throat and said hoarsely, "The news will be on in five minutes, if you want to listen to it." Then as though he might have sounded too cordial (he would not be reduced to toadying to his own boy), "But if you don't want to, don't say you do." Had Cliff seen his glasses slip down his nose? Cliff, no less than the others, would be capable of laughing at him in his infirmity.

"I wouldn't be likely to, would I, Papa?" Cliff had stopped at the doorway and was stifling a yawn as he spoke, half-covering his face with the envelope and the folded sheet of paper. Old Ben nodded his head to indicate that he had heard what Cliff had said, but also, to himself, he was nodding that yes, this was the way he had raised his children to talk to him.

"Just the hourly newscast," Old Ben said indifferently. "But it don't matter."

"Naw, can't make it, Papa. I got to go and write Sue Alice. The stupid woman staying with her while I'm away bores her pretty much." As he spoke, he looked directly into the dark lenses of his father's glasses, and for a brief second he rested his left hand on the door jamb. His manner was self-possessed and casual, but Old Ben felt that he didn't need good sight to detect his son's ill-concealed haste to be off and away. Cliff had, in fact, turned back to the stairs when his father stopped him with a question, spoken without expression and almost under his breath.

"Why did you come at all? Why did you even bother to come if you weren't going to bring Sue Alice and

53

the grandchildren? Did you think I wanted to see you without them?"

Clifford stopped with one foot on the first step of the second flight. "By God, Papa!" He turned on the ball of the other foot and reappeared in the doorway. "Ever travel with two small kids?" The motion of his body as he turned back from the steps had been swift and sure, calculated to put him exactly facing his father. "And in hot weather like we're having in Texas?"

Despite the undeniable thickness in Clifford's hips and the thin spot on the back of his head, his general appearance was still youthful; about this particular turning on the stairs there had been something decidedly athletic. Imperceptibly, behind the dark glasses, Old Ben lifted his eyebrows in admiration. Clifford was the only boy he had who had ever made any team at the university or done any hunting worth speaking of. For a moment, his eyes rested gently on Cliff's white summer shoes, set wide apart in the doorway. Then, jerking his head up, as though he had just heard Cliff's last words, he began: "Two small *kids?* (Why don't you use the word *brats?* It's more elegant.) I have traveled considerably with five—from here to the mountain and back every summer for fifteen years, from my thirty-first to my forty-sixth year."

"I remember," Cliff said stoically. Then, after a moment: "But now I'm going up to my room and write Sue Alice."

"Then go on up! Who's holding you?" He reached for his smoking stand and switched on the radio. It

54

was a big cabinet radio with a dark mahogany finish, a piece from the late twenties, like all the other furniture in the room, and the mechanism was slow to warm up.

Clifford took several steps toward his father. "Papa, we're due to leave for the club in thirty minutes—less than that now—and I intend to scratch off a note to my wife." He held up the writing paper, as though to prove his intention.

"No concern of mine! No concern of mine! To begin with, I, personally, am not going to the club or anywhere else for supper."

Clifford came even closer. "You may go to the club or not, as you like, Papa. But unless I misunderstand, there is not a servant on the place, and we are all going."

"That is, you are going after you scratch off a note to your wife."

"Papa, Ben Junior and I have each come well over five hundred miles—"

"Not to see me, Clifford."

"Don't be so damned childish, Papa." Cliff was turning away again. Old Ben held his watch in his hand, and he glanced down at it quickly.

"I'm getting childish, am I, Clifford?"

This time, Clifford's turning back was not accomplished in one graceful motion but by a sudden jerking and twisting of his shoulder and leg muscles. Behind the spectacles, Old Ben's eyes narrowed and twitched. His fingers were folded over the face of the watch. Clifford spoke very deliberately. "I didn't say *getting*

55

childish, Papa. When ever in your life have you been anything but that? There's not a senile bone in your brain. It's your children that have got old, and you've stayed young—and not in any good sense, Papa, only in a bad one! You play sly games with us still or you quarrel with us. What the hell do you want of us, Papa? I've thought about it a lot. Why haven't you ever asked for what it is you want? Or are *we* all blind and it's really obvious? You've never given but one piece of advice to us, and that's to be direct and talk up to you like men—as equals. And we've done that, all right, and listened to your wrangling, but somehow it has never satisfied you! What is it?"

"Go on up to your letter-writing; go write your spouse," said Old Ben.

The room had been getting darker while they talked. Old Ben slipped his watch back into his vest pocket nervously, then slipped it out again, constantly running his fingers over the gold case, as though it were a piece of money.

"Thanks for your permission, sir." Clifford took a step backward. During his long speech he had advanced all the way across the room until he was directly in front of his father.

"My permission?" Old Ben said. "Let us not forget one fact, Clifford. No child of mine has ever had to ask my permission to do anything whatsoever he took a mind to do. You have all been free as the air, to come and go in this house. . . . You still are!"

Clifford smiled. "Free to come and go, with you

perched here on the landing registering every footstep on the stairs and every car that passed underneath. I used to turn off the ignition and coast through the drive-under, and then think how foolish it was, since there was no back stairway. No back stairway in a house this size!" He paused a moment, running his eyes over the furniture and the other familiar objects in the shadowy room. "And how like the old times this was, Papa—your listening in here in the dark when I came up! By God, Papa, I wouldn't have thought when I was growing up that I'd ever come back and fuss with you once I was grown. But here I am, and, Papa—"

Old Ben pushed himself up from the chair. He put his watch in the vest pocket and buttoned his suit coat with an air of satisfaction. "I'm going along to the club for supper," he said, "since there's to be no-un here to serve me." As he spoke, he heard the clock chiming the half-hour downstairs. And Ben Junior was shouting to Old Ben and Clifford from the foot of the stairs, "Get a move on up there."

Clifford went out on the landing and called down the steps. "Wait till I change my shirt. I believe Papa's all ready."

"No letter written?" Ben Junior asked.

Clifford was hurrying up the second flight with the blank paper. "Nope, no letter this day of Our Lord."

Old Ben heard Ben Junior say, "What did I tell you?" and heard the others laughing. He stood an instant by his chair without putting on a light. Then he reached out his hand for one of the walking canes in

57

the umbrella stand by the radio. His hand lighting on the carved head of a certain oak stick, he felt the head with trembling fingers and quickly released it, and quickly, in three strides, without the help of any cane, he crossed the room to the south window. For several moments, he stood motionless at the window, his huge, soft hands held tensely at his sides, his long body erect, his almost freakishly large head at a slight angle, while he seemed to peer between the open draperies and through the pane of the upper sash, out into the twilight of the wide, shady park that stretched from his great yellow brick house to the Pike. Old Ben's eyes, behind the smoked lenses, were closed, and he was visualizing the ceiling fan in the barber shop. Presently, opening his eyes, he reflected, almost with a smile, that his aunt's cellar was not the only Nashville cellar that had disappeared. Many a cellar! His father's cellar, round like a dungeon; it had been a cistern in the very earliest days, before Old Ben's time, and when he was a boy, he would go down on a ladder with a lantern, and his father's voice, directing him, would seem to go around and around the brick walls and then come back with a hollow sound, as though the cistern were still half-full of water. One time, ah—Old Ben drew back from the window with a grimace—one time he had been so sure there was water below! In fright at the very thought of the water, he had clasped a rung of the ladder tightly with one hand and swung the lantern out, expecting certainly to see the light reflected in the depths below. But the lantern had struck the framework that supported the circular shelves and gone whirling and flaming to the brick floor, which Ben had never before seen. Crashing on the floor, it sent up yellow flames that momentarily lit the old cistern to its very top, and when Ben looked upward, he saw the furious face of his father with the flames casting jagged shadows on the long, black beard and high, white forehead. "Come out of there before you burn out my cellar and my whole damn house to the ground!" He had climbed upward toward his father, wishing the flames might engulf him before he came within reach of those arms. But as his father jerked him up onto the back porch, he saw that the flames had already died out. The whole cellar was pitch-black dark again, and the boy Ben stood with his face against the whitewashed brick wall while his father went to the carriage house to find the old plow line. Presently, he heard his father step up on the porch again. He braced himself for the first blow, but instead there was only the deafening command from his father: "Attention!" Ben whirled about and stood erect, with his chin in the air, his eyes on the ceiling. "Where have you hidden my plow lines?" "I don't know, sir." And then the old man, with his coattails somehow clinging close to his buttocks and thighs, so that his whole powerful form was outlined—his black figure against the white brick and the door—stepped over to the doorway, reached around to the cane stand in the hall, and drew out the oak stick that had his own bearded face carved upon the head. "About face!" he commanded. The boy drew back his toe and made a quick, military turn. The old man dealt him three sharp blows across the upper part of his back. . . . Tears had run down young Ben Brantley's cheeks, even streaking down his neck under his open collar and soaking the neckline binding of his woolen underwear, but he had uttered not a sound. When his father went into the house, Ben remained for a long while standing with his face to the wall. At last, he quietly left the porch and walked through the yard beneath the big shade trees, stopping casually to watch a gray squirrel and then to listen to Aunt Sally Ann's soft nigger voice whispering to him out the kitchen window. He did not answer or turn around but walked on to the latticed summerhouse, between the house and the kitchen garden. There he had lain down on a bench, looked back at the house through the latticework, and said to himself that when he got to be a grown man, he would go away to another country, where there would be no maple trees and no oak trees, no elms, not even sycamores or poplars; where there would be no squirrels and no niggers, no houses that resembled this one; and, most of all, where there would be no children and no fathers.

In the hall, now, Old Ben could hear, very faintly, Ben Junior's voice and Laura Nell's and Katie's and Lawrence's. He stepped to the door and looked down the dark flight of steps at his four younger children. They stood in a circle directly beneath the overhead light, which one of them had just switched on. Their faces were all turned upward in the direction of the open doorway where he was standing, yet he knew in reason that they could not see him there. They were talking about him! Through his dark lenses, their figures were indistinct, their faces mere blurs, and it was hard for him to distinguish their lowered voices one from another. But they were talking about him! And from upstairs he could hear Clifford's footsteps. Clifford, with his letter to Sue Alice unwritten, was thinking about him! Never once in his life had he punished or restrained them in any way! He had given them a freedom unknown to children in the land of his childhood, yet from the time they could utter a word they had despised him and denied his right to any affection or gratitude. Suddenly, stepping out onto the landing, he screamed down the stairs to them, "I've a right to some gratitude!"

They were silent and motionless for a moment. Then he could hear them speaking in lowered voices again, and moving slowly toward the stairs. At the same moment he heard Clifford's footsteps in the upstairs hall. Presently, a light went on up there, and he could dimly see Clifford at the head of the stairs. The four children were advancing up the first flight, and Clifford was coming down from upstairs. Old Ben opened his mouth to call to them, "I'm not afraid of you!" But his voice had left him, and in his momentary fright, in his fear that his wrathful, merciless children might do him harm, he suddenly pitied them. He pitied them for all they had suffered at his hands. And while he stood there, afraid, he realized, or perhaps recalled, how he had tortured and plagued them in all the ways that his resentment of their very good fortune had taught him to do. He even remembered the day

61

when it had occurred to him to build his study above the drive-under and off the stairs, so that he could keep tab on them. He had declared that he wanted his house to be as different from his father's house as a house could be, and so it was! And now he stood in the half-darkness, afraid that he was a man about to be taken by his children and at the same time pitying them, until one of them, ascending the steps switched on the light above the landing.

In the sudden brightness, Old Ben felt that his senses had returned to him. Quickly, he stepped back into the study, closed the door, and locked it. As the lock clicked, he heard Clifford say, "Papa!" Then he heard them all talking at once, and while they talked, he stumbled through the dark study to the umbrella stand. He pulled out the stick with his father's face carved on the head, and in the darkness, while he heard his children's voices, he stumbled about the room beating the upholstered chairs with the stick and calling the names of his children under his breath.

A WIFE
OF NASHVILLE

The Lovells' old cook Sarah had quit to get married in the spring, and they didn't have anybody else for a long time—not for several months. It was during the Depression, and when a servant quit, people in Nashville (and even people out at Thornton, where the Lovells came from) tried to see how long they could go before they got another. All through the summer, there would be knocks on the Lovells' front door or on the wooden porch floor, by the steps. And when one of the children or their mother went to the door, some Negro man or woman would be standing there, smiling and holding out a piece of paper. A recommendation it was supposed to be, but the illegible note scribbled with a blunt lead pencil was something no white person could have written if he had tried. If Helen Ruth, the children's mother, went to the door, she always talked a while to whoever it was, but she hardly ever even looked at the note held out to her. She would give a piece of advice or say to meet her around at the back door for a handout. If one of the boys—there were three Lovell boys, and no girls—went to the door, he

63

always brought the note in to Helen Ruth, unless John R., their father, was at home, sick with his back ailment. Helen Ruth would shake her head and say to tell whoever it was to go away! "Tell him to go back home," she said once to the oldest boy, who was standing in the sun-parlor doorway with a smudged scrap of paper in his hand. "Tell him if he had any sense, he never would have left the country."

"He's probably not from the country, Mother."

"They're all from the country," Helen Ruth said. "When they knock on the porch floor like that, they're bound to be from the country, and they're better off at home, where somebody cares something about them. I don't care anything about them any more than you do."

But one morning Helen Ruth hired a cheerful-looking and rather plump, light-complexioned young Negro girl named Jess McGehee, who had come knocking on the front-porch floor just as the others had. Helen Ruth talked to her at the front door for a while; then she told her to come around to the kitchen, and they talked there for nearly an hour. Jess stayed to fix lunch and supper, and after she had been there a few days, the family didn't know how they had ever got along without her.

In fact, Jess got on so well with the Lovells that Helen Ruth even decided to let her come and live on the place, a privilege she had never before allowed a servant of hers. Together, she and Jess moved all of John R.'s junk—a grass duck-hunting outfit, two mounted stags' heads, an outboard motor, and so on—

from the little room above the garage into the attic of the house. John R. lent Jess the money for the down payment on a "suit" of furniture, and Jess moved in. "You would never know she was out there," Helen Ruth told her friends. "There is never any rumpus. And her room! It's as clean as yours or mine."

Jess worked for them for eight years. John R. got so one of his favorite remarks was, "The honeymoon is over, but this is the real thing this time." Then he would go on about what he called Helen Ruth's "earlier affairs." The last one before Jess was Sarah, who quit to get married and go to Chicago at the age of sixty-eight. She had been with them for six years and was famous for her pies and her banana dishes.

Before Sarah, there was Carrie. Carrie had been with them when the two younger boys were born, and it was she who had once tried to persuade Helen Ruth not to go to the hospital but to let her act as midwife. She had quit them after five years, to become an undertaker. And before Carrie there was Jane Blakemore, the very first of them all, whom John R. and Helen Ruth had brought with them from Thornton to Nashville when they married. She lasted less than three years; she quit soon after John R., Jr., was born, because, she said, the baby made her nervous.

"It's an honorable record," John R. would say. "Each of them was better than the one before, and each one stayed with us longer. It proves that experience is the best teacher."

Jess's eight years were the years when the boys were growing up; the boys were children when she came, and when she left them, the youngest, little Robbie, had learned to drive the car. In a sense, it was Jess who taught all three boys to drive. She didn't give them their first lessons, of course, because, like Helen Ruth, she had never sat at the wheel of an automobile in her life. She had not ridden in a car more than half a dozen times when she came to the Lovells, but just by chance, one day, she was in the car when John R. let John R., Jr., take the wheel. The car would jerk and lunge forward every time the boy shifted gears, and his father said, "Keep your mind on what you're doing."

"I am," John R., Jr., said, "but it just does that. What makes it do it?"

"Think!" John R. said. "Think! . . . *Think!*"

"I *am* thinking, but what makes it do it?"

Suddenly, Jess leaned forward from the back seat and said, "You letting the clutch out too fast, honey."

Both father and son were so surprised they could not help laughing. They laughed harder, of course, because what Jess said was true. And Jess laughed with them. When they had driven another block, they reached a boulevard stop, and in the process of putting on the brake John R., Jr., killed the engine and then flooded the motor. His father shouted, "Well, let it rest! We're just stuck here for about twenty minutes!"

Jess, who was seated with one arm around a big bag of groceries, began to laugh again. "Turn off the key," she said. "Press down on the starter a spell. Then torectly you turn on the key and she'll start."

John R. looked over his shoulder at her, not smiling, but not frowning, either. Presently, he gave the order, "Try it."

"Try what *Jess said?*" John R., Jr., asked.

"Try what Jess said."

The boy tried it, and in a moment he was racing the motor and grinning at his father. When they had got safely across the boulevard, John R. turned around to Jess again. He asked in a quiet, almost humble manner—the same manner he used when describing the pains in his back to Helen Ruth—where she had learned these things about an automobile. "Law," she said, "I learnt them listening to my brother-in-law that drives a truck talk. I don't reckon I really know'm, but I can say them."

John R. was so impressed by the incident that he did not make it one of his stories. He told Helen Ruth about it, of course, and he mentioned it sometimes to his close friends when they were discussing "the good things" about Negroes. With his sons, he used it as an example of how much you can learn by listening to other people talk, and after that day he would permit John R., Jr., to go for drives in the car without him provided Jess went along in his place. Later on, when the other boys got old enough to drive, there were periods when he turned their instruction over to Jess. Helen Ruth even talked of learning to drive, herself, with the aid of Jess.

But it never came to more than talk with Helen Ruth, though John R. encouraged her, saying he thought driving was perhaps a serious strain on his back. She talked about it for several months, but in

67

the end she said that the time had passed when she could learn new skills. When John R. tried to encourage her in the idea, she would sometimes look out one of the sun-parlor windows toward the street and think of how much she had once wanted to learn to drive. But that had been long ago, right after they were married, in the days when John R. had owned a little Ford coupé. John R. was on the road for the Standard Candy Company then, and during most of the week she was alone in their apartment at the old Vaux Hall. While he was away John R. kept the coupé stored in a garage only two blocks east, on Broad Street; in those days traveling men still used the railroads, because Governor Peay hadn't yet paved Tennessee's highways. At that time, John R. had not believed in women driving automobiles, and Helen Ruth had felt that he must be right about it; she had even made fun of women who went *whizzing* about town, blowing horns at every intersection. Yet in her heart she had longed to drive that coupé! Jane Blakemore was working for them then, and one day Jane had put Helen Ruth's longings into words. "Wouldn't it be dandy," she said, "if me and you clomb in that car one of these weekdays and toured out to Thornton to see all the folks—white and black?"

Without a moment's hesitation, however, Helen Ruth gave the answer that she knew John R. would have given. "Now, think what you're saying, Jane!" she said. "Wouldn't we be a fool-looking pair pulling into the Square at Thornton? *Think* about it. What if we should have a flat tire when we got out about as far as Nine Mile Hill? Who would change it? *You* certainly couldn't! Jane Blakemore, I don't think you use your head about anything!"

That was the way Helen Ruth had talked to Jane on more occasions than one. She was a plain-spoken woman, and she never spoke plainer to anyone than she did to Jane Blakemore during the days when they were shut up together in that apartment at the Vaux Hall. Since Jane was from Thornton and knew how plain-spoken all Helen Ruth's family were, she paid little attention to the way Helen Ruth talked to her. She would smile, or else sneer, and go on with her work of cooking and cleaning. Sometimes she would rebel and speak just as plainly as Helen Ruth did. When Helen Ruth decided to introduce butter plates to their table, Jane said, "I ain't never heard tell of no butter dishes."

Helen Ruth raised her eyebrow. "That's because you are an ignoramus from Thornton, Tennessee," she said.

"I'm ignoramus enough to know ain't no need in nastying up all them dishes for me to wash."

Helen Ruth had, however, made Jane Blakemore learn to use butter plates and had made her keep the kitchen scrubbed and the other rooms of the apartment dusted and polished and in such perfect order that even John R. had noticed it when he came on week ends. Sometimes he had said, "You drive yourself too hard, Helen Ruth."

✦

Jess McGehee was as eager and quick to learn new things as Jane Blakemore had been unwilling and slow. She would even put finger bowls on the breakfast table when there was grapefruit. And how she did spoil the three boys about their food! There were mornings when she cooked the breakfast eggs differently for each one of them while John R. sat and shook his head in disgust at the way she was pampering his sons. John R.'s "condition" in his back kept him at home a lot of the time during the eight years Jess was with them. He had long since left off traveling for the candy company; soon after the first baby came, he had opened an insurance agency of his own.

When Jane Blakemore left them and Helen Ruth hired Carrie (after fifteen or twenty interviews with other applicants), she had had to warn Carrie that John R.'s hours might be very irregular, because he was in business for himself and wasn't able merely to punch a time clock and quit when the day ended. "He's an onsurance man, ain't he?" Carrie had asked and had showed by the light in her eyes how favorably impressed she was. "I know about him," she had said. "He's a life-onsurance man, and that's the best kind to have."

At that moment, Helen Ruth thought perhaps she had made a mistake in Carrie. "I don't like my servant to discuss my husband's business," she said.

"No'm!" Carrie said with enthusiasm. "No, *ma'am!*" Helen Ruth was satisfied, but afterward she had often to tell herself that her first suspicion had been right. Carrie was nosy and prying and morbid—and she gos-

siped with other people's servants. Her curiosity and
her gossiping were especially trying for Helen Ruth
during her and John R.'s brief separation. They actually had separated for nearly two months right after
Kenneth, the middle boy, was born. Helen Ruth had
gone to her father's house at Thornton, taking the two
babies and Carrie with her. The boys never knew
about the trouble between their parents, of course,
until Kenneth pried it out of his mother after they
were all grown, and, at the time, people in Nashville
and Thornton were not perfectly sure that it was a real
separation. Helen Ruth had tried to tell herself that
possibly Carrie didn't know it was a real separation.
But she was never able to deny completely the significance of Carrie's behavior while they were at
Thornton. Carrie's whole disposition had seemed to
change the afternoon they left Nashville. Up until
then, she had been a moody, shifty, rather loud-
mouthed brown woman, full of darky compliments for
white folks and of gratuitous promises of extra services
she seldom rendered. But at Thornton she had put the
old family servants to shame with her industriousness
and her respectful, unassuming manner. "You don't
find them like Carrie in Thornton any more," Helen
Ruth's mother said. "The good ones all go to Nashville
or Memphis." But Helen Ruth, sitting by an upstairs
window one afternoon, saw her mother's cook and
Carrie sauntering toward the back gate to meet a
caller. She saw Carrie being introduced and then she
recognized the caller as Jane Blakemore. Presently the
cook returned to the kitchen and Helen Ruth saw

Carrie and Jane enter the servants' house in the corner of the yard. During the hour that they visited there, Helen Ruth sat quietly by the window in the room with her two babies. It seemed to her the most terrible hour of her separation from John R. When Carrie and Jane reappeared on the stoop of the servants' house and Carrie was walking with Jane to the gate, there was no longer any doubt in Helen Ruth's mind but that she would return to her husband, and return without any complaints or stipulations. During that hour she had tried to imagine exactly what things the black Jane and the brown Carrie were talking about, or, rather, *how* and in what terms they were talking about the things they must be talking about. In her mind, she reviewed the sort of difficulties she had had with Jane and the sort she had with Carrie and tried to imagine what defense they would make for themselves —Jane for her laziness and contrariness, Carrie for her usual shiftiness and negligence. Would they blame her for these failings of theirs? Or would they blandly pass over their own failings and find fault with her for things that she was not even aware of, or that she could not help and could not begin to set right? Had she really misused these women, either the black one or the brown one? It seemed to her then that she had so little in life that she was entitled to the satisfaction of keeping an orderly house and to the luxury of efficient help. There was too much else she had not had—an "else" nameless to her, yet sorely missed—for her to be denied these small satisfactions. As she sat alone with her two babies in the old nursery and thought of the two servants gossiping about her, she became an object of pity to herself. And presently John R., wherever he might be at that moment—in his office or at the club or, more likely, on a hunting or fishing trip somewhere—became an object of pity, too. And her two babies, one in his crib and the other playing on the carpet with a string of spools, were objects of pity. Even Carrie, standing alone by the gate after Jane had gone, seemed a lone and pitiful figure.

A few days later, Helen Ruth and Carrie and the two baby boys returned to Nashville.

In Nashville, Carrie was herself again; everything was done in her old slipshod fashion. Except during that interval at Thornton, Carrie was never known to perform any task to Helen Ruth's complete satisfaction. Hardly a meal came to the table without the soup or the dessert or some important sauce having been forgotten; almost every week something important was left out of the laundry; during a general cleaning the upper sashes of two or three windows were invariably left unwashed. Yet never in her entire five years did Carrie answer back or admit an unwillingness to do the most menial or the most nonessential piece of work. In fact, one of her most exasperating pronouncements was, "You are exactly right," which was often followed by a lengthy description of how she would do the thing from then on, or an explanation of how it happened that she had forgotten to do it. Not only that, she would often undertake to explain to Helen Ruth Helen Ruth's reason for wanting it done. "You

are exactly right and I know how you mean. You want
them drapes shut at night so it can seem like we're living in a house out in the Belle Meade instead of this
here Vox Hall flat, and some fool might be able to
look in from the yard."

"Never mind the reasons, Carrie" was Helen Ruth's
usual reply. But her answers were not always so gentle
—not when Carrie suggested that she have the second
baby at home with Carrie acting as midwife, not when
Carrie spoke to her about having the third baby cir-
cumcised. And the day that Helen Ruth began packing her things to go to Thornton, she was certain that
Carrie would speak out of turn with some personal advice. That would have been more than she could bear,
and she was prepared to dismiss Carrie from her service
and make the trip alone. But neither then nor afterward did Carrie give any real evidence of understanding the reasons for the trip to Thornton.

In fact, it was not until long afterward, when Carrie
had quit them to become an undertaker, that Helen
Ruth felt that Carrie's gossip with other Nashville
servants had, by accident, played a part in her separation from John R. She and John R. had talked of separation and divorce more than once during the first
two years they were married, in the era of Jane Blakemore. It was not that any quarreling led to this talk
but that each accused the other of being dissatisfied
with their marriage. When John R. came in from traveling, on a week end or in the middle of the week—
he was sometimes gone only two or three days at a
time—he would find Helen Ruth sitting alone in the

living room, without a book or even a deck of cards to amuse herself with, dressed perhaps in something new her mother had sent her, waiting for him. She would rise from her chair to greet him, and he would smile in frank admiration of the tall, graceful figure and of the countenance whose features seemed always composed, and softened by her hair, which was beginning to be gray even at the time of their marriage. But he had not come home many times before Helen Ruth was greeting him with tears instead of smiles. At first, he had been touched, but soon he began to complain that she was unhappy. He asked her why she did not see something of other people while he was away—the wives of his business and hunting friends, or some of the other Thornton girls who were married and living in Nashville. She replied that she did see them occasionally but that she was not the sort of woman who enjoyed having a lot of women friends. Besides, she was perfectly happy with her present life; it was only that she believed that he must be unhappy and that he no longer enjoyed her company. She understood that he had to be away most of the week, but even when he was in town, she saw very little of him. When he was not at his office, he was fishing out on Duck River or was off to a hunt up at Gallatin. And at night he either took her to parties with those hunting people, with whom she had little or nothing in common, or piled up on the bed after supper and slept. All of this indicated that he was not happy being married to her, she said, and so they talked a good deal about separating.

✦

After the first baby came, there was no such talk for a long time—not until after the second baby. After the first baby came, Helen Ruth felt that their marriage must be made to last, regardless of hers or John R.'s happiness. Besides, it was at that time that one of John R.'s hunting friends—a rich man named Rufus Brantley—had secured the insurance agency for him; and almost before John R. opened his office, he had sold policies to other rich hunting friends that he had. For a while, he was at home more than he had ever been before. But soon, when his business was established, he began to attend more and more meets and trials, all over Tennessee and Alabama and Kentucky. He even acquired a few dogs and a horse of his own. With his friends he began to go on trips to distant parts of the country. It seemed that when he was not deer hunting in the State of Maine, he was deep-sea fishing in the Gulf. Helen Ruth did sometimes go with him to the local horse shows, but one night, at the Spring Horse Show, she had told Mrs. Brantley that she had a new machine, and Mrs. Brantley had thought she meant an automobile instead of a sewing machine. That, somehow, had been the last straw. She would never go out with "people like the Brantleys" after that. She was pregnant again before the first baby was a year old, and this soon became her excuse for going nowhere in the evening. The women she did visit with very occasionally in the daytime were those she had known as girls in Thornton, women whose husbands were bank tellers and office managers and were barely acquainted with John R. Lovell.

After the second baby came, Helen Ruth saw these women more frequently. She began to feel a restlessness that she could not explain in herself. There were days when she could not stay at home. With Carrie and the two babies, she would traipse about town, on foot or by streetcar, to points she had not visited since she was a little girl and was in Nashville with her parents to attend the State Fair or the Centennial. She went to the Capitol, to Centennial Park and the Parthenon, even out to the Glendale Zoo. Once, with Nancy Tolliver and Lucy Parkes, two of her old Thornton friends, she made an excursion to Cousin Mamie Lovell's farm, which was several miles beyond the town of Franklin. They went by the electric interurban to Franklin, and from there they took a taxi to the farm. Cousin Mamie's husband had been a second cousin of John R.'s father, and it was a connection the Thornton Lovells had once been very proud to claim. But for a generation this branch of the family had been in decline. Major Lovell had been a prominent lawyer in Franklin and had been in politics, but when he died, he left his family "almost penniless." His boys had not gone to college; since the farm was supposed to have been exhausted, they did not try to farm it but clerked in stores in Franklin. There was said to be a prosperous son-in-law in St. Louis, but the daughter was dead and Cousin Mamie was reported to have once called her son-in-law a parvenu to his face. Helen Ruth and her friends made the excursion because they wanted to see the house, which was one of the finest old places in the county and full of antiques.

But Cousin Mamie didn't even let them inside the house. It was a hot summer day, and she had all the blinds closed and the whole L-shaped house shut up tight, so that it would be bearable at night. She received them on the long ell porch. Later, they moved their chairs out under a tree in the yard, where Cousin Mamie's cook brought them a pitcher of iced tea. While they were chatting under the tree that afternoon, they covered all the usual topics that are dealt with when talking to an old lady one doesn't know very well—the old times and the new times, mutual friends and family connections, country living and city living, and always, of course, the lot of woman as it relates to each topic.

"Where are you and John R. living?" Cousin Mamie asked Helen Ruth.

"We're still at the Vaux Hall, Cousin Mamie."

"I'd suppose the trains would be pretty bad for noise there, that close to the depot."

"They're pretty bad in the summer."

"I'd suppose you had a place out from town, seeing how often John R.'s name's in the paper with the hound and hunt set."

"That's John R.'s life," Helen Ruth said, "not mine."

"He runs with a fine pack, I must say," said Cousin Mamie.

Nancy Tolliver and Lucy Parkes nodded and smiled. Lucy said, "The swells of Nashville, Miss Mamie."

78

But Cousin Mamie said, "There was a day when they weren't the swells. Forty years ago, people like Major Lovell didn't know people like the Brantleys. I think the Brantleys quarried limestone, to begin with. I guess it don't matter, though, for when I was a girl in upper East Tennessee, people said the Lovells started as land speculators hereabouts and at Memphis. But I don't blame you for not wanting to fool with Brantleys, Helen Ruth."

"John R. and I each live our own life, Cousin Mamie."

"Helen Ruth is a woman with a mind of her own, Miss Mamie," Nancy Tolliver said. "It's too bad more marriages can't be like theirs, each living their own life. Everyone admires it as a real achievement."

And Lucy Parkes said, "Because a woman's husband hunts is no reason for her to hunt, any more than because a man's wife sews is any reason for him to sew."

"Indeed not," Cousin Mamie said, actually paying little attention to what Lucy and Nancy were saying. Presently, she continued her own train of thought. "Names like Brantley and Partee and Hines didn't mean a thing in this state even thirty years ago."

What Lucy and Nancy said about her marriage that day left Helen Ruth in a sort of daze and at the same time made her see her situation more clearly. She had never discussed her marriage with anybody, and hearing it described so matter-of-factly by these two women made her understand for the first time what a special sort of marriage it was and how unhappy she was in it. At the time, John R. was away on a fishing

79

trip to Tellico Plains. She did not see him again before she took the babies and Carrie to Thornton. She
sent a note to his office saying that she would return
when he decided to devote his time to his wife and
children instead of to his hounds and horses. While
she was at Thornton her letters from John R. made
no mention of her note. He wrote about his business,
about his hounds and horses, about the weather, and
he always urged her to hurry home as soon as she had
seen everybody and had a good visit. Meanwhile, he
had a room at the Hermitage Club.

When Helen Ruth returned to Nashville, their life
went on as before. A year later, the third boy, Robbie,
was born, and John R. bought a large bungalow on
Sixteenth Avenue, not too far from the Tarbox School,
where they planned to send the boys. Carrie was with
them for three years after the separation, and though
her work did not improve, Helen Ruth found herself
making excuses for her. She began to attribute Carrie's garrulity to "a certain sort of bashfulness, or the
Negro equivalent to bashfulness." And with the three
small boys, and the yard to keep, too, there was so
much more for Carrie to do than there had been before! Despite the excuses she made for her, Helen
Ruth could see that Carrie was plainly getting worse
about everything and that she now seemed to take
pleasure in lying about the smallest, most unimportant
things. But Helen Ruth found it harder to confront
Carrie with her lies or to reprimand her in any way.

During the last months before Carrie quit, she
would talk sometimes about the night work she did

for a Negro undertaker. To make Helen Ruth smile, she would report things she had heard about the mourners. Her job, Carrie always said, was to sweep the parlors after the funeral and to fold up the chairs. It was only when she finally gave notice to Helen Ruth that she told her what she professed was the truth. She explained that during all those months she had been learning to embalm. "Before you can get a certificate," she said, "you has to handle a bad accident, a sickness, a case of old age, a drowning, a burning, and a half-grown child or less. I been waiting on the child till last night, but now I'll be getting my certificate."

Helen Ruth would not even let Carrie go to the basement to get her hat and coat. "You send somebody for them," she said. "But *you*, you get off these premises, Carrie!" She was sincerely outraged by what Carrie had told her, and when she looked at Carrie's hands she was filled with new horror. Yet something kept her from saying all the things that one normally said to a worthless, lying servant who had been guilty of one final outrage. "*Leave*, Carrie!" she said, consciously restraining herself. "*Leave* this place!" Carrie went out the kitchen door and down the driveway to the street, bareheaded, coatless, and wearing her kitchen slippers.

After Carrie, there was old Sarah, who stayed with them for six years and then quit them to get married and go to Chicago. Sarah was too old to do heavy work even when she first came, and before she had been there a week, John R. had been asked to help

81

move the sideboard and to bring the ladder up from the basement. He said it seemed that every minute he was in the house, he was lifting or moving something that was too much for Sarah. Helen Ruth replied that perhaps she should hire a Negro man to help in the house and look after the yard. But John R. said no, he was only joking, he thought Sarah far and away the best cook they had ever had, and besides business conditions didn't look too good and it was no time to be taking on more help. But he would always add he did not understand why Helen Ruth babied Sarah so. "From the first moment old Sarah set foot in this house, Helen Ruth has babied her," he would say to people in Helen Ruth's presence.

Sarah could neither read nor write. Even so, it took her only a short while to learn all Helen Ruth's special recipes and how to cook everything the way the Lovells liked it. For two weeks, Helen Ruth stayed in the kitchen with Sarah, reading to her from *How We Cook in Tennessee* and giving detailed instructions for every meal. It was during that time that her great sympathy for Sarah developed. Sarah was completely unashamed of her illiteracy, and it was this that first impressed Helen Ruth. She admired Sarah for having no false pride and for showing no resentment of her mistress's impatience. She observed Sarah's kindness with the children. And she learned from Sarah about Sarah's religious convictions and about her long, unhappy marriage to a Negro named Morse Wilkins, who had finally left her and gone up North.

While Sarah was working for them, John R. and

Helen Ruth lived the life that Helen Ruth had heard her friends describe to John R.'s Cousin Mamie. It was not until after Sarah had come that Helen Ruth, recalling the afternoon at Cousin Mamie's, identified Lucy Parkes's words about a wife's sewing and a husband's hunting as the very answer she had once given to some of Carrie's impertinent prying. That afternoon, the remark had certainly sounded familiar, but she had been too concerned with her own decision to leave her husband to concentrate upon anything so trivial. And after their reconciliation, she tried not to dwell on things that had led her to leave John R. Their reconciliation, whatever it meant to John R., meant to her the acceptance of certain mysteries—the mystery of his love of hunting, of his choice of friends, of his desire to maintain a family and home of which he saw so little, of his attachment to her, and of her own devotion to him. Her babies were now growing into little boys. She felt that there was much to be thankful for, not the least of which was a servant as fond of her and of her children as Sarah was. Sarah's affection for the three little boys often reminded Helen Ruth how lonely Sarah's life must be.

One day, when she had watched Sarah carefully wrapping up little Robbie in his winter play clothes before he went out to play in the snow, she said, "You love children so much, Sarah, didn't you ever have any of your own?"

Sarah, who was a yellow-skinned woman with face and arms covered with brown freckles, turned her gray eyes and fixed them solemnly on Helen Ruth. "Why,

I had the cutest little baby you ever did see," she said, "and Morse went and killed it."

"Morse *killed* your baby?"

"He rolled over on it in his drunk sleep and smothered it in the bed."

After that, Helen Ruth would never even listen to Sarah when she talked about Morse, and she began to feel a hatred toward any and all of the men who came to take Sarah home at night. Generally, these men were the one subject Sarah did not discuss with Helen Ruth, and their presence in Sarah's life was the only serious complaint Helen Ruth made against her. They would come sometimes as early as four in the afternoon and wait on the back porch for Sarah to get through. She knew that Sarah was usually feeding one of them out of her kitchen, and she knew that Sarah was living with first one and then another of them, but when she told John R. she was going to put her foot down on it, he forbade her to do so. And so through nearly six years she tolerated this weakness of Sarah's. But one morning in the late spring Sarah told her that Morse Wilkins had returned from up North and that she had taken him back as her husband. Helen Ruth could not find anything to say for a moment, but after studying the large diamond on her engagement ring for awhile she said, "My servant's private life is her own affair but I give you fair warning now, Sarah, I want to see no more of your men friends—Morse or *any other*—on this place again."

From that time, she saw no more men on the place until Morse himself came, in a drunken rage, in the

middle of a summer's day. Helen Ruth had been expecting something of the sort to happen. Sarah had
been late to work several times during the preceding
three weeks. She had come one morning with a dark
bruise on her cheek and said she had fallen getting
off the streetcar. Twice, Helen Ruth had found Sarah
on her knees, praying, in the kitchen. The day Helen
Ruth heard the racket at the back-porch door, she
knew at once that it was Morse. She got up from her
sewing machine and went directly to the kitchen.
Sarah was on the back porch, and Morse was outside
the screen door of the porch, which was hooked on
the inside. He was a little man, shriveled up, bald-
headed, not more than five feet tall, and of a complexion very much like Sarah's. Over his white shirt
he wore a dark sleeveless sweater. "You come on
home," he was saying as he shook the screen door.

Helen Ruth stepped to the kitchen door. "Is that
her?" Morse asked Sarah, motioning his head toward
Helen Ruth.

When Sarah turned her face around, her complexion
seemed several shades lighter than Morse's. "I got to
go," she said to Helen Ruth.

"No, Sarah, *he's* got to go. But *you* don't."

"He's gonna leave me again."

"That's the best thing that could happen to you,
Sarah."

Sarah said nothing, and Morse began shaking the
door again.

"Is he drunk, Sarah?" Helen Ruth asked.

THE WIDOWS OF THORNTON

"He's so drunk I don't know how he find his way here."

Helen Ruth went out onto the porch. "Now, you get off this place, and quick about it," she said to Morse.

He shook the screen door again. "You didn't make me come here, Mrs. Lovellel, and you can't make me leave, Mrs. Lovellel."

"I can't make you leave," Helen Ruth said at once, "but there's a bluecoat down on the corner who can."

Suddenly Sarah dropped to her knees and began praying. Her lips moved silently, and gradually she let her forehead come to rest on the top of the rickety vegetable bin. Morse looked at her through the screen, putting his face right against the wire. "Sarah," he said, "you come on home. You better come on now if you think I be there."

Sarah got up off her knees.

"I'm going to phone the police," Helen Ruth said, pretending to move toward the kitchen.

Morse left the door and staggered backward toward the driveway. "Come on, Sarah," he shouted.

"I got to go," Sarah said.

"I won't let you go, Sarah!"

"She can't make you stay!" Morse shouted. "You better come on if you coming!"

"It will be the worst thing you ever did in your life, Sarah," said Helen Ruth. "And if you go with him, you can't ever come back here. He'll kill you some-day, too—the way he did your baby."

Sarah was on her knees again, and Morse was out

of sight but still shouting as he went down the driveway. Suddenly, Sarah was on her feet. She ran into the kitchen and on through the house to the front porch.

Helen Ruth followed, calling her back. She found Sarah on the front porch waving to Morse, who was halfway down the block, running in a zigzag down the middle of the street, still shouting at the top of his voice. Sarah cried out to him, "Morse! Morse!"

"Sarah!" Helen Ruth said.

"Morse!" Sarah cried again, and then she began mumbling words that Helen Ruth could not quite understand at the time. Afterward, going over it in her mind, Helen Ruth realized that what Sarah had been mumbling was, "If I don't see you no more on this earth, Morse, I'll see you in Glory."

Sarah was with the Lovells for four more months, and then one night she called up on the telephone and asked John R., Jr., to tell his mother that she was going to get married to a man named Racecar and they were leaving for Chicago in the morning.

Jess McGehee came to them during the Depression. Even before Sarah left the Lovells, John R. had had to give up all of his "activities" and devote his entire time to selling insurance. Rufus Brantley had shot himself through the head while cleaning a gun at his hunting lodge, and most of John R.'s other hunting friends had suffered the same financial reverses that John R. had. The changes in the Lovells' life had come so swiftly that Helen Ruth did not realize for awhile what the changes meant in her relationship with John R. It seemed as though she woke up one day and discovered that she was not married to the same man. She found herself spending all her evenings playing Russian bank with a man who had no interest in anything but his home, his wife, and his three boys. Every night, he would give a brief summary of the things that had happened at his office or on his calls, and then he would ask her and the boys for an account of everything they had done that day. He took an interest in the house and the yard, and he and the boys made a lily pool in the back yard, and singlehanded he screened in the entire front porch. Sometimes he took the whole family to Thornton for a week end, and he and Helen Ruth never missed the family reunions there in September.

In a sense, these were the happiest years of their married life. John R.'s business got worse and worse, of course, but since part of their savings was in the bank at Thornton that did not fail, they never had any serious money worries. Regardless of their savings, however, John R.'s loss of income and his having to give up his friends and his hunting wrought very real, if only temporary changes in him. There were occasions when he would sit quietly and listen to his family's talk without correcting them or pointing out how foolish they were. He gave up saying "Think!" to the boys, and instead would say, "Now, let's see if we can't reason this thing out." He could never bring himself to ask for any sympathy from Helen Ruth for his various losses, but as it was during this time that he

88

suffered so from the ailment in his back (he and Helen Ruth slept with boards under their mattress for ten years), the sympathy he got for his physical pain was more than sufficient. All in all, it was a happy period in their life, and in addition to their general family happiness they had Jess.

Jess not only cooked and cleaned, she planned the meals, did the marketing, and washed everything, from handkerchiefs and socks to heavy woolen blankets. When the boys began to go to dances, she even learned to launder their dress shirts. There was nothing she would not do for the boys or for John R. or for Helen Ruth. The way she idealized the family became the basis for most of the "Negro jokes" told by the Lovells during those years. In her room she had a picture of the family, in a group beside the lily pool, taken with her own box Brownie; she had tacked it and also a picture of each of them on the wall above her washstand. In her scrapbook she had pasted every old snapshot and photograph that Helen Ruth would part with, as well as old newspaper pictures of John R. on horseback or with a record-breaking fish he had caught. She had even begged from Helen Ruth an extra copy of the newspaper notice of their wedding.

Jess talked to the family a good deal at mealtime, but only when they had addressed her first and had shown that they wanted her to talk. Her remarks were mostly about things that related to the Lovells. She told a sad story about a "very loving white couple" from Brownsville, her home town, who had been drowned in each other's arms when their car rolled off the end of a river ferry. The point of the story was that those two people were the same, fine, loving sort of couple that John R. and Helen Ruth were. All three of the boys made good grades in school, and every month Jess would copy their grades in her scrapbook, which she periodically passed around for the family to appreciate. When Kenneth began to write stories and articles for his high-school paper, she would always borrow the paper overnight; soon it came out that she was copying everything he wrote onto the big yellow pages of her scrapbook.

After three or four years, John R. began to say that he thought Jess would be with them always and that they would see the day when the boys' children would call her "Mammy." Helen Ruth said that she would like to agree with him about that, but actually she worried, because Jess seemed to have no life of her own, which wasn't at all natural. John R. agreed that they should make her take a holiday now and then. Every summer, they would pack Jess off to Brownsville for a week's visit with her kinfolks, but she was always back in her room over the garage within two or three days; she said that her people fought and quarreled so much that she didn't care for them. Outside her life with the Lovells, she had only one friend. Her interest was the movies, and her friend was "the Mary who works for Mrs. Dunbar." Jess and Mary went to the movies together as often as three or four times a week, and on Sunday afternoons Mary came to see Jess or Jess went to see Mary, who lived over the Dunbar's garage. Jess always took along her scrapbook and her most recent movie magazines. She and Mary swapped movie magazines, and it was apparent from Jess's talk on Monday mornings that they also swapped eulogies of their white families.

Sometimes Helen Ruth would see Mrs. Dunbar downtown or at a P.-T.A. meeting; they would discuss their cooks and smile over the reports that each had received of the other's family. "I understand that your boys are all growing into very handsome men," Mrs. Dunbar said once, and she told Helen Ruth that Jess was currently comparing one of the boys—Mrs. Dunbar didn't know which one—to Neil Hamilton, and that she was comparing Helen Ruth to Irene Rich, and John R. to Edmund Lowe. As the boys got older, they began to resent the amount of authority over them— though it was small—that Jess had been allowed by their parents and were embarrassed if anyone said Jess had taught them to drive the car. When John R., Jr., began at the university, he made his mother promise not to let Jess know what grades he received, and none of the boys would let Jess take snapshots of them any more. Their mother tried to comfort Jess by saying that the boys were only going through a phase and that it would pass in time. One day, she even said this in the presence of Robbie, who promptly reported it to the older boys, and it ended with John R., Jr.'s, complaining to his father that their mother ought not to make fun of them to Jess. His father laughed at him but later told Helen Ruth that he thought she was making a mistake, that the boys were getting big enough to think about their manly dignity, and that she would have to take that into consideration.

She didn't make the same mistake again, but although Jess never gave any real sign of her feelings being hurt, Helen Ruth was always conscious of how the boys were growing away from their good-natured servant. By the time Robbie was sixteen, they had long since ceased to have any personal conversation with Jess, and nothing would have induced Robbie to submit to taking drives with her but the knowledge that his father would not allow him to use the car on dates until he had had months of driving practice. Once, when Robbie and Jess returned from a drive, Jess reported, with a grin, that not a word had passed between them during the entire hour and a half. Helen Ruth only shook her head sadly. The next day she bought Jess a new bedside radio.

The radio was the subject of much banter among the boys and their father. John R. said Helen Ruth had chosen the period of hard times and the Depression to become more generous with her servant than she had ever been before in her life. They recalled other presents she had given Jess recently, and from that time on they teased her regularly about how she spoiled Jess. John R. said that if Jess had had his back trouble, Helen Ruth would have retired her at double pay and nursed her with twice the care that he received. The boys teased her by saying that at Christmas time she reversed the custom of shopping for the servant at the ten-cent stores and for the family at the department stores.

Yet as long as Jess was with them, they all agreed that she was the best help they had ever had. In fact, even afterward, during the war years, when John R.'s business prospered again and his back trouble left him entirely and the boys were lucky enough to be stationed near home and, later, continue their education at government expense, even then John R. and the boys would say that the years when Jess was with them were the happiest time of their life and that Jess was the best servant Helen Ruth had ever had. They said that, and then there would be a silence, during which they were probably thinking about the summer morning just before the war when Jess received a telephone call.

When the telephone rang that morning, Helen Ruth and John R. and the boys had just sat down to breakfast. As was usual in the summertime, they were eating at the big drop-leaf table in the sun parlor. Jess had set the coffee urn by Helen Ruth's place and was starting from the room when the telephone rang. Helen Ruth, supposing the call was for a member of the family, and seeing that Jess lingered in the doorway, said for her to answer it there in the sun parlor instead of running to the telephone in the back hall.

Jess answered it, announcing whose residence it was in a voice so like Helen Ruth's that it made the boys grin. For a moment, everyone at the table kept silent. They waited for Jess's eyes to single out one of them. John R., Jr., and Kenneth even put down their grapefruit spoons. But the moment Jess picked up the in-

93

strument, she fixed her eyes on the potted fern on the window seat across the room. At once her nostrils began to twitch, her lower lip fell down, and it seemed only an act of will that she was twice able to say, "Yes, ma'am," in answer to the small, unreal, metallic voice.

When she had replaced the telephone on its cradle, she turned quickly away and started into the dining room. But Helen Ruth stopped her. "Jess," she asked, her voice full of courtesy, "was the call for you?"

Jess stopped, and they all watched her hands go up to her face. Without turning around, she leaned against the door jamb and began sobbing aloud. Helen Ruth sprang up from the table, saying, "Jess, honey, what *is* the matter?" John R. and the boys stood up, too.

"It was a telegram for me—from Brownsville."

Helen Ruth took her in her arms. "Is someone dead?"

Between sobs, Jess answered, "My little brother—our baby brother—the only one of 'em I cared for." Then her sobs became more violent.

Helen Ruth motioned for John R. to move the morning paper from the big wicker chair, and she led Jess in that direction. But Jess would not sit down, and she could not be pulled away from Helen Ruth. She held fast to her, and Helen Ruth continued to pat her gently on the back and to try to console her with gentle words. Finally, she said, "Jess, you must go to Brownsville. Maybe there's been some mistake. Maybe he's not dead. But you must go, anyway."

Presently, Jess did sit in the chair, and dried her eyes on Helen Ruth's napkin. The boys shook their heads sympathetically and John R. said she certainly must go to Brownsville. She agreed, and said she believed there was a bus at ten that she would try to catch. Helen Ruth patted her hand, telling her to go along to her room when she felt like it, and said that *she* would finish getting breakfast.

"I want to go by to see Mary first," Jess said, "so I better make haste." She stood up, forcing a grateful smile. Then she burst into tears again and threw her arms about Helen Ruth, mumbling, "Oh, God! Oh, God!" The three boys and their father saw tears come into Helen Ruth's eyes, and through her tears Helen Ruth saw a change come over their faces. It was not exactly a change of expression. It couldn't be that, she felt, because it was exactly the same on each of the four faces. It hardly seemed possible that so similar a change could reflect four men's individual feelings. She concluded that her own emotion, and probably the actual tears in her eyes, had made her imagine the change, and when Jess now pulled away and hurried off to her room, Helen Ruth's tears had dried and she could see no evidence of the change she had imagined in her husband's and her sons' faces.

While Jess was in her room preparing to leave, they finished breakfast. Then Helen Ruth began clearing the table, putting the dishes on the teacart. She had said little while they were eating, but in her mind she was all the while going over something that she knew she must tell her family. As she absent-mindedly stacked the dishes, her lips moved silently over the simple words she would use in telling them. She knew

95

that they were watching her, and when Robbie offered to take Jess to the bus station, she knew that the change she had seen in all their faces had been an expression of sympathy for *her* as well as of an eagerness to put this whole episode behind them. "I'll take Jess to her bus," he said.

But Helen Ruth answered, in the casual tone she had been preparing to use, that she thought it probably wouldn't be the thing to do.

"Why, what do you mean, Helen Ruth?" John R. asked her.

"It was very touching, mother," Kenneth said in his new, manly voice, "the way she clung to you." He, too, wanted to express sympathy, but he also seemed to want to distract his mother from answering his father's question.

At that moment, Jess passed under the sun-parlor windows, walking down the driveway, carrying two large suitcases. Helen Ruth watched her until she reached the sidewalk. Then, very quietly, she told her family that Jess McGehee had no baby brother and had never had one. "Jess and Mary are leaving for California. They think they're going to find themselves jobs out there."

"You knew that right along?" John R. asked.

"I knew it right along."

"Did she know you did, Helen Ruth?" he asked. His voice had in it the sternness he used when questioning the boys about something.

"No, John R., she did not. I didn't learn it from her."

96

"Well, I don't believe it's so," he said. "Why, I don't believe that for a minute. Her carrying on was too real."

"They're going to California. They've already got their two tickets. Mrs. Dunbar got wind of it somehow, by accident, from Mrs. Lon Thompson's cook, and she called me on Monday. They've saved their money and they're going."

"And you let Jess get away with all that crying stuff just now?" John R. said.

Helen Ruth put her hands on the handle bar of the teacart. She pushed the cart a little way over the tile floor but stopped when he repeated his question. It wasn't to answer his question that she stopped, however. "Oh, my dears!" she said, addressing her whole family. Then it was a long time before she said anything more. John R. and the three boys remained seated at the table, and while Helen Ruth gazed past them and toward the front window of the sun parlor, they sat silent and still, as though they were in a picture. What could she say to them, she kept asking herself. And each time she asked the question, she received for answer some different memory of seemingly unrelated things out of the past twenty years of her life. These things presented themselves as answers to her question, and each of them seemed satisfactory to her. But how little sense it would make to her husband and her grown sons, she reflected, if she should suddenly begin telling them about the long hours she had spent waiting in that apartment at the Vaux Hall while John R. was on the road for the Standard Candy

97

Company, and in the same breath should tell them about how plainly she used to talk to Jane Blakemore and how Jane pretended that the baby made her nervous and went back to Thornton. Or suppose she should abruptly remind John R. of how ill at ease the wives of his hunting friends used to make her feel and how she had later driven Sarah's worthless husband out of the yard, threatening to call a bluecoat. What if she should suddenly say that because a woman's husband hunts, there is no reason for *her* to hunt, any more than because a man's wife sews, there is reason for him to sew. She felt that she would be willing to say anything at all, no matter how cruel or absurd it was, if it would make them understand that everything that happened in life only demonstrated in some way the lonesomeness that people felt. She was ready to tell them about sitting in the old nursery at Thornton and waiting for Carrie and Jane Blakemore to come out of the cabin in the yard. If it would make them see what she had been so long in learning to see, she would even talk at last about the "so much else" that had been missing from her life and that she had not been able to name, and about the foolish mysteries she had so nobly accepted upon her reconciliation with John R. To her, these things were all one now; they were her loneliness, the loneliness from which everybody, knowingly or unknowingly, suffered. But she knew that her husband and her sons did not recognize her loneliness or Jess McGehee's or their own. She turned her eyes from the window to look at their faces around the table, and it was strange to see that they were still thinking in the most personal and particular terms of how they had been deceived by a servant, the ignorant granddaughter of an ignorant slave, a Negro woman from Brownsville who was crazy about the movies and who would soon be riding a bus, mile after mile, on her way to Hollywood, where she might find the friendly faces of the real Neil Hamilton and the real Irene Rich. It was with effort that Helen Ruth thought again of Jess McGehee's departure and the problem of offering an explanation to her family. At last, she said patiently, "My dears, don't you see how it was for Jess? How else can they tell us anything when there is such a gulf?" After a moment she said, "How can I make you understand this?"

Her husband and her three sons sat staring at her, their big hands, all so alike, resting on the breakfast table, their faces stamped with identical expressions, not of wonder but of incredulity. Helen Ruth was still holding firmly to the handle of the teacart. She pushed it slowly and carefully over the doorsill and into the dining room, dark and cool as an underground cavern, and spotlessly clean, the way Jess McGehee had left it.

THE DEATH
OF A KINSMAN

Cast of Characters
Robert Wade
Margie, his wife
Aunt Lida Wade
Miss Bluemeyer, their housekeeper
Myra Willis, family servant
Lennie, upstairs maid, Myra's niece
Paris, houseboy, Myra's nephew
The Wade children
   James
   Nancy
   Alfred
   Charles William
   Lida Sue

SCENE I

*It is long before daybreak, but in the Wade house
lights have been put on in the halls and in the pantry
and in the upstairs sitting room and in nearly every
room in the whole house and on the side porch as well.*

*Nobody has been left sleeping. The curtain rises on
the scene in the upstairs hall. It is a rectangular room
running the entire width of the stage. A large stair well
is in the center and back of the stage. On the wall
beyond the balustrade which guards the descending
stairs is an enormous mirror. Doors to the bedrooms
are at either end of the hall. A door at the extreme
right in the back wall opens into the service hall where
there is presumably another stairway. The door at the
head of the stairs (left, back) leads to the bedroom of
Mr. and Mrs. Wade. The general effect is that all of
the wall space, except that beyond the stair well, is
taken up by the doorways. The elaborate door facings
and the oak balustrade and the pilasters at the four
corners of the stair well indicate that the house is one
of those mansions put up in Midwestern cities during
the early part of the present century. The floor is not
carpeted, but it is partly covered by two large rugs.
The one on the left is a handsome, though rather worn
and faded, Oriental rug. On the right is an obviously
new imitation of the same thing, with extremely bright
colors and a general effect of silkiness. The end of the
hall to the left (and front) is furnished as an upstairs
sitting room. There are several upholstered chairs, a
footstool, a small table and lamp. The only other furnishings are a table and chair at the right (front) corner of the balustrade. The table is an old-fashioned
card table, the typical Southern antique, and the chair
a ladder-back imitation antique with a cushion on the
seat. On the table are an electric clock, a modern
French-style telephone, and an ultra-modern desk lamp*

*which, except for the dimly lit table lamp, is the only
light burning as the curtain rises.*

*Simultaneously two Negro maids enter from doors
at opposite ends of the hall. One is a tall, thin, stooped
woman with a good deal of gray in her hair. The other
is a somewhat more than plump young woman. Both
are black. They advance hurriedly toward the middle
of the room until simultaneously children's voices call
from the rooms they have just quitted. "Myra, where
are my good socks? What did you do with . . ."
"Lennie, where's the brush I put . . ." The two
women halt, exchange first exasperated grimaces and
then indulgent smiles, and return to the children.
Aunt Lida Wade appears from one of the doors at the
left. Her thin white hair is in rollers and she is at-
tired in a cinnamon-colored kimono. As she enters she
is addressing her great-niece Nancy over her shoulder:
"No, I don't know which dress you mean, Nancy, but
it must be one of those in the back hall closet." Nancy's
eleven-year-old whine can be heard from within: "You
know the one, Aunt Lida; the one with the long sash."
Aunt Lida answers in an impatient but conciliating
voice: "I'll see. I'll see." She closes the door behind
her and moves across the stage taking the small, practiced ladylike steps of a long-legged woman who would
naturally move with great strides. She goes into the
service hall, closing the door behind her. Now quick
footsteps are heard on the dark stairway, and presently
a Negro houseboy, wearing an unbuttoned white
jacket, dashes up into the hall. He places a pair of
highly polished brown shoes by the door at the head*

of the stairs and turns at once to descend the stairs. Seeing the dark stair well before him, he inadvertently reaches out and flicks the light switch on the wall beside him. The light does not come on, and grinning at himself he says, "Ah, shoot!" Meanwhile, the older Negro woman has entered from a door at the right; she addresses him contemptuously: "Ain't fix 'at even yit, have you, Paris?" His grin broadens into a big, silly smile, showing a mouth full of gleaming white teeth: "I cain't fix it, Aunt Myra." He puts his hand on the rail and disappears down the stairway. Now Aunt Lida enters from the service hall with three of Nancy's dresses over her arm. She passes Myra, who is moving slowly toward the head of the stairs.

AUNT LIDA: What an hour of the day to be gotten up, eh, Myra?

MYRA: Ain't it the truth, Miss Lida? An' him not on this place more'n three times in ten year.

AUNT LIDA: But he was the only relative any of us have in Detroit, Myra.

MYRA: Not much kin. An' getting all them chillun up.

AUNT LIDA: I don't see why the children should be gotten up, but you know Mr. Robert.

MYRA: I know white folks.

AUNT LIDA: Listen here, don't you talk about white folks to me, Myra Willis. If it were *your* Cousin Harry, you'd be off work for a week. (*She has now opened the door to Nancy's room.*)

MYRA (*at the head of the stairs, looking down into the darkness; still addressing Aunt Lida*): Nobody ain't fix 'at light yit.

AUNT LIDA: Mr. Robert said he would do it today.

MYRA: He say.

AUNT LIDA: I know, I know. (*Closing the door behind her.*)

Mr. Wade opens the door of his room to fetch his shoes. Myra looks over her shoulder at him.

MR. WADE: Morning, Myra.

MYRA: It's still night to me. An' this here light ain't fix yit.

MR. WADE: By George, it's not. You tell Paris to bring the ladder up, and we'll fix it right now.

MYRA: Now? This now? At five o'clock in the mornin'? (*He picks up his shoes and closes the door.*)

MYRA: Lord God.

Miss Bluemeyer, the housekeeper, enters from the service hall. She is a large woman dressed in navy blue with tiny white ruffles at the collar. Her hair, cut like a man's, has obviously not been combed this morning, and she is still wearing her flat-heeled bedroom slippers. She is carrying a small tray with one cup of coffee and a silver sugar and cream set.

MISS BLUEMEYER: Are you in a great rush, Myra?

MYRA: Not me.

MISS BLUEMEYER: Then I would like to see you a minute, please. About something.

MYRA: Yassum.

Meanwhile, the housekeeper strides across the hall and knocks at the door at the head of the stairs.

MRS. WADE (*from within*): Just a minute! Who is it?

MISS BLUEMEYER: It is I. . . . Miss Bluemeyer.

Mrs. Wade opens the door. She is an extremely small woman of about forty. Her long brown hair falls about the shoulders of her negligee. She is pregnant.

MRS. WADE: Oh, I'm *so* much obliged to you, Miss Bluemeyer. You know that I'm not a bit of good till I've had my coffee. I'll just bet you had to make it yourself.

MISS BLUEMEYER: I did, Misses Wade. But that's all right; I made a cup for myself too.

MRS. WADE: Isn't it a hideous hour? (*Beginning to close the door.*)

MISS BLUEMEYER: Yes, it is, but I am awfully sorry about your cousin.

MRS. WADE: Yes, it is sad of course. He was very old, you know, and we knew him very little, really.

MISS BLUEMEYER: I see.

Mrs. Wade closes the door, and Miss Bluemeyer turns to Myra. With a movement of her head she indicates that Myra should follow her. Then she crosses the stage and seats herself at the telephone table. Myra follows and stands before Miss Bluemeyer, with her hands folded and resting against her white apron.

MISS BLUEMEYER (*smiling intimately and a little sadly*): Myra, tell me, did you ever know their Cousin Harry?—Mr. Wilson, that is.

MYRA: Yassum, oh, yassum. (*Casually.*) My sister Cora used to work for his own sister, Miss Jamie, in Nashville, way back yonder. Most of them Wilsons is dead though. He muss be the lass of 'em, I reckon.

MISS BLUEMEYER: That is not what I mean, Myra. I know that all of you knew one another back in Tennessee, but that is ten years or more—

MYRA: Yassum, we been in Deetroit ten year. Now, the two oldest chillun was born'd in Tennessee, but—

MISS BLUEMEYER: That is not what I mean, Myra. I mean—that is, I have been keeping house for Misses Wade nearly a year now and had never heard Cousin Harry's name—Mr. Wilson, that is to say—mentioned until his stroke a few weeks ago.

MYRA: No'm. He never come aroun' here much. He warn't congenial with 'em; that's all.

MISS BLUEMEYER: I . . . I did not mean to imply that there was more to it, Myra. I only mean that they are such wonderful people to feel so responsible for a person they hardly know.

MYRA (*quickly*): Yes'm, but he *war* kin to 'em.

MISS BLUEMEYER: Yet he never came to see them.

MYRA: It warn't because he warn't invited. (*Resentfully.*) He didn't care nothin' bout kinfolks. Stuck off to hisself and worked down in the depot up here. He was jess— (*Breaks off suddenly, and begins again with an entirely different tone.*) Well, anyhow, he 'uz kin to 'em, and the only one here kin to 'em. That's all.

MISS BLUEMEYER: I did not mean to be prying, you understand, Myra. It is only that it seems odd that they should make such to-do over a man they knew so slight.

MYRA: He didn't have no money, sho God.

MISS BLUEMEYER: That, Myra, is not what I meant.

MYRA: I don't know what you been meanin', Miss Bloomer, but he's daid an he war kin to 'em.

From the left the voice of Charles William, aged five and a half, is heard calling, "Myra! Myra!" A door is thrown open and a towheaded little boy rushes into the hall with his shoestrings flopping about.

CHARLES WILLIAM: Myra, Alfred won't tie my bows!

MYRA (*who has turned around and advanced several steps in his direction*): I'll buss his back wide op'n.

CHARLES WILLIAM: You tie 'em, Myra.

MYRA (*already on her knees before him*): Come here, chile.

CHARLES WILLIAM: Is Cousin-Harry-Wilson dead, Myra?

MYRA: Sho.

CHARLES WILLIAM: Was he eighty-three years old?

MYRA: 'Course he was, C.W.

CHARLES WILLIAM: Still?

MYRA: He'll be eighty-three from here out, C.W.

CHARLES WILLIAM (*obviously comforted, he places his hand on the head bent over before him*): I love you, Myra.

Myra lifts her dark oval face and grins broadly at him. He whispers to her, "You haven't got your teeth in, Myra." She bends with laughter as Charles William runs back to his room. During their conversation Miss Bluemeyer examines her wristwatch and the electric clock very closely. She dials a number on the telephone and says after a moment, "Will you repeat that? Will you repeat that?" She dials the number again and then sets her watch and moves the hand of the clock a frac-

tion of an inch. When Charles William is gone, she says:

Miss Bluemeyer: Myra—

Myra *(rising and moving toward the dark stairs)*: I got go fetch Paris an the ladder for Mista Robert. This here light!

Miss Bluemeyer: You *could* use the back stair, Myra.

Myra: Not me. Not them straight-up-and-down steps. (*She goes down the steps.*)

Miss Bluemeyer rises and strides toward one of the doors at right. Aunt Lida Wade opens the door from Nancy's room, left, and the two women face each other in silence a moment. "Oh," says Aunt Lida, "I thought you were my nephew, Mr. Wade." Miss Bluemeyer makes her exit, and Aunt Lida remains a moment to giggle girlishly. Then she withdraws into Nancy's room again and closes the door. Lennie enters from door at right and moves sluggishly across the hall to head of stairs. Aunt Lida opens her door again and says, "Oh, I thought you were my nephew Mr. Robert." Lennie answers, "No'm, it's jess me." Aunt Lida closes her door again, but before Lennie has begun to descend the stairs Mr. Robert Wade, master of the house, opens the door to his room and steps into the hall. Mr. Wade is six feet, three inches in height. His hair and his small mustache are dark. The belt to his silk dressing robe is tied, but the robe is not brought together in front; and so his dark trousers and white shirt and his bow tie may be seen. He wears usually a pouty expression on his face and has little to say except when giving directions or explaining some matter to his family.

MR. WADE: Lennie, a full half hour ago I sent word for Paris to bring me the ladder.

Lennie makes no answer but fairly dives down the dark stair well. Her feet on the steps make a frightful racket. Aunt Lida opens her door again.

AUNT LIDA: Well, now, did you ever? No wonder the women in the house have been insulted when I mistook their steps for yours. How do you do it?

MR. WADE: That was Myra's little niece descending the stair. (*He walks around to the front balustrade and leans out over the stairs to peer up at the fixture.*)

AUNT LIDA: Ah! the dungeon stair. This is the moment I've been waiting for. Rumor has got around that my nephew has roused his family at five A.M. to watch him change light bulbs over the stairway.

MR. WADE: True . . . true. (*Still looking up at the fixture.*) And, incidentally, my wife's cousin is dead.

AUNT LIDA (*matter-of-factly*): Poor Harry. You ought, in all conscience, to have made him come live with us years ago, Robert.

MR. WADE: He wouldn't live with his own sister, much less us. He had an allergy to the very idea of blood relations. (*Turning to Aunt Lida.*) You know, one of the few times I saw him he asked me how I could stand living under the same roof with you.

AUNT LIDA: I'm sure he did. And he told me that he left Tennessee to get away from his own flesh and blood, and that you and Margie and your younguns had to pursue him up here. (*They laugh merrily.*)

While they talk, the top of a ladder rises from the stair well.

AUNT LIDA: But we ought to have gotten him to come here and live, somehow.

MR. WADE: He'd have been miserable here, Aunt Lida. And he'd have made us more than miserable. He wouldn't have fitted in.

AUNT LIDA: Pooh! That's why it would have been all right. (*She whispers.*) When I selected Miss Blue-meyer for Margie's housekeeper I was careful to choose someone who wouldn't fit in. If she were congenial with us, her presence here would be an intrusion. That's why my presence is an intrusion, don't you see?

MR. WADE: Tut-tut, Auntie. (*Pronounced "ontee."*)

The head and shoulders of Paris have now appeared from the top landing where he is setting up the ladder. The ladder leans backward and forward, backward and forward, and Paris can be heard panting and grunting.

AUNT LIDA: Oh, but what I say about Miss Blue-meyer is really pretty true, Robert. She's always happy when we're sad, and sad when we're happy; and that's right convenient. This morning, for instance— Well, notice for yourself.

MR. WADE: Aunt Lida, you're just awful! The poor woman.

AUNT LIDA: Why, I'm crazy about her. She's perfect. And have you seen her this morning? She's mourning your Cousin Harry, as none of us would think of do-ing— Poor old codger's got his blessed relief at last— and, Robert (*rolling her eyes thoughtfully*), she never even saw him once, did she? Once even? No! . . . But if she were showing the kind of relief that we feel for him, it *would* be kind of bad, now. You see!

MR. WADE: Oh, what difference does it make that she's— (*Breaking off.*) What *in* the devil?

He whirls about. Paris, having steadied the ladder and having climbed uneasily to the top of it, has been sitting there tapping first his lip and then his forehead with his finger, trying hard to think of something, then with a stupid but still speculative expression on his face he has reached down and brought up a long broom with the handle of which he has now bent forward and poked (between the balusters) the back of Mr. Wade's knee. Mr. Wade's knee bends slightly. He whirls about, saying, "What in the devil." Paris jerks back the broom, gives a short, hysterical laugh, and splutters out:

PARIS: Mista Robert!

MR. WADE: What in the name of sin do you mean by that, boy!

PARIS (*solemnly*): Somehow, I couldn't call yo name, Mista Robert, why you reckon? Couldn't think of it till you whull aroun an say, "Whut *in* de debil?" (*Catching Mr. Wade's exact intonation.*)

MR. WADE (*leaving Aunt Lida, who stands in openmouthed wonder and amazement at Paris's behavior, and going round the balustrade to the head of the stair*): Come down off that ladder! Did you bring the screw driver and the bulb?

PARIS: I brung the screw driber, Mista Robert.

MR. WADE: Well, go brung me a big bulb and a dust rag from the pantry.

Paris disappears from the ladder and down the stairs. Mr. Wade has now come down the stairs to the landing and climbed to the top of the ladder. The ladder shakes violently, and Aunt Lida cries out in a voice unlike her rather deep speaking voice:

AUNT LIDA: Robert, mind; do be careful, honey!

MR. WADE: Careful, hell! (*He clambers down the ladder.*) Paris! Paris, you come hold this ladder for me!

At the sound of Aunt Lida's voice doors from both right and left and from the back are opened. Now the children come one by one to the head of the stairs and watch their father who is climbing the ladder again. The two older children come first and watch their father in silence; they are Nancy, from left, and James, from right—aged eleven and twelve respectively. Quick on James's heels come Charles William who is five and a half, and behind him Alfred, aged nine, still wearing the "niggery" stocking cap he sleeps in. Then the fifth child, Lida Sue, the youngest of all, comes chattering. No one can understand what she says, for she has been slow learning to talk and now at four she stammers and lisps alternately. When the doors to the children's rooms opened, the door to their parents' room, at the head of the stairs, opened also; and Mrs. Wade, having glanced at her husband and smiled at Aunt Lida, has turned back into her room, leaving the door open. Her hair is now pinned up, and she wears a maternity dress. She can be seen moving about the room, making up the bed, etc. During the conversation that follows, Lida Sue, instead of watching her father, as she has sat down to do, allows her attention to be distracted by the glimpse she has had of her mother, and lying back on the floor and rolling on her left side she watches her mother's movements in the room. Aunt Lida, still wearing her cinnamon-colored kimono, has moved away from the balustrade on which the children are now leaning. She stands, arms akimbo, in the center of the hall with the back of her head of sparse, uncombed, gray hair to the audience.

AUNT LIDA (*to Mrs. Wade in a loud voice*): Margie, he's taking the whole business apart, screw by screw.

MRS. WADE (*from the bedroom*): It's the only way to do it, Aunt Lida.

AUNT LIDA: He has poor Paris holding the ladder, who ought to be down setting the table.

MRS. WADE: There's plenty of time. (*Still from the bedroom.*)

AUNT LIDA: I should say plenty of time. The greatest plenty. There was no earthly reason in his getting the whole house up at this hour.

MRS. WADE: No sense, I admit. (*Only slight interest.*)

AUNT LIDA: And did you ever in your life hear of a man's choosing such a time for such a job?

MRS. WADE: Never in my life. (*Complete indifference.*)

AUNT LIDA: I've been after him for weeks to do it, myself, and I know you have. There's really no earthly reason why Paris shouldn't learn to take down a chandelier. Otherwise, let's take him back to Tennessee and bring Mamie's brother up here. Or let Paris learn to drive, and bring Sellars in the house. Sellars's too old

113

to drive, anyway. (*She pauses. All of this is being deliv-ered in a shaky but resonant voice that Mrs. Wade and possibly even the servants in the kitchen can hear.*) Sellars can do anything if you show him once. But the main thing, though, is the time for such a job, the un-heard of hour of the morn . . .

MR. WADE (*interrupting with a booming voice, his early morning hoarseness adding to the onomatopoeic effect*): Thunderation, Aunt Lida!

Aunt Lida seems only to have been waiting for this; immediately she dismisses from her mind the problem of the light fixture and all of this business in the hall. She raises her little right forefinger to her chin and frowns meditatively, trying to recollect for what she has originally come into the hall. Then of a sudden she turns and goes out the door leading to the service hall.

MR. WADE: Now, you see, children, this is not a very simple undertaking. Each of the glass sections must be removed separately, and for each there are three screws. Observe: one at the top and one on each side. Now, this protector must be broken down into its five com-ponent parts, and to do this you must understand the real structure of the fixture. Mind, now. *All* of the five pieces must be removed before the bulb—because of its large size—can be inserted. Once the bulb is in, each piece must be dusted and cleared of all dead bugs, lint, dust, trash, et cetera before being replaced.

Mr. Wade works in silence for several moments. Then suddenly the light shines brightly above the stair well. Mr. Wade, atop the ladder in a white shirt and

114

a polka-dot bow tie with a sprinkling of dust on his black mustache, is a bright figure of enchantment for the five children who all fix a charmed gaze upon him, like five little green-eyed kittens. The spell is so absolute that they are momentarily blind and deaf to the sudden hilarious commotion on the part of Paris. This lantern-jawed houseboy, whose complexion is a dull copper color, who is supposed to be giving support to the unsteady ladder, has become so convulsed by laughter that he has thrown his whole weight against the ladder. One stern word of rebuke from Mr. Wade, however, makes Paris jump back from the quivering ladder.

MR. WADE: Get away from this ladder, you idiot!

Paris runs up the steps until he is in plain view of the audience. He continues to cavort about, twisting and bending his body, completely unable to restrain himself, giggling and pointing to the mirror on the wall beyond the stairs. All the while he is sputtering, "Look-a-there! Look-a-there!" and pointing to the mirror. Mr. Wade sits uneasily atop the ladder, staring at Paris in exasperation. As Paris runs up the steps, the children by the balustrade all turn their faces toward him but move not a muscle in their bodies.

PARIS: Do y' see what I see, Mista Robert? Look-a-there, Mista Robert.

Slowly the five children move their eyes from the houseboy to the mirror opposite them. Then Mr. Wade, steadying himself on the ladder, looks in the mirror too. What he sees there are the eight brown-

115

stockinged legs of the four older children and the row of brown balusters interspersed with the legs.

PARIS: I thought them posts was movin'! They's jest alike—all of them legs and all them little stair posts, Mista Robert. In the mirror they all seem alike—posts and legs. Same size an same color. (*His words are interrupted now and again by his own giggling.*)

Mr. Wade's mustache twitches involuntarily, and his eyes narrow into little slits. Then he looks into the mirror for the first time. Recognizing the ridiculous likeness of the legs to the balusters, he tosses back his head and laughs aloud. And the children one by one, even down to Lida Sue, who has picked herself up from the floor, join in the laughter. Their mirth has just reached its peak when Miss Bluemeyer, the house-keeper, appears from left. Her short hair is now combed, and she has exchanged her slippers for a pair of oxfords. She advances toward the head of the stairs without showing any interest in the cause of their mirth. She passes the children with a tolerant smile, affecting to be absorbed in her own thoughts. When she reaches the head of the stairs, Lida Sue and Paris step to one side; and Lida Sue reaches for the Negro man's hand which she holds until the housekeeper has passed. Miss Bluemeyer descends the first three or four steps and then stops as she addresses Mr. Wade.

MISS BLUEMEYER: If you will pardon me, Mr. Wade, I would like to try and get by. I am going to run down and see how breakfast is going.

MR. WADE: Good morning, Miss. Isn't that a sight up there in the mirror?

MISS BLUEMEYER (*glancing briefly in the general direction of the glass*): Oh, yes, isn't it? (*She takes another step as she speaks.*) I was going to say— (*She begins, but finding Mr. Wade's eyes fastened on her she hesitates.*) If you will pardon me, Mr. Wade, I must ask you to let me pass. (*Fearlessly, courageously.*)

MR. WADE (*sternly*): I suggest that you use the back stairs since we haven't quite finished operations here, Miss Bluemeyer.

Miss Bluemeyer gazes defiantly at Mr. Wade for a moment, then at Paris and Lida Sue, then at the four children who are lined up along the balustrade and who, like sheep, have drawn closer together, their slight movement having been almost imperceptible to the audience.

MISS BLUEMEYER (*utterly without expression, as though answering a question about the day of the week or the title of a book*): Good morning, kiddies. (*Presently she retreats to the head of the stairs, at which point she stops to address Mr. Wade again.*) I was going to say that when Paris has put away the ladder, it will be time to set the table for breakfast. That is, if you have an early breakfast in mind, Mr. Wade.

MR. WADE: I had an early breakfast in mind, Miss Bluemeyer, for there is a busy day ahead for us all.

MISS BLUEMEYER (*in a sympathetic stage whisper*): The funeral won't be until tomorrow, I presume, Mr. Wade?

MR. WADE: Well . . . there'll be a little service in the undertaker's chapel today. I'm taking the body back to Tennessee on the train tonight.

MISS BLUEMEYER: I see . . . I see. (*In a gentle voice, full of sentimentality.*) He must have been a fine old man—Mr. Wilson. The few times I saw him he seemed very, very polite. I imagine to ladies especially, being Southern.

MR. WADE: I suppose so. . . . Yes, I suppose he was. (*He turns his attention back to the light fixture for a moment, and then as though only now realizing what she has said he turns again to her with a little jerk of his head.*) Did I understand you to say you had seen him? But I didn't know you had ever seen our cousin, Miss Bluemeyer.

MISS BLUEMEYER: Oh, really? (*Significantly, as though perceiving that there had been some conversation about her not having seen Mr. Wilson.*)

MR. WADE: Yes, indeed . . . really. (*With parts of the fixture in his hands he goes down several rungs of the ladder, then jumping nimbly off onto the stairs and coming up into the hall he hands these pieces to Paris. Miss Bluemeyer has meanwhile moved past the children and as far as the telephone table in the direction of the door to the service hall.*) I don't recall Mr. Wilson's having been to see us since you came, Miss Bluemeyer.

MISS BLUEMEYER: That is quite right.

MR. WADE (*his usually direct manner exaggerated somewhat*): Miss Bluemeyer, I think you are behaving and speaking in a mighty strange manner.

MISS BLUEMEYER: I am sorry if that is your opinion, Mr. Wade.

MR. WADE: Well, I think . . .

MISS BLUEMEYER: Remember, I am not one of the servants, Mr. Wade, not one of your servants.

When Mr. Wade came up into the hall, all of the children turned about and faced him and Miss Bluemeyer; and now he turns and gives them a "look" which sends them off quietly but quickly to their rooms, the older ones leading the younger. Paris, who has until this time been standing on the stairs with the parts of the light fixture in his hands, now moves down toward the ladder, ascends it, and begins hurriedly and skillfully to reassemble the fixture.

MR. WADE: I am aware that you are not one of the servants, and I am not speaking to you as such. In fact, I don't mean to provoke any unpleasantness this morning.

MISS BLUEMEYER (*repentantly, mournfully*): And *I* am truly sorry to have been any bother this morning, Mr. Wade—this morning of all mornings. The truth is I used to see Mr. Wilson elsewhere. I never met him, you understand.

MR. WADE: I see. But you never mentioned having seen him to my wife or my aunt?

MISS BLUEMEYER: I didn't know the family would be interested that I had seen him. You understand, he lived a door from a lady with whom I am great friends.

MR. WADE: I see, I see.

MISS BLUEMEYER: He was a solitary figure, Mr. Wade, and this friend of mine had noticed him. She is an invalid, you understand, and when I was staying with her she would sometimes look out the window and say, "There goes that old Mr. Wilson. He seems to be an independent sort like us, Madge." That is all there was to it, Mr. Wade, and I used to notice him quite of-ten.

MR. WADE: But this happened when you were staying with your invalid friend?

MISS BLUEMEYER: Yes. You will think it is odd, I know, but that was before I even came here, Mr. Wade.

MR. WADE: I was thinking just that. And when was it you first made the connection between your Mr. Wilson and our Cousin Harry Wilson? That is, when did you discover that the old man you watched from your friend's window was my wife's cousin?

MISS BLUEMEYER: Only the shortest time ago, Mr. Wade, only a few weeks. Only when I happened to mention to this friend of mine that Misses Wade's only relative in Detroit had had a stroke. "What is his name, Madge?" she asked me. I told her his name and she said, "Why, Madge, that must be the same old Mr. Wilson I have pointed out to you. They tell me *he's* had a stroke," she said. It quite struck me at the time, Mr. Wade, that it was quite a coincidence, but I didn't want to bother the family at the time in their grief with idle, outside talk.

MR. WADE: Of course not. I'm sure you didn't. And it was very considerate of you.

A pause, during which Mr. Wade straightens his tie and casts his eyes about the room as though trying to decide how this conversation should be concluded.

MISS BLUEMEYER: If you would not think it was too odd, Mr. Wade, would you mind telling me to what funeral home the remains will go?

MR. WADE: Why! (*Taken aback.*) Of course I wouldn't mind. To Lewis Brothers, I believe.

MISS BLUEMEYER: Lewis Brothers, you say? I don't believe I have heard of . . . ?

MR. WADE: No, it's a small, uh, shop, uh, concern on the other side of town. But the Lewises were from Tennessee, from my mother's county, and my aunt thought it would be—uh—nice.

MISS BLUEMEYER: I see . . . yes . . . Well I *do* thank you, Mr. Wade. (*Turning quickly to Paris, as though to change the subject.*) Paris, you can set the table now!

She walks rapidly toward the door to the service hall. As she reaches for the door knob, the door opens and Aunt Lida enters with still another dress for Nancy, a black one. Paris has meanwhile reassembled the light fixture. Mr. Wade turns toward him and exclaims in genuine surprise at Paris's achievement, "Say!" Simultaneously Mrs. Wade enters from the door to her room.

MR. WADE: Boy, how did you know how to put that thing together?

PARIS (*giving one glance at Mr. Wade*): I had to do somepn to make myself scass. I thought you gwine eat 'at woman alive, way you come down off 'at ladder.

AUNT LIDA: What in the world do you make of it, Margie?

MRS. WADE: What do you think, Aunt Lida?

The two women have met in the center of the stage, in front of Mr. Wade, and by first addressing each other, instead of Mr. Wade whose conversation has roused their interest, they reveal their mutual sympathy and understanding and their slight regard for

121

any interpretation which Mr. Wade might put upon his own conversation.

MR. WADE (*having completely forgotten the episode with Miss Bluemeyer*): Margie! Aunt Lida! Look what Paris has learned! (*Paris sits beaming atop the ladder.*)

AUNT LIDA (*paying no attention to him*): Did you hear every word of what she said?

MRS. WADE: I think so.

AUNT LIDA: I could hear every word. She said she had watched him from her friend's window even before she came here. All through his sickness she has known he was the man she and her cripple friend watched. She *is* a weird one, now, I'll tell you.

MRS. WADE: It's a curious picture, isn't it—those two lonely women watching that lonely old man. Why hasn't she spoken of it, do you suppose?

MR. WADE: Margie! Aunt Lida! This is a great day. This is important. This is a turning point in Paris's life, in the life of us all. He has learned to put that fixture together. Now he can have a try at the chandelier downstairs. (*When the women continue to take no notice of him, Paris begins to descend the ladder.*)

AUNT LIDA: It's from sheer perversity that she hasn't mentioned it, poor creature. She seems to delight in the dreariness of her own life and in finding other dreary "solitary figures." And I suppose we mustn't begrudge her her greatest pleasure.

Paris has now disappeared down the ladder, and as the ladder is seen being slowly lowered from view, Mr. Wade begins to show interest in what the women are saying.

MR. WADE: Now, Auntie, awhile ago it was her sheer perversity that made Miss Blue so suitable for our household. You know, I think you are downright vicious about that "poor creature."

AUNT LIDA: Why, I'm not at all, Robert Wade!

MR. WADE: Indeed, you are. You seem to have developed a special voice, a special expression, a special vocabulary for talking about her.

MRS. WADE: That's nonsense, Robert. How could you accuse Aunt Lida of being vicious about *any*body, *ever?*

AUNT LIDA: There, you see.

MRS. WADE: A fine way your house would be in if it weren't for Aunt Lida. And your children, and your wife, and yourself!

MR. WADE (*waving his hands before his face*): I didn't mean to start such a furor. I wasn't serious. That is, it's not a very serious crime of Aunt Lida's. That Bluemeyer is a strange duck. Anybody can see that.

AUNT LIDA: Now who's being cruel? I am interested in all people, Robert, and am not without sympathy for . . .

MR. WADE: But this seems a very special—. You have a wonderful interest in the ways and doings of all your friends and especially in your family, in us particularly (*indicating this household, by a gesture*). A kindly, gentle, womanly interest. You have a real knowledge of people, too. You know us all better than we know each other. You are a wonderful, wonderful woman, Aunt Lida, and we couldn't live without you.

But (*holding up one finger*) I still maintain that regarding Miss Blue—

AUNT LIDA: Her name is not . . .

MRS. WADE: Robert! What nonsense!

AUNT LIDA: And at such an hour. (*Unruffled.*)

When interrupted, Mr. Wade turned and began walking toward the door to his room. Now he hesitates at the doorway.

MR. WADE: Has my blue serge come back from the cleaner's, Aunt Lida?

AUNT LIDA: It'll be back today, Robert.

Mr. Wade goes into his room and closes the door. Mrs. Wade moves to the front of the stage and sits down in one of the upholstered chairs, at left.

MRS. WADE: Where are the children, Aunt Lida?

AUNT LIDA (*calling, in a voice almost as deep as Mr. Wade's*): Chill-drun!

Doors on both sides of the stage open. The children peer out at their Aunt Lida.

AUNT LIDA: Come say good morning to your mama-dear.

The children run across the stage to Mrs. Wade, all hugging and kissing her at once, saying, "Good morning, Mama-dear. Good morning, Mama-dear. How pretty you are, Mama." Mrs. Wade kisses each of them, pushing the older ones slightly aside in order to lean over and kiss little Lida Sue who says, "P-p-puhty muh-muh." Aunt Lida watches approvingly. Presently she says:

AUNT LIDA: Not one of you has noticed how charmingly your mama-dear has done up her beautiful hair this morning.

MRS. WADE: Aunt Lida, I declare! (*Smiling and shaking her head.*)

All of the children go behind her chair and admire her coiffure, Nancy lifting Lida Sue up to where she can see.

JAMES: It's all plaited and fixed.

NANCY: It's fixed in a bun. It's charming, Mama-dear.

ALFRED: How long is it now, Mama-dear?

MRS. WADE: Too long, too long. I'm going to cut it again before . . .

CHILDREN: No, no, no.

AUNT LIDA (*coming forward*): We won't let her cut that beautiful hair, will we, children? . . . Nancy, let me fix your sash. It's all twisted.

MRS. WADE: It's impractical. Especially now. It will be too much trouble.

AUNT LIDA: Nonsense. We'll take turns arranging it for you. We'll never let her cut this beautiful hair, will we, children?

CHILDREN: Never, never.

MRS. WADE: I'll do as I like about my hair, thank you, all. You'll some day all be sorry for spoiling me so. I'll be the spoiledest of spoiled women. I'll cut off all my hair and wear a ring in my nose, just to show you I can if I want to.

The children are delighted and they scream with laughter. "No, no, we won't let you, we won't let you."

MRS. WADE: I will. And I'll wear tow sacks for

125

dresses and old tennis shoes with the toes cut out. I'll wear a stocking cap like Alfred's.

The children laugh again and chant, "No, never. No, never. No, never."

AUNT LIDA: Turn around, Charles William. I do believe you've managed to get your bottom rompers on backward again.

CHARLES WILLIAM: I like 'em.

AUNT LIDA: Stand still, child. (*She has got down on one knee and begun unbuttoning his little pants. Without more words about it, she makes him step out of his pants; she turns them around and puts them on properly. Meanwhile, Charles William continues to gaze at his mother.*) (*Addressing the children as she buttons-up Charles William.*) We're going to keep Mama-dear the ornament of this household, aren't we? She ought to let us get her a personal maid, instead of a housekeeper.

MRS. WADE: One day you'll all be sorry. And I can hear you mumbling behind my back about *she.*

AUNT LIDA: Take off that stocking cap, Alfred. You'll be bald before you're in long pants. (*Alfred hesitates, turns his face away and gazes at the wall, pouting.*) Take it off, Alfred, I said. (*He snatches off the cap, revealing a flat pompadour with every hair in place, and continues to stare at the wall, right.*) Look at him pouting, children. Stick a pin in his cheeks and they'd pop like a balloon. (*The children laugh; even Alfred gives up pouting and laughs with them.*) Margie, every one of your children has a different way of pouting while being reprimanded. Only a slightly different way, however, for they are all gazers. Alfred here gazes at a blank wall. James likes to gaze up at the ceiling. (*She mimics each as she describes his form of gazing. The children and Mrs. Wade laugh appreciatively after each piece of mimicry.*) Nancy is a window gazer. Charles William is a hand gazer, or a plate gazer, if we're at the table.

JAMES: What about Lida Sue, Aunt Lida?

AUNT LIDA (*still on one knee after buttoning Charles William's pants, she turns to Lida Sue, who is nearby*): Why, she's the fearless type who stares a hole right through you and makes you feel that you couldn't possibly be right. (*She places her hands on Lida Sue's shoulders and stares, with a ridiculous frown. Lida Sue and the other children laugh hysterically. But Mrs. Wade has become aware of the presence of Miss Bluemeyer who has entered several moments before from the service hall with Mrs. Wade's breakfast on a tray. Mrs. Wade watches the housekeeper whose eyes are fixed on Aunt Lida. During that moment Mr. Wade, now wearing his suit coat, enters from the bedroom.*)

MR. WADE (*observing all that is taking place*): Is there breakfast for the rest of us downstairs, Miss Bluemeyer?

MISS BLUEMEYER: Yes, there is, Mr. Wade.

MR. WADE: Then let's break up this dog and pony show, what say? Breakfast, children! James! Nancy!

The children go frolicking to the head of the stairs and disappear down the steps. Aunt Lida has got to her feet and turned about so quickly that she catches Miss Bluemeyer's gaze still upon her.

AUNT LIDA: Is my petticoat showing, Miss Bluemeyer?

MISS BLUEMEYER: No, Miss Wade, not that I can see.

AUNT LIDA: Then, what is it, please? You were staring so, I thought something must be wrong. (*She pretends to examine her dress.*)

MISS BLUEMEYER: I beg your pardon.

MR. WADE (*coming forward; cordially*): Ah, that's a mighty fine-looking breakfast a certain person's going to get this morning. (*Taking the tray from Miss Bluemeyer.*) Ah, look-a-here. I believe they've got you on double rations, Margie.

MRS. WADE (*clearing the coffee table that Aunt Lida has pushed before her*): Well, I should think so.

Miss Bluemeyer, continuing to scrutinize the group until the very last, has finally retreated down the front stairs. Aunt Lida goes and looks over the balustrade into the stair well. Mr. and Mrs. Wade observe her action and exchange glances.

MR. WADE: Now, Aunt Lida! What is it? What's the matter? If that woman bothers you so, why don't you give her her walking papers?

MRS. WADE: Don't talk so, Robert. Don't make a mountain out of a molehill.

AUNT LIDA: No, dear. He's right. This is more than a molehill. When I looked over the bannister just now I could see Miss Bluemeyer. She was running her hand through her hair, like this, and clenching her other fist with all her might. (*She comes to the front of the stage and speaks, as to herself, while Mr. and Mrs.*

128

Wade look on in wide-eyed amazement.) That poor, embittered creature! My God, my God, when I looked down that stair well I felt that I had been given a quick glimpse of a soul suffering the tortures of hell. (*Turning to Mrs. Wade.*) And it's our happiness that is her hell, mind you, Margie. She can't abide the sight of our family happiness. Particularly not this morning when one of her sort—a man who reveled in his own bitterness and despised all those who tried to make his life a less lonesome, a less dreary business—lies dead in an undertaker's parlor. She cannot endure the presence of our happiness. Particularly not mine. (*Now angrily.*) Can you tell me how the good Lord can endure the existence of such a mean and jealous being in His world? She watched me there on my knees fondling those children, and it filled her with nothing but resentment and hatred. (*Quietly again.*) No, you are right, Robert. She shall have her proverbial walking papers the moment you and the corpse of our Cousin Harry are safely on the night train to Tennessee.

MR. WADE: Aunt Lida, what a tirade! What a fit of temper! And at such an hour of the morning! Who ever heard of making such an important decision before breakfast?

Aunt Lida stares blankly at Mr. Wade for a moment; then she turns her face slowly from him to the audience. She is not smiling and she makes no answer. She doesn't seem to have heard what he said.

CURTAIN

129

SCENE II

*The curtain rises on a second scene in the upstairs hall.
It is the evening of the same day. One table lamp is
lit, front and left, and as the curtain rises Miss Bluemeyer switches on the desk lamp, seats herself, and
begins dialing a number on the telephone. She is alone
in the hall. The Wade family is still at dinner. During
the late afternoon a funeral service has been held in
the undertaker's chapel.*

MISS BLUEMEYER (*speaking into the telephone*):
Merton? It's Bluemeyer speaking. Quite well, thank
you. And you? Oh, that's too bad. (*Pause.*) Well, let
me tell you . . . (*Pause.*) Ah, that's too bad, Merton.
(*Pause.*) I want to tell you . . . (*Pause.*) Well, have
you taken something? (*Pause.*) Merton, I want to tell
you . . . (*Impatiently.*) Of course I am interested in
how you feel, but you said yourself for me to call you
when they got back. Yes, they have been back a couple
of hours, Merton. . . . No. . . . Why, I mean exactly
this: When I talked to you a few hours ago, when they
had just left for the funeral home—all but Misses
Wade. She didn't go; she took her nap.—I said to you
then, you remember, they were sure to guess whose
flowers they were. Yes, I know you thought so too,
Merton, and that is not what I am calling to tell you.
We both knew they would, and I have already heard
all about it, but not the last of it, I am afraid. This is
what I mean: I dreaded, as you said you dreaded for
me, that they would come home all sentimentalized

130

and would gush over me with their thanks. The thing I was afraid of, Merton, was that they would think I was playing up to them. . . . Don't rush me, Merton. I will tell you the whole story right now if there is time. They are all at dinner now, you see, and if I am interrupted I will call you back from the kitchen phone when the Negroes have gone to bed. . . . I *am* going to get on with it, Merton. Don't be rude to your best friend. On the card I sent with the flowers, you remember, I had the young man write, "From Two Friends." Well, when *she* came back with the rest of the family, from the funeral, she had our card tucked in her little gray glove. I was downstairs in the side hall, you understand, when they came in, and she just stopped beside me for a minute as though she were thinking of something. Then she slips the card out, like she was a magician— She had that air, Merton, that I should be surprised where she got it—and says in a deep, businesslike voice, "Many thanks, Miss Bluemeyer, and thank the other friend for the family of the bereaved." Bereaved, indeed! They spent breakfast poking their sly fun at the child Nancy for wanting to wear a black dress. . . . No, that is all there was to it, Merton. No, not a question about who the other friend was. No, not another word, not from any of them. . . . No, I didn't want their thanks any more than you. What I mean is they have hardly spoke another word to me since, except about the usual things. Dinner was just awful, and I left just now without dessert. I couldn't have eat (*pronounced eet*) it, and the children carrying on so as if nobody had ever passed away, much less a poor lonesome old man. But the grownups are all hopping mad, I can tell you. *Mad,* you understand, because we had the presumption to send flowers to somebody who was their relation. Wouldn't you think *she* would understand, though, Merton, how it is. . . . Of course, she does, and she is ashamed. If *he* had been one of those who care to fawn over their relations, as *she* has! Anybody who has so little pride and independence, indeed! Of course, I know you know, but . . . (*Hearing someone on the stairs.*) Well, that will be all. Thank you. Good-by, Merton. (*Sotto voce.*) Of course, I am not angry. Somebody's . . . Yes. Good-by, Merton.

Mr. and Mrs. Wade are ascending the stairs, arm in arm. Miss Bluemeyer moves toward her room, at right. Lennie enters from door to service hall, right and back.

MISS BLUEMEYER (*just before entering her room*): Lennie, you need not turn down my bed tonight. I have some patterns spread out.

LENNIE: Yehsm.

Miss Bluemeyer closes the door behind her. Lennie enters the boys' room through the other door, right. Mr. and Mrs. Wade come forward and take seats in the sitting-room end of the hall, extreme left. They have been talking quietly as they came up the stairs and crossed the hall. Now their words become audible.

MR. WADE: The children couldn't have behaved better. I think even Lida Sue would have behaved all right if I had taken her.

MRS. WADE: I still feel a little as though I should have been there. Mama always felt so sorry for Cousin

Harry. She used to say he was offish and surly even as a child. He never *was* happy.

MR. WADE: God! Eighty-three years of it! . . . Well, did you wire Cousin Lula what time I arrive with the body?

MRS. WADE: Oh, I wired her this morning. They'll want to have a little service in Nashville, I'm sure.

MR. WADE: Oh, I'm *sure* they will. And I suppose I'll have to attend that too?

MRS. WADE: Darling, I hope you will. It'll mean so much to them.

MR. WADE: I know. I know. And it won't be nearly so bad without Aunt Lida there.

MRS. WADE: Did she really behave badly?

MR. WADE: Well, I don't suppose the undertakers noticed, and there was nobody else to notice it. But as soon as they brought in that big wreath—it was a tremendous thing (*he holds his hands out to indicate the size*)—she took herself up to where they set it by the coffin and looked at the card.

MRS. WADE: And just what did the card say?

MR. WADE: "From Two Friends."

MRS. WADE (*smiling*): Isn't that incredible?

MR. WADE: And a strange expression came over Aunt Lida's face that didn't leave it until after we were home. She sat through the whole service as stiff as a broom and didn't sing a word of either hymn.

MRS. WADE: She was obviously making her plans. I doubt if Miss Bluemeyer will still be on the place as late as noon tomorrow.

MR. WADE: Do you think she'll let her stay the night?

MRS. WADE: Aunt Lida ought to restrain herself. The woman is merely peculiar. I wish you would talk to Aunt Lida about it before you go, Robert.

MR. WADE: *You* will have to talk to her, Margie. She has never been known to take a man's advice on anything but money matters.

MRS. WADE: Aunt Lida's a mighty clever woman.

MR. WADE: Be serious, dear. There's more in this than meets the eye.

MRS. WADE: Speak for your own eye, Robert.

MR. WADE: Then, what is it? I know I am a mere unimaginative man, but . . .

MRS. WADE (*casually, as she settles herself in her chair*): You make us out awfully ugly, honey—Aunt Lida and me.

MR. WADE: And how do you two make me out?

MRS. WADE: I really think you are coming to believe literally in our womanly contempt for mankind. I think you're good for lots more than breadwinning, my love. Our contempt is only skin deep. It's only a tiresome old joke that makes life easier for two women under the same roof.

MR. WADE: I wish it made it easier for three. . . . Tell me, then, what is it you see in this business that I don't see? What is it about Miss Bluemeyer's queerness that disturbs Aunt Lida so? Are we only detecting the first signs of old age in her?

MRS. WADE: It has nothing to do with old age. It is simply that someone has entered the field who won't play the game according to Aunt Lida's rules.

MR. WADE: What sort of nonsense is that? You and Aunt Lida are forever . . .

MRS. WADE: Robert Wade, stop linking me with your aunt as though there were no difference between us.

MR. WADE: Then her age . . .

MRS. WADE: I'm not speaking of the difference in our ages. Don't you really know that your wife and your maiden aunt are two quite different people? (*Hotly.*) If you haven't perceived *that* in thirteen years, how can you hope to comprehend the niceties of a problem between your maiden aunt and an old-maid housekeeper?

MR. WADE: What in the devil are you getting so worked up about?

MRS. WADE: Worked up! I say!

MR. WADE: Have you and Aunt Lida been quarreling, too?

MRS. WADE: Have we . . . ? (*Quietly.*) God in heaven, give me strength. For the ten years we have been in Detroit, Robert Wade, your Aunt Lida and I haven't had a cross word; and now you ask me calmly, have we been quarreling!

MR. WADE: And why is that such an outlandish question?

MRS. WADE: Don't you really know why it is? And don't you really know why Aunt Lida and I have such smooth sailing? It's because we have arranged our lives as we have. It's because Aunt Lida and I have played our roles so perfectly, as we've always seen them played in Tennessee: She, the maiden aunt, responsible and

135

capable! I, the beautiful young wife, the bearer of children, the reigning queen! (*She laughs, and Mr. Wade jumps to his feet, obviously alarmed.*) Why, suh, sometimes ah can almos' heah the darkies a-croonin' in the quawtuhs! (*Her laughter is now definitely hysterical.*)

MR. WADE: Margie, I won't have you flying off like this!

MRS. WADE (*coming to her feet*): I may fly off further than you think. (*Then she bursts into tears and throws her arms about his neck, weeping on his shirt front.*) Robert, forgive me. You know I adore Aunt Lida. (*But she continues to weep.*)

MR. WADE (*putting his arms around her*): There, darling. Of course you do.

As he eases her into her chair again, Miss Bluemeyer throws open her door and hurries across the stage.

MISS BLUEMEYER: Oh, the dear thing! She has been such a brave lady up until now. It has been a very sad day for her, and I feel . . .

MR. WADE (*seated on Mrs. Wade's chair arm with his arms still around her; to Miss Bluemeyer*): Hold on, ma'am. You're mistaken.

MISS BLUEMEYER: Indeed, I have been very much mistaken. Grief has strange ways, Mr. Wade. Let me get her a cup of coffee.

She turns and strides toward the door to the service hall. Suddenly she faces Lennie who has been observing events from the door to the boys' room.

MISS BLUEMEYER: Lennie, bring Misses Wade a cup of coffee.

LENNIE: Yehsm, but she's jess having a nachal spell.

MISS BLUEMEYER: A natural spell?

LENNIE (*impatiently*): She's six months gone, Miss Bloomer. (*She goes to fetch the coffee.*)

MISS BLUEMEYER: She's . . . ? Oh, of course.

The housekeeper glances quickly in the direction of Mr. and Mrs. Wade, and her glance is met by Mr. Wade's glare. She turns and makes a hurried exit into her own room. Aunt Lida's voice is heard on the stairs, and the three children come romping up the steps ahead of her.

MRS. WADE (*completely recovered*): How silly of me.

MR. WADE: That Bluemeyer woman *is* morbid, Margie.

MRS. WADE: You mustn't worry yourself about her, Robert. What time does your train leave?

AUNT LIDA (*crossing from head of stairs to sitting room*): Robert, I told Paris to bring up your Gladstone. Isn't that what he should take, Margie?

MRS. WADE: I think so, Aunt Lida.

AUNT LIDA (*standing, hands clasped loosely before her*): You feel like packing for him, don't you, Margie?

MRS. WADE: There, you see, Robert!

AUNT LIDA: See what, Margie?

MR. WADE: Yes, what?

MRS. WADE: *He* knows very well what.

Charles William has now climbed on his mother's knees. Alfred is tugging at his father's hand. Lida Sue is walking round and round Aunt Lida.

AUNT LIDA: You children run and play.

ALFRED: Can we play in your room, Aunt Lida?

AUNT LIDA (*severely*): Yes, but don't touch one thing

137

on my dresser. (*They scamper away to Aunt Lida's room, left.*)

MRS. WADE: I've made a little scene since we came upstairs, Aunt Lida. I've had a good cry and everything.

AUNT LIDA: Are you feeling right tired, honey?

MRS. WADE: I guess I am. I must be awfully tired, for I was protesting Robert's linking our names so eternally.

MR. WADE: Jealous of you, Aunt Lida!

AUNT LIDA: Pshaw! It *is* tiresome of you, Robert.

MRS. WADE: And what I was just now pointing out to him was an example of how well we know our roles and how clearly defined are our spheres of authority. (*Turning to Mr. Wade.*) Aunt Lida saw to it that your bag should be brought up, but she would leave the packing of it to me.

AUNT LIDA (*in good nature*): Now, if I am to be embarrassed by your referring to your private conversations about me, be good enough to explain what set you off on the subject.

There is a moment's silence.

MR. WADE: We were trying to fathom the reasons for your sudden strong feelings against the housekeeper.

There is another moment of silence. Aunt Lida puts her hand self-consciously to her string of pearls. Lennie enters from service hall with coffee.

AUNT LIDA: Oh, I see.

MRS. WADE (*uncertain of what she is going to say*): Robert . . .

138

AUNT LIDA: Put the tray on the table here, Lennie. Are you right sure you want to drink coffee at this hour of the night, Margie?

MRS. WADE: Come to think of it, I guess I won't.

AUNT LIDA: Leave it there, Lennie, and I'll drink it.

LENNIE: Yehsm. (*She goes into the girls' room, left.*)

AUNT LIDA: What time is your train, Robert?

MR. WADE: I've got just about an hour. (*Looking at watch.*)

AUNT LIDA: Then you'd better set about packing. Margie's plainly not up to it.

MR. WADE (*rising from chair*): You're dead right.

MRS. WADE: Do you mind?

MR. WADE: Not a bit, honey. (*He goes into his bedroom.*)

Aunt Lida sits down in the chair that Mr. Wade was occupying a few minutes before. With her foot she draws a footstool in front of her and rests her feet on it. She rests her head on the chair back and with her elbows raised she interlocks her fingers and places her hands over her eyes.

AUNT LIDA: Margie, I'm right tired, myself.

MRS. WADE: Poor dear, I know you are. It's been an awful strain on you, Aunt Lida.

AUNT LIDA: What has, Margie?

MRS. WADE: Oh, all of Cousin Harry's illness, with me in this condition, and the funeral today especially.

AUNT LIDA: Margie, I hope you don't ever think I underestimate you.

MRS. WADE: How so?

139

AUNT LIDA: I mean your powers of perception and understanding.

MRS. WADE: I'm a simple, artless little mother-woman from upper Middle-Tennessee.

AUNT LIDA: And I, I am a pore relation, a maiden aunt from the Cumberland Plateau. (*They laugh, and Aunt Lida removes her hands from before her eyes.*)

AUNT LIDA: That's how your Cousin Harry saw us to the very end, you know.

MRS. WADE: That's how we *are* to the very end, isn't it, Aunt Lida?

AUNT LIDA: I don't know, Margie. It's sometimes hard, isn't it?

MRS. WADE: Aunt Lida, it's great fun mostly. And what else is there better, with the given circumstances? When I was a girl I used to think . . .

AUNT LIDA: Yes, and so did I, even I, even then. But what chance has a person? It's like throwing away money, the horrid stuff. Yet it's the coin of the realm, and you'd best use what you have of it.

MRS. WADE: But I also thought . . .

AUNT LIDA: Ah, and so did I. But that part was harder for me, not being the pretty little thing.

MRS. WADE: Now, Aunt Lida, I was always told at home that you were a mighty attractive young girl.

AUNT LIDA: Well, as your husband's great-aunt Rhody Baird from East Tennessee used to say of herself (*in the voice of a crone*), "Like any other, I had my little lovyer. Hee-he-he—hee." And let me tell you I made them step and fetch for me; but I used to hate myself. Sometimes I hate myself now and think that

140

your Cousin Harry was right about it all. People like him, and like her (*pointing with her thumb in the direction of Miss Bluemeyer's room*) make it hard. They point an accusing finger.

MRS. WADE: I know what you mean.

AUNT LIDA: Yes, I thought you did. And that's how we began this conversation.

Mr. Wade appears at the door of his room.

MR. WADE: Aunt Lida, does Paris think I'm not leaving till midnight?

AUNT LIDA (*rising from chair*): I told that boy . . .

MR. WADE (*seeing Lennie as she comes out of the girls' room*): Never mind, Aunt Lida. Lennie, you tell Paris to get up here with my Gladstone!

LENNIE (*stepping into the hall*): Yehsuh, he's on the back stair, wipin' it. You wouldn't-a tetched it the way it wuz.

AUNT LIDA (*to Mrs. Wade*): Lennie *always* has to add her nickel's worth.

LENNIE: Aw, Miss Lida, I got beds to tunn back.

AUNT LIDA: Girl, that sounded to me just this side of uppity. I'll have to speak to *your* Aunt Myra.

LENNIE: Wull, there's uppitier niggers than I be in this house.

MR. WADE (*coming forward*): By George, this isn't getting me my Gladstone.

At this moment Paris enters from the service hall, and Lennie turns toward Aunt Lida's room. Simultaneously Myra appears on the stairway with a stack of clean, highly starched rompers and dresses for the smaller children piled high in her arms. She is mouth-

141

ing over her shoulder at James and Nancy who are behind her: "Wull, make hase! Come ohn by me if y'aim to come, and mine these-here close." Nancy and James brush past her and gallop up the few remaining steps before her. Each carries a large walking cane with a crook handle. Meanwhile, Mr. Wade addresses Paris the length of the hall, "Paris, is that the bag Miss Lida told you to bring me?" Paris replies, "Yessuh, it the Glodstone." And Aunt Lida is saying to Lennie whom she has called back from her room, "You can leave my bed; the children are playing in there. And if you're going to change Miss Margie's sheets tonight, get Nancy to help you. I want her to learn to look after things."

MR. WADE (*still to Paris, who has stopped in his tracks at the far end of the hall*): It's a Glodstone, I'll grant you. It's the one Miss Margie's papa took to the Tennessee Centennial in 1896.

AUNT LIDA (*turning toward Paris*): What's this about the Gladstone?

MR. WADE (*to Aunt Lida*): Do you think I'm going to travel with that old carpetbag? Did you tell Paris . . . ?

AUNT LIDA: I *did* not!

MRS. WADE (*whose attention has been attracted by the noise of the children, James and Nancy, behind her—looking over her shoulder to Myra*): Myra, the clothes look lovely. Come let me see them.

MYRA: Yassum. 'At James come mighty nigh spillin' 'um "lovely close."

JAMES: I did not, Myra. It was Nancy.

142

AUNT LIDA: Don't contradict Myra, James.

LENNIE: Come ohn, Nancy.

AUNT LIDA: Paris, you march right back down there and get the new Gladstone.

MRS. WADE (*holding up one of Lida Sue's dresses*): They're positively lovely, Myra. Look, Aunt Lida! Of course, these ruffles here ought to be pressed over this way.

NANCY: Aunt Lida, I know how to turn back an old bed! Don't make me do it tonight, Aunt Lida. James and I want to roll back the big rug yonder and play slide-on-the-rag-rug.

MR. WADE: You *are not* going to play that game while I'm in this house. Do as your Aunt Lida says; and James, put that walking cane down and come help me pack.

PARIS: I don't know which-a-one you mean, Miss Lida.

AUNT LIDA (*stepping nearer to Mrs. Wade and examining the dress she holds up*): Of course, it should be over that way. I told you so, explicitly, Myra; and you knew how I wanted it. (*Suddenly laughing.*) Myra Willis, admit it! You just liked it better this way.

MYRA (*bending forward and laughing*): Aw, Miss Lida, ain't you a sight.

PARIS: I don't know which-a-one you mean, Miss Lida.

NANCY: Aunt Lida, don't make me . . .

MR. WADE: For God's sake, tell him the right one, Auntie.

LENNIE: She ain't comin', Miss Lida.

MRS. WADE: Aunt Lida . . .

AUNT LIDA (*raising her voice*): Now, see here, all of you . . .

At this moment Aunt Lida realizes that Miss Blue-meyer is standing in the open doorway to her room, right. Since Mr. Wade came from his room saying, "Does Paris think I'm not leaving till midnight?" she has been standing there, watching.

MISS BLUEMEYER: Mr. Wade.

MR. WADE (*furiously*): Yes—ma'am!

MISS BLUEMEYER: I will see that you get the right luggage. (*Taking a step in the direction of door to service hall.*) Come with me, Paris.

AUNT LIDA: That won't be necessary, Miss Blue-meyer. Paris knows the suitcase we mean now.

PARIS (*quickly*): Yessum, I suhtnly do.

He hurries through the service hall doorway, clos-ing the door after him. At the same moment Lennie takes Nancy's hand and pulls her into her parents' room. "Come ohn, Nancy!" As they are closing the door, James rushes after them, pushing his way through the half-closed door and then closing it after him. Miss Bluemeyer begins walking slowly across the hall toward Aunt Lida who watches her intently.

MRS. WADE (*pushing the child's dress at Myra and nodding her head significantly toward the girls' room*): Here, Myra. (*Half-whispering.*) Robert, you will miss that train if you don't hurry.

MR. WADE: By George, yes! (*Looking at his watch.*)

Paris now runs up the stairs with a yellow-brown Gladstone bag. Myra goes into the girls' room.

PARIS: Here, Mista Robert. (*He sets the bag down at the head of the stairs.*)

MR. WADE (*striding in the direction of Paris*): Tell Sellars to bring the car round.

PARIS: Sellars waitin' in the potecoshay.

Paris glances at Miss Bluemeyer, who has now reached the center of the hall, and runs down the stairs. Mr. Wade goes into his room and closes the door. Miss Bluemeyer suddenly turns about face and hastens to her room, leaving the door ajar.

MRS. WADE (*in alarm*): Aunt Lida!

AUNT LIDA (*reassuringly, in her deepest voice*): She's only going to fetch her hat and coat. She's quitting. She's not going to stay the night.

MISS BLUEMEYER (*enters with a light coat thrown over her left arm, a handbag in her left hand, and a soft felt hat in her right hand; with the latter she gesticulates rather wildly as she speaks in a loud masculine voice*): No, not another hour in the house with such as you. (*Striding the length of the hall to face Aunt Lida.*) My conscience would burn me out before morning.

AUNT LIDA (*sternly, calmly*): Just leave us your address, Miss Bluemeyer. We'll send your things tomorrow.

MISS BLUEMEYER: Send 'em or not, Miss Wade, as you like. Do I care if I never see them again? Not one thing that will remind me . . .

MRS. WADE (*rising from chair*): Good night, Miss Bluemeyer! (*Miss Bluemeyer turns submissively and goes to the head of the stairs.*)

AUNT LIDA: Wait a moment.

MRS. WADE: No, Aunt Lida!

AUNT LIDA: Miss Bluemeyer, can't you calm your-self sufficiently to tell me what you have to say in a civilized manner? You and I will never see each other again, and you might be glad some day that you told me. (*Miss Bluemeyer laughs ironically.*)

MRS. WADE: Good *night,* Miss Bluemeyer.

MISS BLUEMEYER: No, Misses Wade, I will stay a bit. (*She returns to the group of chairs.*) I want to talk to you about your husband's aunt.

MRS. WADE (*turning her back and taking several steps in the direction of her room*): I have no interest in what you may say. Good night.

MISS BLUEMEYER: Ah, shame, Misses Wade. You who are so kind to your husband's aunt ought to be kind to other lonesome beings in this world. (*Mrs. Wade stops and turns halfway round.*) Doesn't it seem maybe that's what is wrong with all the family falderal your sort go in for?

AUNT LIDA: It was not to hear your criticism of my niece that I called you back, Miss Bluemeyer.

MISS BLUEMEYER: It was not to criticize her I am staying. . . . (*Mr. Wade enters with his Gladstone. He pulls the door to behind him and stands listening.*) Misses Wade, I have a thing or two to say. . . .

MRS. WADE: If those things concern my aunt . . .

AUNT LIDA: Miss Bluemeyer, I asked you to stop a moment because I thought you had something to say about our late cousin, Mr. Wilson.

146

MISS BLUEMEYER (*suddenly, with emotion*): Mr. Wilson! Mr. Wilson! Your *cousin,* Mr. Wilson! (*Then speaking in a hoarse monotone, obviously making a conscious effort at self-restraint.*) Can you not hear yourselves? Aunt! Niece! Nephew! Father! Son! Daughter! Cousin! *Cousin!* I can see the poor old fellow now tramping past Merton's window to the lunchroom or going up to the corner with a little package of laundry under his arm.

AUNT LIDA: Are you accusing us of unkindness to Cousin Harry?

MISS BLUEMEYER: Not to Cousin Harry, but to Mr. Wilson.

MR. WADE: I thought it had been definitely established that Cousin Harry *was* . . .

AUNT LIDA: Your distinction isn't quite clear, Miss Bluemeyer.

MISS BLUEMEYER: Oh, it is clear enough!

AUNT LIDA (*calmly*): If only you could calm yourself. I do think you may have a point to make.

MRS. WADE: Aunt Lida, this whole interview is uncalled-for. . . . Even if you have no respect for our family, Miss Bluemeyer, remember that one near to us has died this day. We simply do not understand each other. Please say no more and go.

MISS BLUEMEYER: Do we not understand each other, Misses Wade? I understand a good deal of how this family business works. It makes a woman safe and sure being related this way and that way to everybody around her. And it keeps you from having to bother about anybody else, since they are not "kinfolks." I

147

understand how it works, for I was one of nine, and I saw the women in my family making the most of it too. And I might have done the same, but I was a queer sort who couldn't make herself do it.

AUNT LIDA: Is that all, Miss Bluemeyer?

MISS BLUEMEYER: Not quite all. For a solid year I have watched you here giving directions and making this house your own. And I have seen it right along that you are really the same as I in lots of your feelings, Miss Wade, that you are really lost and alone in the world, but you would not have it so, you just wouldn't. All along I have seen you are really a brainy woman and yet to see you here saying the things you say and play-acting all the time! And then when the old man Wilson was dying, you, like the rest of 'em, talked of nothing but that he was kin, kin, kin. You have mocked and joked all this day and gave him a funeral only because he was a kinsman.

MR. WADE: Miss Bluemeyer.

MISS BLUEMEYER: I am going now, Mr. Wade. (*She goes to the head of the stairs where he is standing by the door.*) Good-by, Mr. Wade.

MR. WADE: Good-by, ma'am. And believe me, to us all our Cousin Harry was just a poor, lonely old man that we would have befriended if he had let us.

MISS BLUEMEYER: I know your feelings are good, Mr. Wade. But you are a man. For a man it is easier. (*She goes down the stairs. There is a moment's silence when each of the three persons present seems to be concerned with his own thoughts.*)

148

MRS. WADE: What could have so embittered a person?

MR. WADE: Why, the woman's crazy, and naturally Aunt Lida was the first to make it out. How long have you known she was insane, Aunt Lida?

AUNT LIDA: I don't know.

MR. WADE (*taking several steps forward, slowly*): What do you mean?

MRS. WADE: She means that she doesn't know when she realized it.

MR. WADE: By the way she said it, I thought she meant she wasn't sure she was crazy.

MRS. WADE (*taking his arm*): Oh, could a sane person possibly have been so critical and questioning of a happy family life?

AUNT LIDA: Robert, aren't you going to miss your train?

MR. WADE: By George! Well, aren't the children going to tell me good-by?

AUNT LIDA (*calling*): Chill-drun!

Mr. Wade kisses Mrs. Wade.

MR. WADE: So long, Auntie.

AUNT LIDA (*casually*): Toodle-loo. Hurry back, Robert.

The children have now appeared in the doorways from Aunt Lida's room and their parents' room. "Yes, ma'am!" "What, Aunt Lida?"

AUNT LIDA: Tell your daddy good-by. (*Slowly letting herself down into chair.*)

NANCY: Oh, of course!

JAMES: Sure!

149

All of the children rush toward their father to be kissed. As he bends and stoops to kiss each of them, he is saying, "Good-by, Alfred. Good-by, Nancy. Good-by, Lida Sue. Good-by, James. Good-by, Charles William." But Mrs. Wade is watching Aunt Lida, who, as the curtain falls, sits with her hands over her face, as before.

CURTAIN

COOKIE

Two nights a week, he *had* to be home for supper, and some weeks, when his conscience was especially uneasy, he turned up three or four times. Tonight, she had a dish of string beans, cooked with cured side meat, on the table when he came in. The smoky odor of the fat struck him when he opened the front door, but he couldn't believe it until he went back to the dining room and saw the dish on the table. "Good God!" he said to himself. "That's fine. Where did she get fresh beans at this time of year?"

Presently his wife, who was, like himself, past fifty, came through the swinging door from the pantry.

"Ah," she said, "my husband is right on time tonight." She came to him and undid the buttons of his overcoat, as she used to undo the children's. It was his lightweight "fall coat," which she had brought down from the attic only two weeks before. She took it and folded it over the back of a dining-room chair, as she would have a visitor's. She knew that he would be leaving right after coffee.

He leaned over the dish and smelled it, and then sat down at the place that was set for him. It was directly across the round dining-room table from her place. She stepped to the pantry door and called: "Cookie, we're ready when you are." She pulled out her chair and sat down.

"Shall we have the blessing tonight?" she said, with some small hope in her smile.

"Oh, let's not." He smiled back. It was a cajoling smile.

"All right, then." She smoothed the tablecloth with her fingers.

He served himself from the dish of beans and selected a piece of the side meat. He bent his head over and got one whiff of the steaming dish. "You're too good to me," he said evenly. He pushed the dish across the table to within her reach.

"Nothing's too good for one's husband."

"You're much too good to me," he said, now lowering his eyes to his plate.

Cookie came through the swinging door with a vegetable dish in each hand. She was a brown, buxom Negro woman, perhaps a few years older than her mistress. She set the dishes on the table near her mistress's plate.

"Good evenin', Cookie," he said to her as she started back to the kitchen.

"Yessuh," she said, and went on through the doorway.

His wife was serving herself from a dish. "Here are some of your baked potatoes," she said.

"Ah!" he said. "You *are* too good . . ." This time he left the sentence unfinished.

She passed him the dish. "And here are simply some cold beets."

"Fine . . . fine . . . fine."

"Do you think we would like a little more light?" she said. She pushed herself back from the table.

"We might. We might."

She went to the row of switches by the doorway that led to the hall. She pushed the second switch, and the light overhead was increased. She pushed the third, and the wall lights by the sideboard came on. With each increase of light in the room her husband said, "Ah . . . fine . . . ah . . . fine." It was a small dining room—at least, it seemed so in the bright light, for the house was old and high-ceilinged. The woodwork was a natural pine, with heavy door facings and a narrow chair rail. The paper above the chair rail was a pale yellow, and no pictures were on the walls. There were two silver candlesticks and a punch bowl on the sideboard. Through the glass doors of the press the cut-glassware showed. The large light fixture, a frosted glass bowl, hung from a heavy "antiqued" chain low over the table, and the bright light brought out a spot here and there on the cloth.

She was taking her seat again when Cookie pushed through the door with the meat and the bread.

"What's this? A roast? You're outdoing yourself tonight, Cookie," he said.

"Y'all want all iss light?" Cookie said, blinking, and she set the meat down before him.

"Well, it's—well, it's cold-water cornbread!" He took

two pieces of bread from the plate that Cookie held to him.

"Y'all want all iss light?" Cookie said to her mistress, who was selecting a small piece of bread and smiling ingenuously at her husband.

"Yes, Cookie," she said, "I think so. I thought I'd turn 'em up some."

"Wull, I could a done it, Mizz."

"It's all right, Cookie. I didn't want the bread burned."

"Wull, it ain't Judgment Day, Mizz. Y'all could a waited. I'd a done it, stead of you havin' to do it." She put the bread on the table and covered it with the napkin that she had held the plate with.

"It's all right, Cookie."

Cookie opened the door to go back to the kitchen. As she went through, she said, "Lawd a *mercy!*"

His wife pushed her plate across the table, and he put on it a slice of roast that he had carved—an outside piece, because it was more done. He cut several slices, until he came to one that seemed rare enough for himself. "Any news from the chillun?" he said.

"Yes," she said. "Post cards from all three."

"Only post cards?"

She began to taste her food, taking so little on her fork that it was hardly visible.

"Now, that's just rotten!" he said. He brought a frown to his face. "They ought to write you letters. They ought to write you at least once a week! I'm going to write the boys tomorrow and tell 'em."

154

"Now, please, honey! Please don't! They're well. They said so, and that's all I need to know. They're just busy. Young people don't have time for letters." She eased her knife and fork down on her plate. "They're young!"

"What's that got to do with it?" he said. "They ought always to have time for *you*." He went on eating and talking at the same time. "These beets are fine," he said. Then, after swallowing, "I won't have that! They ought to write their mother once a week. When I was in med school, you know how much I wrote Mama. Father would have beaten me, I believe, and taken me out, if I hadn't. I ought to take them out just once." He stopped eating for a moment, and shaking his fork at her, he spoke even more earnestly: "And just one month I should forget to send *her* that check."

His wife sat, somewhat paled, making no pretense of eating. "Now, please, honey," she said. "She has two little children and a husband who is far from well. I had a letter from her last week, written while the children were taking a little nap. Remember that she has two little children to look after." Her lips trembled. "There's nothing for the boys to write. They say on every single card they miss being home."

He saw that her lips were quivering, and he began eating again. He frowned. Then he smiled suddenly and said, as if with relief, "I'll tell you. Yes. You ought to go up and see 'em. You haven't been to Nashville since they were *both* in med."

She wiped her mouth with her napkin and smiled.

155

"No, there's no need in my going," she said. And she began to eat her dinner again.

Cookie came in with a small pan of hot bread, holding it with a kitchen towel. She uncovered the plate of bread on the table and stacked the hot bread on top of what was there. With her free hand, she reached in front of her mistress and felt the untouched piece of bread on her plate. " 'S got cole on ya," she said. She picked it up in her brown hand and threw it on the cooking pan. She placed a piece of hot bread on her mistress's plate, saying, "Now, gwine butter't while 't's hot."

Her mistress pushed the bread plate across the table toward her husband. She said to him, "Cookie and I are going to get a box of food off to 'em next week, like we used to send 'em in military school. Aren't we, Cookie?"

"Fine . . . fine . . . fine," he said. He took a piece of the cornbread and began to butter it.

Cookie nodded her head toward him and said to her mistress, *"He* hear from 'em?" Then she took several steps around the table, picked up the bread plate, and returned it to its former place. She was tucking the napkin about its edges again.

"No, I have *not!"* He brought the frown to his face again. "They ought to write their mammy, oughtn't they, Cookie?"

"Sho-God ought. 'S a shame," Cookie said. She looked at her mistress. And her mistress put her knife and fork down again. Her lips began to quiver. She gazed tearfully at her husband.

He looked away and spoke out in a loud voice that seemed almost to echo in the high-ceilinged room: "What are you goin' to send 'em? What are you going to send them youngons, Cookie?"

Cookie looked at him blankly and then at the butter plate, which was in the center of the table. "Whatever she say."

"Well, what do you say, Mother?"

She cleared her throat and ran her hand in a series of pats over her thick and slightly graying hair that went in soft waves back over her ears. "I had thought that we might get hold of two fat guinea hens," she said.

"Fine . . . fine."

"I thought we might get some smoked sausage, not too new and—"

"Ah . . . fine."

"And we might spare one of the fruitcakes we've got soaking."

"How does that suit you, Cookie?" he said.

Cookie was on her way toward the kitchen again. "Yessuh," she said.

He ate in silence for several minutes, took a second helping of string beans, and another piece of bread. She nibbled at a piece of bread. She put more salt and pepper on her meat and ate a few bites. And then she arranged her knife and fork on her plate. Finally, he put his knife and fork down on his empty plate and, with his mouth still full, said, "There's not more, surely?"

She smiled, nodding her head. "Pie."

"No! What kind!"

"I cooked it myself." She picked up a little glass call bell beside her plate and tinkled it. He sat chewing his last bite, and presently Cookie appeared in the doorway with two plates of yellow lemon pie topped with an inch of white meringue.

"This is where she can beat you, Cookie," he said as the cook set the piece of pie before him.

Cookie made a noise that was somewhat like "Psss." She looked at her mistress and gave her a gold-toothed smile. She started to leave with the dinner plates.

"Wait a minute, Cookie," he said. She stopped and looked at him, with her lower lip hanging open. He was taking big bites of the pie. "Cookie, I've been wantin' to ask you how your 'corporosity' is."

"M'whut, Boss-Man?"

"And, furthermore, I understand from what various people are saying around that you have ancestors." He winked at his wife. She dropped her eyes to her plate.

"Whut's he mean, Mizz?" Cookie asked, standing with the two dinner plates in hand.

"Just some of his foolishness, Cookie," she said, with her eyes still on her plate.

He thought to himself that his wife was too good to tease even Cookie. He said to himself, "She doesn't realize that they really eat it up."

"M' coffee's bilin'," Cookie said, and she went through the swinging door.

His wife looked up from her plate. "You know Cookie never has liked to joke. Now, please, honey, don't tease her. She's getting along in her years now. Her temper's quicker than it used to be."

He had finished his pie when Cookie brought in the coffee. She brought it on a tray—two cups and a kitchen pot. She set a cup at each place, filled them, and set the pot on the tablecloth.

"How's that church of yours comin', Cookie?" he said.

"It's makin' out, Boss-Man."

"Haven't you-all churched nobody lately?"

"No, suh, not us."

"How about Dr. Palmer's cook, Cookie? Is she a member in standing?"

"Sho. Mean 'at gal Hattie?" She looked at her mistress and smiled.

He looked at his wife, who he thought was shaking her head at Cookie. Then he looked at Cookie. "Yes," he said, almost absent-mindedly. "He brought her in from the country. That's it—Hattie! That's her name."

"Yessuh. She's from out on Pea Ridge."

"She's givin' 'im some trouble. Drinkin', ain't she, Cookie?"

" 'Cep' *he* didn't get her from Pea Ridge."

"No, Cookie?"

"She put in a year for some ladies he know out near the sand banks, and—"

"She's a drinker, ain't she, Cookie?"

"Yessuh. I *reckon* she is." She tilted her head back and gave him her gold-toothed laugh, which ended in a sort of sneer this time. "She uz dancin' roun' outside

159

chuch las' night an' say to me she want to teach me
how to do dat stuff. I tell huh she's drunk, an' she say,
'Sho I is. I teach you how to hit de bottle, too!' "

He pushed his chair away from the table, still holding his coffee, and laughed aloud. He saw that his wife
was looking threateningly at Cookie. "What else did
she say, Cookie?" he pressed her.

"Oh, dat gal's a big talker. She's full of lies. De way
she lies 'bout huh boss-man's terble. She lie 'bout
anybody an' everybody in Thornton. She call names
up an' down de street."

"What sort of lies?" He leaned forward, smiling,
and winked at his wife.

"Them ladies from the sand banks—she say they's
in an' out his place mos' any night. Doc Palmer's a
bachlorman, sho, but Hattie say hit ain't jus' Doc
Palmer! They comes there to meet the ladies—all sorts
of menfolks, married or not. She say she see 'em *all*
'bout his place sooner later."

His wife had quit sipping her coffee and was staring
at Cookie.

"Who, for instance, Cookie? Let us in on it," he said.

The cook turned to him and looked at him blankly.
"You, Boss-Man."

His wife stood up at her place, her napkin in her
hand. Her eyes filled with tears. "After all these years!"
she said. "Cookie, you've forgotten your place for the
first time, after all these years."

Cookie put her hands under her apron, looked at
her feet a moment, and then looked up at him, her
own eyes wet. Her words came almost like screams.

160

"Hattie say she *seen* ya! But she's a liar, ain't she, Boss-Man?"

Her mistress sat down, put one elbow on the table, and brought her napkin up to cover her face. "I'm disappointed in you, Cookie. Go to the kitchen."

Cookie went through the swinging door without looking at her mistress.

In a moment, his wife looked up at him and said, "I'm sorry. I'd not thought she was capable of a thing like that."

"Why, it's all right—for what she said. Doctors will get talked about. Even Cookie knows the girl's a liar."

His wife seemed, he thought, not to have heard him. She was saying, "A servant of mine talking to my husband like that!"

"It's only old-nigger uppitiness," he reassured her.

"I shall speak to her tonight," she said. "I promise you."

"Oh, I suppose you'll think you have to fire her."

She looked at him, her features composed again. She ran her hand over her hair in a series of pats. "No, no," she said. "I can't fire Cookie. I'll speak to her tonight. It'll never happen again."

"Now I think of it, perhaps she ought to be sent on her way after talking like that."

"I'll look after the matter."

He poured himself a second cup of coffee and, as he drank it, he watched his wife closely. He frowned again and said, "Why, she might talk to *you* that way someday. That's all I thought."

She smiled at him. "There's no danger. I'll have a talk with her tonight."

She helped him on with his overcoat. He said, "Got to see some country people tonight. Might even have to drive over to Huntsboro." She was buttoning his coat. "There's a lot of red throat over there."

"I can't have her talking that way to my husband," she said aloud, yet to herself. "But I won't fire her," she told him. "She's too much one of us—too much one of the family, and I know she'll be full of remorse for speaking out of turn like that."

He looked directly into her eyes, and she smiled confidently. She told him she would leave the back light on, because lately the nights had been cloudy and dark. As he stopped in the hall to pick up his hat and his case, he heard Cookie come through the swinging door.

"Now, Cookie, I want to have a little talk with you," his wife said, and Cookie said, "Yes'm, Mizz."

He went out, closing the door softly behind him, and as he crossed the porch, he could still hear their voices inside—the righteousness and disillusion of Cookie's, the pride and discipline of his wife's. He passed down the flight of wooden steps and stepped from the brick walk onto the lawn. He hesitated a moment; he could still hear their voices indistinctly— their senseless voices. He began walking with light, sure steps over the grass—their ugly, old voices. In the driveway, his car, bright and new and luxurious, was waiting for him.

TWO LADIES
IN RETIREMENT

Some Nashville wit had once said, "When I look at Miss Betty Pettigru, I'm reminded of an old, old baby." Others thought she looked more like the Home-Run King himself. She was a short, plump woman, not fat but with an individual plumpness to all her limbs and to her torso, her breasts, her hands, and even to the features on her moon-shaped face. She was a lady well known in Nashville, during a period of twenty-five years, for her Sunday-night parties and for her active role in the club life of the city. Miss Betty's face and figure and her parties and her active role seemed so much a part of Nashville that hardly anyone could believe it when, in the spring of 1926, word finally got around that she was definitely going to move away and go to live in St. Louis.

At first they all said, oh, it would be merely another of her protracted visits to St. Louis, and she would come back talking of nothing but her little nephews, who, of course, weren't really her nephews at all. She was only going for another stay with some of that Tolliver family she was kin to. Miss Betty's enemies were particularly skeptical. "Miss Betty Pettigru leave Nashville? The scene of all her victories? Nonsense! Never!" And they kept asking what on earth made her even talk of leaving. "I think I am going to St. Louis to watch my irresistible nephews grow up," she said. "But you know me. Woman-like, I seldom know my own mind or what my reason is for doing anything."

By everyone, her talk of leaving Nashville was considered "completely and entirely absurd." But then it came out in the Sunday paper that Miss Betty Pettigru had sold her house on West End Avenue—came out not on the society page but in the real-estate section. And it was this—its appearance in the real-estate section—that convinced everybody. Soon they learned that she had actually sold her lovely big limestone house, disposed of all but a few pieces of her furniture, and had left for St. Louis in the company of her cousin and close companion of many years, Mrs. Florence Blalock. In Nashville, it seemed the end of an era!

During ten years, Miss Betty and Mrs. Blalock had been paying visits together to their St. Louis relatives, the James Tollivers. Their visits were frequent and long, yet as guests they had always had to have their stockings "rinsed out" by the maid and their breakfasts brought to their rooms, and had to be given little parties, which had been made up of mothers and aunts of the Tollivers' friends. At last, and quite unexpectedly, too, they had been told by Mr. James Tolliver himself that their visits were a bad length. Either they should come for shorter visits or they should come and live the year around as members of the household. Miss Betty had burst into tears on the spot—from pure shock, as she said afterward. James Tolliver, a very gentle and businesslike man of about forty, had tried immediately to relent. But there was no relenting once such a thing was said, and the decision had to be made.

How could anyone who had followed Miss Betty's social career imagine that she would make the choice in favor of St. Louis? The answer, of course, was that nobody but her cousin Mrs. Blalock could. Mrs. Blalock remembered the warmth with which Miss Betty had welcomed her into her house thirty years before, how she commenced calling her Flo Dear at once, how she talked of the longing she had always felt for a sister whom she could love. And, what was more, Flo Dear remembered how Miss Betty's kindness and generosity toward her continued even after she realized that her poor cousin could not supply the sort of family affection that she craved. Flo Dear knew that at the Tolliver fireside it would be a different story.

To the Tolliver boys, it seemed that Auntie Bet and Flo Dear had always lived in St. Louis and occupied those two rooms at the end of the upstairs hall. Before the two ladies had resided in the Tollivers' house six months, the boys would speak of something that had happened during last year's visit as though their "aunts" had already been living with them then, and they would have to be reminded that it was otherwise.

It wasn't long before the boys' aunts seemed to feel,

with the boys, that they had always lived there. Reaching back into the days of their visits for anecdotes, they managed to vest each of the three little boys with a highly individual character. There was little Jimmy, who had a natural bent for arithmetic and knew his multiplication tables before he ever went to school a day. They stood in awe of his head for figures and wondered what it would be like to have a scientist in the family. They said proudly that they hated to think of what out-of-the-way opinions he might come to hold. Jimmy's birthday came on January 8, and when he was "just a little fellow," he had figured out that if Christmas comes on a Sunday, then so must New Year's Day, and so must the eighth day of January, and then he had calculated how many times in his life Sunday was bound to ruin those three best days of the year. His aunts marveled at him. He was the second boy and in some ways the brightest. Vance was the oldest, and about him they said, "He is a very sober child, so respectful—and beautifully mannered." As for little Landon, they felt that one could not help adoring him, because of his sweet, dreamy nature and because he was the baby.

Vance was certainly the best mannered. But not their favorite. They had no favorite. Miss Betty and Flo Dear were impartial, utterly and completely. If one of Mr. Tolliver's business friends said to them, "Tell me about your little nephews; I understand you're very fond of them," they would hardly know where to begin. Finally Flo Dear might say, "Well, Vance is the oldest."

"Yes, Vance is getting so grown up it frightens one," Miss Betty would add, as though she had been with him every minute since he was born.

All in all, the move to St. Louis gave Miss Betty Pettigru just the new start in life that it had seemed to promise. She and her cousin had a small circle of acquaintances among the mothers and aunts of the Tollivers' friends, but they seldom went anywhere or saw anyone except the members of their own family. Almost at once, Flo Dear had set up her drawing board in her room (she practiced the ancient art of blazonry), and very soon had completed a Tolliver coat of arms, which was hung in the library. Before long, she was accepting commissions from various friends of the Tollivers. Miss Betty assumed just as many household duties as Amy Tolliver would allow her to. But Amy, despite her easygoing nature, was too efficient and farseeing a family manager to leave an opening for trouble in that quarter. Miss Betty, in the end, was left free during almost all her waking hours to be of service to her little nephews. It was the new start in life she had hoped for, and yet, almost upon her arrival, there began an unfortunate episode that threatened to demolish all this happiness. Within a matter of weeks after the two ladies were installed, a terrible competition for the boys' favor developed between Miss Betty and Vennie, the Tollivers' aging cook.

At first glance, it would seem that Miss Betty had all the advantages in the struggle with Vennie. She lived in the same part of the house the boys did; she ate at the table with them, was treated with respect by their parents, was at their service any and every hour of the day, not excluding Saturday and Sunday, when her chaperonage and financial backing were needed for excursions to the ice-skating rink or to the amusement parks and movie houses. Plainly, she was willing to throw into the battle the entire fortune old Major Pettigru, her father, had left her. She even went so far as to replace the town car she had sold upon leaving Nashville with a sea-green touring car, whose top could be put back in pleasant weather, and she added half again to the houseboy's salary in order that he might look after the car and drive her and Flo Dear and the boys on their expeditions.

Vennie's advantages were different, but they were real ones and were early recognized by Miss Betty. Vennie lived in the basement. She had not just a room there but an apartment, complete with an outside entrance, living room, kitchen, et cetera. One reached it by descending from the back hall to a long, narrow, poorly lit passage flanked by soapy-smelling laundry rooms, a tightly locked wine cellar, and the furnace room and coalbin. Her quarters were at the end of the passage. Miss Betty was destined never to go there, but in her mind she carried a picture of it that was as clear and accurate as if she had once occupied the rooms herself. The clearness was due to her knowledge of other such quarters she had visited in years gone by, but the accuracy of detail was due to the accounts her little nephews supplied. Landon told about the pictures on Vennie's walls: pictures of Negro children in middy blouses and other absurdly old-fashioned clothes you never thought of Negroes as wearing, pictures of Negro sergeants and corporals who had actually gone to France in the Great War (they all wore spectacles and looked, somehow, very unlike Negroes), pictures of Landon's mother and father and of other white people Vennie used to work for, in Thornton, and pictures of those other white people's children. Jimmy told about the horn on Vennie's old-timy phonograph and about the player piano and how it stretched and tired your legs to pedal it. Vance never said much about how things looked down there, but he talked about Vennie's "magic stove." Nothing cooked on the gas stove upstairs ever tasted like things cooked on that little coal range in Vennie's kitchen. And not one of the boys had failed to mention the dark scariness of the passage and how safe and bright Vennie's place always seemed when you got there.

Vennie's cooking, naturally, was a big advantage, but not such a serious one in itself. Auntie Bet could treat the boys to all manner of good things to eat when they went out. And what sort of handsome presents might she not have made them if it had been permitted! But it wasn't permitted, and Miss Betty didn't have to be told but once by Mr. James Tolliver that Christmas was the time—and the only time—when boys should receive expensive presents like bicycles and motor scooters. Amy and James were quick to shake their heads accusingly at her if one of the boys came back from Forest Park Highlands with even just a toy pistol he had won in a chance game. But when a three-layer chocolate cake was discovered in the lower compartment of the sideboard, and there was every reason to think other cakes had been kept there before and partaken of at will by the boys, despite all the rules against eating between meals, no more than a teasing, jovial finger was shaken at Vennie. Miss Betty protested that it really ought to be stopped, because Vance already had hickeys all over his face from so many sweets between meals. "But what can one do?" replied James Tolliver, shrugging his shoulders. "Vennie's like somebody's old granny, and since the world began, grannies have been hiding cooky jars for youngons."

Certainly James Tolliver would not have made that casual remark if he had known the pain it would cause Miss Betty. It came on a day when the boys had been repeating to her some of the stories they liked to hear Vennie tell, stories about the old times at Thornton and in the country along the Tennessee River where it flows north up from Mississippi. How Uncle Wash got lost in the snowy woods and slept in a hollow log for two nights, and how Mr. Ben Tolliver found him there and thought he was "dead and maybe murdered." How little Jane Pettigru fell down the old well and Vennie's blind dwarf brother, whose name was Pettigru, too—Jules Pettigru—was the only one small enough to be let down on a rope to bring the baby out. Vennie's stories and her way of telling them were surely her greatest advantage. Or, at least, it was the thing that most unnerved Miss Betty and made her feel useless to her little nephews. Occasionally, she had heard Vennie telling some old anecdote to the whole Tolliver family. Vennie would take her stance just inside the dining-room door, arms akimbo, her head thrown back, and wearing a big smile that grew broader and broader until she finished the story in a fit of laughter. Her stories were mostly about the Tolliver family and the Tolliver Negroes, about the wondrous ways they were always rescuing each other from dangers great and small, usually ending with some fool thing a field hand Negro had said, or with Mr. Jeff Tolliver quoting the law to a pickaninny who had snatched an apple from the back porch. The really bad thing was that Miss Betty so often recognized Vennie's stories, remembered hearing other versions of them in her youth. Yet she could not tell the stories herself, or even think of them until something Vennie had told the boys reminded her. Sometimes she would recall a very different version of a story Vennie had told, but the boys were not impressed by Auntie Bet's corrections.

When the very first newness of Miss Betty's "treats" wore off, there would be times when she got all dressed and ready to take the boys somewhere and found that they were down in the basement with Vennie. Instead of sending for them, she would go to her room in a fit of depression, asking Flo Dear to tell the boys she had a headache and that they would go another day.

James and Amy Tolliver were apt to say of almost anyone, "He is a genuine, intelligent, thoroughly sane person and has a fine sense of humor." They said some-

171

thing of the sort about Miss Betty and Flo Dear, and added that they were also "characters," which was the final term of approval. Amy especially was inclined to think everyone had a fine sense of humor. She herself saw what was funny in any situation and was wonderfully responsive to other people's humor, frequently inspiring them to say something quite beyond their ordinary wit. She would laugh heartily at things the two aunts said, though at least half the time James would say afterward that he didn't think she had been supposed to laugh. But Amy would reply, "Why, Flo Dear has a fine sense of humor," or "You don't do the boys' Auntie Bet justice, James."

No one was funnier to Amy than her own servants. She was forever laughing either at them or with them about something. But whereas many a Southern woman in a Northern city will get to be on rather intimate terms with her Southern servants, Amy never did. To some extent, she treated them with the same mixture of cordiality and formality that she used with her next-door neighbors. She nearly always liked her servants but never hesitated to "send them on their merry way" when there was reason to. "There are no second chances in Amy's service," her husband once said. "One false step and you are cast into the pit."

"Oh, stuff!" said Amy. "This house serves as a sort of immigration office for Tennessee blacks in St. Louis. We bring them up here and train them, and when they leave us, they always go to something better. You *know* that's so."

James laughed and said, "Only old Vennie is a permanent fixture here, I guess."

"Ah, have no illusion about that," said Amy. "Vennie's time is bound to come. And when it does, we'll be liberated from a very subtle tyranny. When Vennie is gone, I tell you, the turnover among the others won't be nearly so fast."

It seemed too funny for words when the current maid and houseboy could not get used to the fact that Flo Dear and Miss Betty were no longer to be regarded as guests. Despite all Amy could do, Emmaline would put only company linen on their beds, and every few mornings she would slip upstairs with their breakfasts on a tray. One morning, in an effort to put a stop to that, the two ladies came marching down the stairs carrying their trays, and they proceeded, amid general hilarity, to transfer their breakfast dishes to their regular places at the table. Emmaline was called in to witness it, and Bert, the houseboy, was also present. The two Negroes laughed more heartily than even the little boys at the two aunts' clowning. Amy seemed almost hysterical. "I laughed so hard I thought I was going to have hysterics," she said afterward.

But Miss Betty said, "The only signs of hysteria I saw were in Bert and Emmaline. They seemed downright scared to me." Half an hour later, when she went upstairs, she didn't stop a second in her own room but passed right on through it and through the bathroom into Flo Dear's room. Flo Dear had preceded her upstairs by some fifteen or twenty minutes and was already at work at her drawing board. Miss Betty knew

173

that her cousin hated being interrupted, but what she had to say could not wait. "I am now convinced," she announced, "that all this politeness is that old Vennie's doing."

Flo Dear raised her eyes and stared at Miss Betty.

"It is now plain to me," said Miss Betty, "that Bert and Emmaline are taking orders from two mistresses."

Presently Flo Dear gave three quick, affirming little nods and said, "Yes, you're probably right. But you and I must not give them still two more mistresses." She and Miss Betty looked into one another's eyes for a moment, and then Miss Betty turned and retreated into the bathroom, closing the door behind her.

Yet very soon Bert and Emmaline began to have small pieces of change thrust into their hands at the oddest moments—when Bert forgot to put the pillow in Miss Betty's chair at table or when Emmaline put frayed and faded towels in the ladies' bathroom. Within a few weeks, the difficulty with the two younger servants was past.

Miss Betty's three "nephews" went to a school on Delmar Boulevard, only a few blocks from home. School was out at one o'clock on Wednesdays, and it was their privilege that day to bring home as many as four guests to lunch. Since Wednesday also happened to be Emmaline's day off, it was Vennie's privilege not only to cook but to serve the meal to the boys. It was a privilege and an advantage of which she made the most. By a ruling of Vance's, none of the white adults were allowed to be present at that meal, and Vance often directed what the menu should be and even what china and glassware should be used. He always saw to it that Landon asked the blessing at that meal, and there was no horseplay whatsoever at the table. Vennie served in a black uniform with white cap and apron, and she never said a word until spoken to by Vance. But Vance, seated at the head of the table with his black hair slicked down on his head, the part glistening like a white scar, would faithfully begin addressing remarks to Vennie when dessert was about over. He did it in just the manner that his father did it whenever Vennie appeared at the evening meal, and Vennie responded with the same show of modesty and respect. "Oh, come on, Vennie," Vance would say. "Tell us about Uncle Wash's fight with the bear when they were laying the railroad to Texas."

Vennie would demur, saying, "Those boys don't want to hear my old-nigger talk." But finally she would be brought around by the insistence of all the boys, and never were her tales so exciting as then, and never so full of phrases like "plantation roads" and "ol' marster" and "befo' freedom." While she talked, Vance would sit winking at the other boys, just as his father would do. Vennie's favorite way of beginning was to say, "Now, every Tolliver, black or white, know this story and know it be true." It was a convincing way to begin and usually removed all doubt from the minds of her listeners. But on a Wednesday in the fall after the boys' aunts had come there to live, one long-faced little friend of Jimmy's stopped Vennie with the question "How do you mean 'black or white'? Are there black Tollivers?"

"What you think my name is?" Vennie asked, annoyed by the interruption.

"Your name is Vennie."

"My name's Vennie Tolliver," Vennie said. Her name indeed was Tolliver, since she had once been married to one of the Negro Tollivers at Thornton. The Negro Tollivers, like the Negro Pettigrus and Blalocks, had kept the name of their former masters after emancipation, and most of them had continued in service to the Tollivers. But Vennie's husband, like Flo Dear's, had long before "disappeared off the face of the earth."

The four luncheon guests all broke into laughter, because they thought Vennie was joking. Landon and Jimmy laughed, too. But Vance began to blush. His whole face turned red; even the part in his hair changed color. Vennie looked at him a moment in bewilderment, and then suddenly she began to laugh herself. "Didn't you-all know I was kin to Vance?" she said in a shrill voice. "Why, sho, I'm his cousin!" Her voice, which normally was rather deep and hoarse, grew clearer and higher. "'Course it ain't really the truth, 'cause I 'uz only *married* to a sort of cousin of his. But I'm his old Auntie Vennie, all right. Ain't that so, Cousin Landon?"

Landon smiled sweetly and said he guessed it was so. Vennie never did tell her story that day. Under her breath she kept laughing so hard that she couldn't have told it if she had tried. And the boys—all but Vance—

kept giggling until they finished their dessert and left the table.

Worst of all for Vance was the laughter that night from the grown people. Landon told all about it at the dinner table, right where Vennie could hear every word of it. Vance at first managed to smile halfheartedly, but in the midst of all the talk and laughter he observed that there was no shade of a smile on his Auntie Bet's face. His own halfhearted smile vanished, and he and Auntie Bet exchanged a long look, which —in Vance's mind, at least—may have constituted some sort of pledge between them.

It was Vance, with his sense of what the grownups liked, who had invented the pet name Auntie Bet, and he would have said Auntie Flo, except that Flo Dear had discouraged it. Instead, she had asked the boys just to call her Flo Dear, the way their Auntie Bet did. She was ever considerate of Miss Betty's prerogative as a blood relation, despite all of Amy's and James's impartiality. In her consideration, she went so far as to try to accept Miss Betty's views on every important thing that happened in the house. When the first complaints against Vennie were made to her by Miss Betty, she tried to admit their justice, while at the same time minimizing their importance. She imagined she saw seeds of Miss Betty's ruin in the struggle, and events pointed more and more in that direction.

By Miss Betty's "ruin" she didn't mean that Vennie would remain and Miss Betty would go; she knew that Vennie would finally be sent away, but Miss Betty's ruin would lie in her very condescension to this struggle and in the means she would use to dispose of Vennie. If only Flo Dear could delay action on Miss Betty's part, then soon enough Vennie would be discharged for reasons that wouldn't involve anyone else, because Flo Dear knew, without listening at the hot-air register in the shut-off card room downstairs, that if Vennie entertained and cooked on her magic stove for the boys in her basement rooms, she also entertained and cooked for a large number of those colored people, or their like, whose pictures hung on her walls, and the food, of course, all came out of Amy's kitchen. She knew there would be a last time for Amy's saying, "My grocery bills are outrageous! I don't understand where the leak is. That is, I'm not sure yet."

Miss Betty's complaints were not all of indirect thrusts through the boys and the other servants, for after Bert and Emmaline had been neutralized, Vennie began, herself, a series of personal affronts. If Miss Betty crossed the threshold of the kitchen, she put down whatever she was doing and retired to the basement. If the two were about to meet in the narrow upstairs hall or on the stairs, Vennie would turn back and manage to get out of sight before Miss Betty could call to her. Miss Betty did try to call to her sometimes, or at least to speak to her—there was a period when she imagined it was not too late to make friends and join forces with her adversary—but Vennie would have none of it. At last, Miss Betty trapped her one day in the pantry and said, "Why don't you and I plan a surprise dessert for the family tonight? You make us

178

a cake—one of your good devil's-food cakes—and I'll set us up to a wonderful new sort of ice cream they're making at a place I know out on De Baliviere."

Vennie rared back and her voice became shrill: "I been making the cream since before you-all come here, and I'll be making it when you and her's both gone."

When Flo Dear heard about this, her heart went out to Miss Betty in a way it seldom did. But she was also frightened by the look in Miss Betty's eyes. Ruin seemed inevitable at that moment—spiritual ruin, or, more specifically, spiritual *relapse.* Flo Dear's life in Nashville had been as quiet as Miss Betty's had been active. She knew that some people in Nashville had called her "Miss Betty Pettigru's silent partner." She had overheard people speaking of her that way, but she had said to herself, "I live this way because I have *chosen* to live this way." It was true that if she had wished, she could have shared all of Miss Betty's activities, for that was what Miss Betty had once hoped she would do. But the choice had been made long before she came to live on West End Avenue. She didn't herself pretend to know when she had made the choice, but it was made before she ever married Tolliver Blalock and became a part of his huge family connection. In the big country family that she was born into, they had always told her she was by nature a mouse, to which she had replied (silently), "If I am a mouse, at least I am a principled mouse." But when she was twenty-two and already considered an old maid, she had been swept off her feet by Tolliver Blalock, the black sheep of his family and widely known as a rascal with women. He had left her after only two months, "disappeared off the face of the earth," leaving his hat and coat on the bank of the Tennessee River, more as a sign that he would never return than as any real pretense that he had drowned. As his widow, Flo Dear was taken to the bosom of the Tolliver-Pettigru-Blalock connection as no other in-law ever was. For years, she lived with first one of her in-laws and then another. They quarreled over who was to have the privilege next. Apparently there had never been a mouse in any of those families, or at least not a *silent* mouse, and they delighted in how she would sit and listen to what *any* one of them said. She listened, and listened especially to the old ones, and then, one day, thinking it would help her forget for a while the loneliness and humiliation she felt in the bosom of her husband's fine family, she sat down and wrote out all she had heard about their splendid history. As much as anything, it was to clear her head of the stuff. The manuscript was discovered and she became known as the finest living authority on the history of the Tollivers, Blalocks, and Pettigrus. After ten years of this life in the vicinity of Thornton, there came a letter to her from Miss Betty Pettigru, whose wealthy old father had taken her up to Nashville in the vain hope of finding her a suitable husband. Miss Betty was then seeking membership in the Colonial Dames of America and she wanted Flo Dear's help in that cause. It ended, of course, by Flo Dear's moving up to Nashville.

Searching through Nashville libraries for proof of

Miss Betty's eligibility, Flo Dear found her true vocation, discovered the one passion of her life. It happened in a single moment. She was standing—tiny, plain, dish-faced creature that she was—in the dark and towering library stacks of what is surely the mustiest, smelliest, dirtiest, ugliest of state capitol buildings in the Union. In her pawlike little hands she held a book whose faded title she was trying to read on the mildewed binding. Presently, she opened the book with an impatient jerk. It came open not at the title page but at the plates of two brightly emblazoned fifteenth-century escutcheons. They were the first coats of arms Flo Dear had ever seen, and the beauty of their joyful colors seemed suddenly to illuminate her soul and give her a first taste of the pure joy of being alive. Needless to say, the joy and inspiration she received from her discovery made the matter of talent an unimportant one. In practically no time at all, she became a modern master in the art of blazonry, and by the time she left Nashville, thirty years later, there was hardly a nice house in town on whose walls a piece of her work was not hung.

Flo Dear's work became the absorbing interest of her life. Yet it wasn't entirely her fault or her work's fault that she and Miss Betty could not become "as close as sisters." At first, Flo Dear was guilty of suspecting Miss Betty of disingenuousness. She could not see why Miss Betty made over her so and she felt that she was being "cousined" to death. Outside her profession, Flo Dear soon got so she could not abide the word "cousin." She felt that if she allowed it, Miss

181

Betty would smother her with confidences. More than her time, somehow her small supply of energy seemed to disappear when she listened to her cousin. She simply could not afford the intimacy and dependency that was being asked of her.

There was more explanation than this: When old Major Pettigru was on his deathbed, he had said to Miss Betty, who was his only child, "It's a shame and a scandal, Bet. Since I brought you to Nashville, you've expended your time making a place for yourself among strongheaded women whiles you ought to have been making your place in the heart of some gentle, honest man." He had said that to her in the presence of two doctors and a nurse, and so almost immediately it had become known all over town. To most people it was an amusing story, but not to Flo Dear. She felt, exactly as Major Pettigru had, that Miss Betty had expended foolishly not merely her time but her invaluable, marvelous energy as well. Perhaps, with her unprepossessing appearance and her lack of small talk, finding a husband was not feasible for Miss Betty, but something—surely *something*—better than a life of social climbing could be found. It was worse than a shame and a scandal in Flo Dear's eyes; it was a sin. She had never told Miss Betty so in as many words, but she knew that Miss Betty knew what she thought, and she knew that Miss Betty acknowledged in her heart that she was right. Else why had Miss Betty always made a point of matching each social victory with some act of charity? When she succeeded in having Mrs. John O'Neil Smith impeached as madam presi-

182

dent of the Corinne Society (for having sat down to dinner with the president of a Negro college), she immediately gave a formal luncheon for the homeliest, least eligible debutante of the season. After she had blackballed every candidate for membership in the West End Book Club until the other members accepted an ambitious but illiterate satellite of her own, she paid a formal call on a notorious lady in town and went about saying that she, for one, thought that that lady's "adopted" child looked nothing in the world like its foster mother. Surely, in Nashville, Miss Betty's life had been all sin and expiation, sin and expiation, but with never a resolution to sin no more.

"They have big get-togethers down there," Vance said.

"Big get-togethers?" said Miss Betty.

"Yes, ma'am. Sometimes there's a whole crowd and sometimes not so many. We used to always listen to them through the radiator in here, till we got tired of it. Listen! That's Vennie's cousin who works out at the Florisant Valley Club. He's from Thornton, too, and used to work for us. Listen to them! They think they're whispering now. But you can hear them just as plain."

"Yes, you can almost hear them breathing," said Auntie Bet.

"And they can't hear you at all unless you really holler."

Vance and his Auntie Bet were in the card room, behind the drawing room. It was a room that Amy kept shut off, because she and James were not card players and it was only another room for Bert to keep clean. It was a tiny room, and the furniture had been left there by the former occupants. There was a built-in game cabinet with a dozen different size pigeon-holes and compartments, and a "stationary card table," and some chairs. It all went with the house, the former occupants had said.

It was a Sunday afternoon and Vance and Auntie Bet were playing checkers. He had come back from a long walk in the park and had found her arranging some flowers in a vase on the hall table. When he invited her to go with him to the card room and have a game of checkers, she looked at him wonderingly, because she could tell that he had something on his mind. When they were in the room, with the door closed, and had begun to play, it occurred to her that perhaps the boys weren't supposed to play games like checkers on Sunday. And in the *card* room, too. Then she began to notice the Negro voices coming through the hot-air register in the corner of the room. She was so distracted by her thoughts and by those voices that almost before she knew it, the game was over and she was badly beaten.

"Oh, you weren't even trying, Auntie Bet," said Vance.

She smiled—or, rather, she turned up the corners of her mouth self-consciously. "I tried, but I got to listening to the Negroes' voices in the radiator," she said. "We must be right above Vennie's living room." And then Vance told her about the get-togethers down there.

"It's rather eerie, isn't it?" she said. "I mean how we can hear their voices and they can't hear ours."

Vance began arranging the checkers for a new game. "Sometime," he said, not looking at her, "you might just come in here—you and Flo Dear, that is—when Jimmy and Landon and I are down in Vennie's rooms." He raised his eyes and said in a grave, reflective tone of voice, "Auntie Bet, that Vennie says the darnedest things to us children. You should just hear her."

"Why, *what*, Vance?" But before he could answer, Miss Betty had suddenly understood what sort of plot he was suggesting, and she abruptly got up from the table.

Vance instantly grew pale. "What's the matter, Auntie Bet?"

"Nothing's the matter, my darling," she said. "But I—I left half my flowers out of water." She was opening the door into the drawing room, but she glanced back at Vance and saw him still sitting with the checkerboard before him and with the bare light of the overhead lamp shining on his black hair, which looked rather too soft and too thick for a boy, and on the mottled complexion of his forehead, on the widespread nares of his nose. And silently Miss Betty Pettigru was saying to the oldest of her three Tolliver nephews, "Poor wounded, frightened child! What thoughts have you had of me? What thoughts?"

As she passed through the hall, she was surprised to see that she had indeed left some of her flowers lying on the big console table. She had bought them at a florist's on the way home from church that morning but had waited till Vennie left the kitchen to select her vase and arrange them. She snatched the flowers from the table and went upstairs.

In her room, she dropped the flowers in her wastebasket and, without taking off her daintily pleated dress, she lay down across the bed. This time, she was not up pacing the floor after fifteen or twenty minutes. She was still lying there when Flo Dear called her to go down to supper.

As she lay on her bed this Sunday afternoon, she thought of the life she had left in Nashville. Her life there had never in her eyes been one of sin and expiation. It had just been life, plain and simple, where you did what good things you could and what bad things you must. As she looked back, it seemed that it had been hard for her to decide to leave Nashville only because it had meant facing the fact of the worthlessness of the goal she had set herself many years before—the goal set *for* her, really, by circumstances and by her personal limitations. What else could she have done with her life? She had not asked to be born in the days when Victoria was queen of England, when Southern womanhood was waited upon not by personal maids but by personal slaves. She had not asked to be born the unbeautiful, untalented heiress of a country family's fortune, or to grow up to find that the country town that gave that fortune its only meaning was decaying and disappearing, even in a physical sense. The men of her generation, and of later generations, had gone to Nashville, Memphis, Louisville, and even to St. Louis, and had used their heads, their connections, and their genteel manners to make their way to the top in the new order of things. And wasn't that all *she* had done, and in the only way permissible for a Miss Pettigru from Thornton? Once the goal was defined, was it necessary that she should be any less ruthless than her male counterparts? In her generation, the ends justified the means. For men, at least, they did. Now, at last, Miss Betty saw how much like a man's life her own had been. She saw it in the eyes of the wounded, frightened child. She saw how it was that every day of her adult life had made her less a woman instead of more a woman. Or less somebody's old granny instead of more somebody's old granny. Wrong though it seemed, the things a man did to win happiness in the world—or in the only world Miss Betty knew—were of no consequence to the children he came home to at night, but every act, word, and thought of a woman was judged by and reflected in the children, in the husband, in all who loved her. "If only Flo Dear had not been so embittered before she ever came to my house," Miss Betty thought miserably, "maybe my instincts would not have died so dead."

She had done nothing to bring on Vennie's dismissal, and yet Vance had seen that she was capable of doing that something and had thought she might enter into a conspiracy with little children in the house of her kinspeople. If he condemned old Vennie for saying things to "us children" that she ought not to say, what thoughts must he have of *her?* All was lost, and in the morning she would go—not back to Nashville but perhaps to Thornton itself.

Flo Dear knocked on Miss Betty's door from the hall. "It's almost supper time," she said.

"Well, I'll be along soon," Miss Betty answered, not suggesting that Flo Dear open the door and come in.

"It's Bert's Sunday on," Flo Dear reminded her, "and Amy and James are going out to dinner."

Its being Bert's Sunday on meant that Bert would prepare and serve the cold supper and that someone must check closely to see that he washed the lettuce for the salad and that the table was set properly. Amy's and James's going out to dinner meant that the check on Bert would be Miss Betty's and Flo Dear's responsibility.

Flo Dear inferred from Miss Betty's being alone for so long in her room that there had been another incident. She had heard Miss Betty come upstairs an hour earlier, and although she had not put down her book, her mind had wandered more than once from the subject of heraldic symbolism to all the incidents of recent weeks. Miss Betty had managed to make it plain enough to her, in the way she reported the incidents, that Vennie's antagonism was directed equally at both of them. It was really Flo Dear, wasn't it, Miss Betty had asked her one day, that Vennie had made fun of to the boys and their Wednesday guests? During all their thirty years together, Flo Dear felt, this was the first deliberate unkindness Miss Betty had shown her. Yet she interpreted it as a "sign of nerves." It was

188

so unreasonable that she could not really resent it. It was as though Miss Betty expected *her* to do something about Vennie. Even in Nashville, Miss Betty had never tried to involve *her* in her petty wars with womankind. She stood outside Miss Betty's door now, shaking her head and saying to herself, "Well, it can't go on. It can't go on. We must leave. We must leave Amy and James and their children to their peace. If we can't go back to Nashville, we—or I—can go back to Thornton." But the very thought of that prospect made Flo Blalock clasp her hands and shudder inwardly. Spending her last days among the remnants of the Tolliver-Blalock-Pettigru clan! Moving from garrulous house to garrulous house! She, the pitiable woman whom one of them had wronged. She hurried along the hall, past the room where Amy and James were dressing, down the stairs, and into the dining room to see how things were going with Bert. The light was on, but there were not even place mats on the table yet. "I declare," she whispered, "that Negro Bert is not worth his salt." She went into the pantry and into the kitchen. The rooms were empty. There was no light on in the kitchen, but one of the gas jets of the stove was burning, though no pot or pan was on the stove, or even a coffeepot.

And then, through the back door and vestibule, she heard Bert's footsteps on the cement driveway. She stepped to the back door and saw him, in his white coat, coming through the twilight from the garage— the old carriage house, where he had his room, in the coachman's loft. She could see that he saw her, and that he hesitated. "What's the matter, Bert?" she asked.

He came on up the steps. He was a tall, brown-skinned Negro and walked with a peculiar gait. Amy said he picked his feet up slew-foot and put them down pigeon-toed. As he came inside the door, he pretended to laugh. "You know what I done, Miss Flo? When I left out of here, I aimed to turn off the stove, but I turned off the light instead." He switched on the light and went to the table where the coffeepot and the open coffee can were sitting.

"And now you've left the light on in your room." She was still looking out toward the garage.

"Is I now?" He was filling the coffeepot.

Flo Dear was trembling. When she spoke, she hoped her voice would sound like Miss Betty's or Amy's or James's, or Vennie's, or *anybody's* but her own. "Somebody's out there, Bert, who hasn't any business out there. Is that so, Bert?"

Bert put the coffeepot on the stove and then looked at Miss Flo, but not in his usual simple big-eyed way. "Yes, ma'am, they is. It's Vance."

Flo Dear couldn't find the words she wanted, but she continued to stare at Bert, and she knew that even with just a stare she was taking a hand in things. And now Bert, too, knew that she was taking a hand, and when he saw that, every last bit of foolishness seemed to go out of his face.

"I'm just going to tell you about it, Miss Flo," he said. "Vance come down here in the kitchen and he was crying around and wanted to talk to me. He said he had hurt Miss Betty's feelings and wouldn't never git over it, and he was scared to talk to his daddy or Miss Amy about it. He wanted to go out younder to my old rooms to talk with me, so I just taken him on out there, Miss Flo, and he and me had it all out. He'll be along in the house directly."

Flo Dear sat down on a chair beside the table. "Tell me how he hurt Miss Betty's feelings, Bert."

Bert, looking right into Miss Flo's eyes, stood before her and told her how Vance had got Miss Betty to go in the card room and all they had said there and finally how Miss Betty wouldn't really listen to Vennie and her company and wouldn't "be conniving with any little old Vance."

When he had finished, Flo Dear made no move to go. "You begin setting the table, Bert," she said. "I want to just sit here a while."

Amy and James came downstairs in evening clothes. They were going first to a cocktail party and then to a large supper party honoring the debutante daughter of two of their friends. They knew that Miss Betty always liked to see them when they were "dressed," particularly if they were going out among people whom she considered "prominent in an important way."

Amy went to the dining-room door to see if the two ladies were in there. Bert was just beginning to set the table. "You're late getting started with that, Bert," she said.

"Yes'm, ain't I, though? I got behind." He was all big-eyed simpleness again.

"Well, have you gotten Mr. James's car out?"

"Yes'm, it's at the side."

"Hasn't Miss Betty or Miss Flo come down?"

"Miss Flo's back here," he said, and he dashed off toward the kitchen. Amy stood watching the swinging door until Flo Dear appeared.

"How lovely you look, Amy," said Flo Dear, coming into the dining room. "Nothing so becomes you as green, Amy." Compliments from her were rare but not unheard of. Such compliments on Amy's appearance were Miss Betty's prerogative, but now and then, when Miss Betty was not present, Flo Dear would say something like this.

"Why, I thank you, Flo Dear," Amy said. "A compliment from you really sets me up. You're not the wicked flatterer Aunt Betty is."

"She's just more articulate than I, Amy."

"Pooh," said Amy, turning back into the hall. "Where is she, anyway?"

"Here she comes from upstairs now," James said. He was standing near the foot of the stairs, his derby on his head, his overcoat over one arm and Amy's white *lapin* wrap over the other.

"Take off your hat in the house, James," Amy said. "What will your aunts think of you?"

"It's time we're going," James said, holding up Amy's wrap for her.

"Do wait and let me see Amy's dress," called Miss Betty from the stairs, rather spiritlessly.

The others looked up at her. "Aunt Betty, you don't sound like yourself," Amy said.

"I've been taking a nap," she said. "You look lovely, Amy. It's a stunning dress."

Amy's dress was of a dark green silk, with a long waist, a very low back, and a hemline just at her knees. Her hair was not bobbed, but tonight she had it arranged in a way that made it at first glance look so.

"She looks sixteen, doesn't she?" said Flo Dear.

Suddenly Amy called out, "Boys! Boys! We're going!"

Landon and Jimmy came racing down from upstairs, and in a moment Vance appeared in the doorway from the dining room, looking solemn and dejected. Miss Betty went to him and put an arm about his shoulders.

Amy, seeing that all that was going to be said about her new dress had been said, allowed James to put the wrap about her shoulders.

"If you boys behave and mind your aunts," James Tolliver said, getting into his coat, "I'll take you to East St. Louis with me next Saturday. I'm going out to see old Mr. Hendricks at the stockyards."

Jimmy was standing on the bottom step of the stairs. Partly, no doubt, because he didn't like to go to East St. Louis but mostly because he wished to satisfy his thirst for scientific truth, he asked, "Why do you say 'our aunts' when Flo Dear is not our aunt or even related to us and Auntie Bet isn't really our aunt, either?"

Jimmy's mother and father looked at him as though he had spoken an obscenity. "Jim, are you asking to be punished?" his father said. "Do you want me to take you upstairs in my dress clothes and punish you?"

Amy dropped her velvet evening bag on the console table and sat down in one of the high-backed hall chairs. This was her usual way of saying she wouldn't go somewhere until the boys stopped misbehaving. It was also a way of emphasizing her speechlessness. After a moment, she said, "Just what do you mean by that, James Junior? What earthly power made you ask that?"

Flo Dear glanced at Miss Betty and saw that she had managed to catch Vance's eye and was shaking her head at him warningly. Jimmy was blushing and carefully avoiding the eyes of his aunts. He kept looking first at his mother and then at Landon. After a moment, Landon, who was always the one most moved by his mother's threats, said to Jimmy, "Go ahead and tell, Jimmy. It's just Vennie, and she always says she doesn't care who you tell." Then, turning to his mother, he said, "Vennie's always saying we aren't a bit of kin to Flo Dear, and not much to Auntie Bet. And she thinks they ought not to live with us unless they are close kin."

But Jimmy still had not told when his father pulled the derby off his head and was saying, "You boys—all of you—get upstairs to your rooms and get up there quick."

The three boys were upstairs and in their rooms almost before their father had taken off his overcoat. He removed the coat with great care and folded the sleeves and the collar as though he were about to pack it in a traveling bag. Then he handed it and his derby to Amy.

"Oh, James," said Miss Betty in a hoarse whisper, "don't punish the boys."

"I'm not going to punish the boys," he said. "I'm going downstairs before I leave this house and give Amy's notice to Vennie."

"No," Miss Betty said, "don't do that, James!"

But Amy said, "Tell her she needn't even come up in the house again."

"I'll meet you at the car, Amy," he said to her, and as he went out through the dining room, he called back, "I'll tell Bert to stay in the house all evening, till we come home."

When he was gone, Amy tried to smile. "I don't know why he couldn't wear his overcoat to fire Vennie," she said. "A sign of special respect, I suppose."

Miss Betty, wearing a dazed expression, said, "This won't do, Amy. It just won't do."

"Oh, it'll do fine, Aunt Betty," said Amy. "Don't you think I know what's been going on in my own house? It was James who had to be shown. He has been Vennie's protector since long before this business. And Emmaline and Bert both gave me notice a week ago; I've been sick about it. Why, for a houseboy, you just can't beat that simple-minded Bert. No, my dears, Vennie's days of usefulness in this house are past. Her superannuation is long overdue."

Supper for Miss Betty and Flo Dear and the boys was delayed for three-quarters of an hour that Sunday night. Bert was an eternity getting the food on the table, but none of them was hungry, and so it did not matter. Not long after their parents were out of the house, Vance and his brothers came downstairs and into the living room, where the two aunts were sitting together. But before the boys came down, Flo Dear and Miss Betty had exchanged a few words, and each had had a great many thoughts that were not exchanged, at least not in words.

They were seated directly opposite each other on either side of the fireplace, in two little Windsor chairs that were the only uncomfortable chairs in the room. Last embers of the usual Sunday fire were smoldering in the wood ashes between the andirons. When first they sat down, there was a long silence, with each of them staring into the embers, watching an occasional flame spring up and then die almost at once. Miss Betty's small, pudgy nose seemed swollen and her eyes were two glazed buttons. She sat with her feet placed far apart, her ankles looking swollen like her nose, and on her knees her hands rested, the ten fingers spread out like so many wrinkled little sausages. Flo Dear sat crossing and uncrossing her narrow ankles, fingering the buttons that ran from the high neck to the waist of her dress, and blinking her eyes at the fire.

At last, without changing her expression or moving a muscle of her body, Miss Betty said, "We should go on back to Nashville, I think, Flo Dear, or maybe to Thornton." She wanted to tell Flo Dear that she had had no hand in Jimmy's outburst, but it would be useless and somehow not entirely truthful to say that. Yet at the very moment she was saying that they must leave and thinking that they must, she was also thinking that if they could stay, if they could only stay, she might, with her new insight, begin to be of some use to the Tolliver boys. After all, they were rich children, just as she had been a rich child, and the world was still changing, preparing people for one thing and giving them another. And poor little Vance—what problems would be his! Not excelling in his schoolwork, certainly not good-looking, with only that one terrible talent that she, too, had—the talent for observing what things the world valued and making the most of *that*.

But she knew that she could not spend the last years of her life with Flo Dear sitting there so straight in the Windsor chair, accusing her with every crossing of her ankles and every blinking of her eyes.

All that Flo Dear said before the boys came down was, "We must do whatever seems the right thing to you and the best thing for the boys." From this, Miss Betty took hope. She detected a new softness in Flo Dear's voice. It was a softness that must have come from Flo Dear's own reassessment of things. Whether it was the thought of Thornton or her thoughts in the dark kitchen or the knowledge that Miss Betty had been truly hurt by Vance's proposal, something was making her question her old judgments of Miss Betty Pettigru. It seemed to her that perhaps to do anything at all in the world was to do wrong to *someone*. She thought of Vennie and of what would become of her now. Perhaps it was fair and just that Miss Betty should have the affection the boys gave to Vennie. Perhaps Vennie had nieces and nephews of her own. She could go and live with them or with some of her many friends.

197

There must be many of her relatives who loved and needed old Vennie. And yet perhaps she didn't really have a family of her own. Or perhaps none of them would find her so lovable and attractive when she no longer had this good job and could make them presents and cook them meals on her little coal range. But already Flo Dear could hear Vance and Jimmy and Landon coming down the stairs into the hall.

When the boys came into the living room, with their hair combed and wearing fresh shirts, Miss Betty and Flo Dear stood up and greeted their nephews as though it were after long months of separation. And the boys seemed equally glad to see their aunts. There was even kissing and hugging, and there were some tears shed. Supper was still not on the table, and though Miss Betty complained about Bert's being "so mortally slow," Flo Dear did not say again that he wasn't worth his salt. Instead, she gathered the three boys about her chair and commenced explaining to them, as no one else in the world was so well qualified to do, just exactly what her family connection was with them, and in even greater detail she described the blood ties that existed between them and their Auntie Bet. There was a certain hollowness in her voice, and as she spoke she stared somewhat vacantly into the dying embers of the Sunday fire. The boys, however, did not notice any of this. They listened attentively to the facts she was presenting, as though they were learning life's most important lessons.

For a while, Miss Betty watched this scene with

tears in her eyes. But then she went and lay down on the sofa. It would be no mere protracted visit to St. Louis; she was here for life. And when, finally, Bert announced supper, Vance had to go and touch Auntie Bet's hand to wake her from a deep, dreamless slumber.

BAD DREAMS

The old Negro man had come from somewhere in West Tennessee, though certainly not from the Tollivers' home town. Mr. James Tolliver had simply run across him in downtown St. Louis and had become obligated or attached to him somehow. For two or three years, Mr. James had kept him as a hand around his office there, no doubt believing every day he would discover some real use for him. Then one evening, without a word to his wife or to anybody else, he brought the old fellow home with him and installed him in an empty room above the garage.

Actually, this was likely to make little difference to Mrs. James Tolliver, whom everybody called Miss Amy. It would concern Miss Amy hardly at all, since the old fellow was clearly not the house-servant type. He might do for a janitor (which was Mr. James's plan) or even a yardman (under Mr. James's close supervision), and he could undoubtedly pick up odd jobs in the neighborhood. But his tenure of the room above the garage was bound to go almost unnoticed by Miss Amy and by her three half-grown sons and two elderly female relatives. They would hardly know he was on the place. They hardly knew the room he would occupy was on the place. Yet during the first few minutes after his arrival the old Negro must have supposed that Miss Amy was a nervous and exacting fussbudget and that every member of the family had a claim on that unoccupied servant's room above the garage.

The Tollivers' garage, having been designed originally as a carriage house and stable, was of remarkable amplitude. When the Tollivers' two Lincolns were in their places at night, there was space enough for two more cars of the same wonderful length and breadth. And on the second floor, under the high mansard roof, the stairway opened onto an enormous room, or area, known as the loft room, in one end of which there was still a gaping hay chute, and from the opposite end of which opened three servant's rooms. The Tollivers' housemaid, Emmaline, and her husband, Bert, shared with their infant daughter a suite of two rooms and bath. The third room had been unoccupied for several years and was furnished only with an iron bedstead and a three-legged chest of drawers.

It happened that Emmaline was in her quarters on that late afternoon in October when Mr. James arrived with the old Negro. Her husband, who was houseboy and butler, was in the house setting the table for dinner, and she herself had just hurried out for one reassuring glance at their four-month-old baby, for whom they had not yet agreed upon a name. When the sounds of Mr. James's car reached her ears, Emmaline was in the room with the sleeping baby. She had no idea that

anything unusual was astir, but at the first sound of
the Lincoln motor she began moving away from the
baby bed and toward the door to the loft room. It was
almost dark, but, craning her neck and squinting her
eyes, she gave a last loving and protective look toward
the dark little object in its cagelike bed. Then she
went out, closing the door behind her. She had taken
only two steps across the rough flooring of the wide,
unlighted loft room when she saw Mr. James ascending
the stairs, followed by an old Negro man whom she
had never seen before.

The Negro man halted at the top of the steps to get
his breath, and, catching sight of Emmaline, he
abruptly jerked the tattered felt hat from his head.
Emmaline, at the same moment, commenced striding
with quickened step toward him and Mr. James.

"Is that somebody you aim to put up out here, Mr.
James?" she asked in a loud and contentious whisper
as she approached the two men.

"Is there no electric light in this room?" Mr. James
said sternly.

He had heard Emmaline's question distinctly
enough, and she knew that he was not pretending he
had not. Mr. James was, after all, Emmaline's and
Bert's landlord, the master of the house where they
worked, and a Tolliver of the pre-eminent Tolliver
family of Thornton, Tennessee, where she and Bert
were born; and this was merely his way of saying that
he did not desire to have any conversation with her
about the old fellow. But why didn't he? Why could it
be, Emmaline asked herself. Then the truth about the

whole situation came to her, and as she recognized the true picture of what was happening now and of what, indeed, had been happening for several months past, she began uttering a volley of objections that had no relation to any truth: Why, now, Mr. James ought to have given Miss Amy some warning of this, oughtn't he? Miss Amy was going to be right upset, wasn't she, being taken by surprise, with Mr. James's moving somebody or other into her good storeroom where she was planning to put the porch furniture any week now? And besides, weren't the two old aunts expecting some of their antiques sent up from Tennessee? And where else *could* the aunts store their antiques? And wasn't it a shame, too, how crazy about playing in that room James, Jr., and little Landon always had been? Why, the room was half-full of basketballs and bows and arrows and bowie knives this minute unless the boys had moved them this very day!

She was addressing this collection of untruths not to Mr. James but frankly to the old Negro, who stood with his hat in one hand and a knotty bundle of clothes under the other arm. The old man gave no sign either that he recognized Emmaline's hostility or that he really believed his moving in would cause a great stir in the family. He stood at the top of the steps gazing with respect at the great, dark, unceiled loft room, as though it might be a chapel of some kind. So little, his manner seemed to say, such a one as he knew about even the loft rooms of the rich.

Mr. James, in the meantime, was walking heavily across the floor in the direction of the empty servant's room. Suddenly Emmaline turned and ran on tiptoe after him. "Mr. James!" she whispered rather frantically.

Mr. James stopped and did a soldierly about-face. "Emmaline," he said, "I want some light in this place."

In a single moment, total darkness seemed to have overcome the loft room. And at that same moment came the waking cry of Bert's and Emmaline's baby. With her next step Emmaline abandoned her tiptoeing and began stabbing the floor with her high heels. As she passed Mr. James, she reached one arm into the empty room to switch on a light and said, "Now that's what I been afraid of—that we would go and wake that baby of mine before I help Bert serve supper."

"In here," Mr. James said to the old Negro, and gestured toward the room. "And we'll have you a stove of some sort before winter sets in."

The weak light from inside the bedroom doorway only made the wide loft room seem darker. Mr. James remained completely beyond the reach of the light. "Is there no electrical outlet in this loft room, Emmaline?" he said.

The baby had set up a steady, angry wailing now. "No, sir," Emmaline replied softly.

"In here," Mr. James's voice repeated. This time the words came plainly as an order for the old man to advance. At once there was the sound of the old man's shambling across the rough flooring, and presently there was the sound of Mr. James's heavy footsteps as he went off toward the stairs. Somewhere in the darkness the two men passed each other, but Emmaline knew they made no communication as they passed. She heard Mr. James's firm footsteps as he descended the dark stairs, but still she didn't go to the baby, who was crying now in a less resentful manner. She waited by the open door until the old man came into the light.

"Who are you, old fellow?" she asked when he shuffled past her into the room. "Who are you?" As though who he was were not the thing Emmaline knew best in the world at this moment! As though guessing who the old fellow was hadn't been what gave her, a few minutes before, the full, true picture of what was now happening and of what had been happening for several months past. Ever since the baby came, and before too, she had been trying to guess how the Tollivers felt about her and Bert's living here on the place with a baby. Did they want them to get rooms somewhere else? Did they want her to take the baby down to her mama's, in Tennessee, and leave her there? She had talked to Miss Amy about the first plan and then the second, hoping thus to find out just what the Tollivers thought. But Miss Amy had always put her off. "We'll talk about it later, Emmaline, after Mr. James decides what he thinks is best," she would say, or, "I'll have to discuss it with Mr. James some more." Day after day Emmaline had wondered how much talk there had already been about it and what had been said. For some reason it had all seemed to depend on Mr. James.

And now she knew why. Mr. James had been waiting to spring *this* on them. It would be all right about the baby if she and Bert would take on this old grand-daddy to look after for as long as he lived. Ah, she and Bert hadn't thought of that! They had known about the old fellow ever since Mr. James first found him, and Bert had seen him a good many times, had even talked to him on various occasions at Mr. James's office. But he was such a dirty, ignorant old fellow that Bert had sheered away from much conversation or friend-liness with him. Both Bert and Emmaline had even sheered away from any talk with Mr. James *about* him. They didn't like to have Mr. James connecting them in his mind with such a dirty old ignoramus just be-cause they happened to be colored people.

But here the dirty, ignorant old fellow was, standing in the very room that Emmaline had come to think of as her baby's future nursery. Here he had come—him-self to be nursed and someday, no doubt, to die on her hands. She studied the room for a moment, mocking her earlier appraisals of it as a possible nursery. What mere trash all her thoughts about it had been. When she had not even *known* that she could keep the two rooms she had, she had been counting on a third. She had been going to make the room that the baby slept in now into a sort of living room. Oh, the window-shopping she had already done for living-room furni-ture! For some reason, the piece she had had her heart most set on was a drop-leaf table. And how she had pictured the new baby's room, as it would have been— painted the same pink as the old nursery in the Tol-livers' house!

206

Emmaline looked at the room more realistically now than she ever had done before. There was no door connecting it with hers and Bert's room, as there was between their room and the baby's. There was but the one door and one small window, and it really wasn't finished nearly so well as the two other servant's rooms. The walls were of rough sheathing, not plaster, and it would be harder to heat. In the neighborhood, there was a German washwoman who had been washing for people hereabouts since long before the Tollivers bought their place, and she had told Emmaline how the coachman used to sleep in this room and how the very finest carriage harness had always hung on the walls there under his protection. The massive hooks, which evidently had held the harness, were still on the walls and they caught Emmaline's eye momentarily. They were the hardware of a barn.

She and Bert were still living, after all, in a barn. And yet she had named this room a nursery. It was the plaster on the walls of her own two rooms that had deceived her. She realized that now, and realized that those rooms might never look the same to her again, just as her life here with Bert and the baby would hardly be the same while this old Tennessee hobo was present to be a part of it—to eat with them in the house (it was bad enough eating with the grouchy, complaining, overpaid cook, Nora Belle) and to share their bathroom (he would have to pass through her very own bedroom to reach the bathroom; she resolved that instant to make him use a chamber and to permit him to empty it only once a day). The ill-furnished bedroom and the old man standing in the center of it, now dropping his bundle on the lumpy mattress, brought back to her all the poverty and nigger life she had known as a girl in Tennessee, before the Tollivers had sent back for her. And this unwashed and ragged old man was like the old uncles and cousins whom she had been taught to respect as a little girl but whom she had learned to despise before she ever left home. While she stared at him, the old man replaced and then removed his hat at least three or four times. Finally, he hung the hat over one of the big harness hooks.

The hat hanging on the wall there seemed an all too familiar sight to Emmaline, and the uncovered head and the whole figure of the old man seemed just as infuriatingly familiar. Perhaps she had thought she would never set eyes again on such a shiftless and lousy-looking creature. Certainly she had thought she would never again have to associate such a one with herself and with the place she lived in. His uncut and unkempt white hair was precisely like a filthy dust mop that ought to be thrown out. Even the whites of his eyes looked soiled. His skin was neither brown nor black but, rather (in this light, at least), the same worn-out gray as his overcoat. Though the evening was one in early autumn, and warm for the season, the old fellow wore a heavy overcoat that reached almost to his ankles. One of the coat's patch pockets was gone; the other was torn but was held in place with safety pins and was crammed full of something—probably his spare socks, and maybe his razor wrapped in a newspaper, or a piece of a filthy old towel. God knew what all. The coat was buttonless and hung open, showing the even more disreputable rags he wore underneath. For a moment Emmaline wondered if it was really likely that Mr. James had let the old fellow hang around his office for two or three years looking like that. And then she reflected that it was a fact, and characteristic of Mr. James.

But now the old Negro was hers, hers and Bert's. Miss Amy wouldn't so much as know he was on the place. It was Miss Amy's policy not to know janitors and yardmen existed. And Mr. James—he, too, was out of it now. The final sound of Mr. James's footsteps on the stairs seemed to echo in her ears. The old fellow was nobody's but hers and Bert's.

The baby continued to wail monotonously, and rather dispassionately now, as though only to exercise her lungs. Suddenly, Emmaline said to the old man, "That's *my* baby you hear crying in there." The old man still had not spoken a word. Emmaline turned away from him abruptly. She went first to the door of the room where she and Bert slept, and then to that of the baby's room. She opened each door slightly, fumblingly took the key from the inside, and then closed and locked the door from the loft side. When she had locked both doors and tried them noisily and removed the keys, and while the baby cried on, Emmaline took her leave. She went down the steps, through the garage, and across the yard toward the house. Just before she reached the back porch, she began hurrying her steps. Bert would be wondering what had kept her so long, and she could hardly wait to tell him.

It was nine o'clock. Emmaline had made a half-dozen trips back to see about the baby. At seven-thirty she had offered her breast, and the baby had fed eagerly for several minutes and then dozed off. It was not unusual that Emmaline should make so many trips when the baby was fretful, except that she could usually persuade Bert to go for her at least once or twice to the foot of the steps and listen. Tonight, however, Bert had seemed incapable of even listening to her reports on how the baby was crying—whether "whining sort of puppy-like" or "bawling its lungs out." When she first came in from the garage, he had asked her in his usual carefree, good-natured way if "that little old sweet baby was cutting up." But when she told him about the old fellow's being out there, all the good cheer and animation habitual to Bert seemed to go out of him for a while. In the dining room, he was as lively and foolish-talking as ever when one of the boys said something to him, but in the pantry he listened only absent-mindedly to what she said about the old fellow and not at all to her reports on the baby. Then, as soon as dinner was over and the dishes were brought out, he took off his white coat and, without stopping to eat any supper, lit into washing the table dishes in the pantry sink.

At nine o'clock, the two of them went up the steps into the loft room. There was no sound from the baby. They crossed in the darkness to the door of the room where they slept. Emmaline was turning the key in the lock when the door to the old man's room opened. In his undershirt and galluses, and barefoot, he showed himself in the doorway. Presently, he made a noise like "pst" and beckoned with one hand. Bert went over to him. There was a brief, whispered exchange between them, and Bert returned to where Emmaline was waiting. He told her that the old fellow wanted to use the toilet. Emmaline stepped inside the room and switched on the light. With her finger still on the switch she looked searchingly into Bert's eyes. But his eyes told her nothing. She would have to wait a little longer to learn exactly what was going on in his head.

Then, upon hearing the old man's bare feet padding over the floor of the loft, Emmaline stepped to the door that joined her room to the baby's room, opened it softly, and went in there and waited in the dark, listening to the baby's breathing. She did this not out of any delicacy of feeling but because she felt she could not bear another sight of the dirty old man tonight. When he had been to the toilet and she had heard him go away again, Emmaline went back into their bedroom. She found Bert seated on the bed with one shoe already removed and his fingers casually unlacing the string of the other.

"Is *that* all you care?" she said belligerently. He seemed to be preparing for bed as though nothing extraordinary had happened.

"Just what you mean 'care'?" Bert answered in a whisper.

Emmaline's eyes widened. When Bert whispered, it

wasn't for the baby's sake or for anybody else's but because he was resenting something some white person had said or done. It was a satisfaction to her to know he was mad, yet at the same time it always roiled her that he whispered at times when her impulse would be to shout. Bert would whisper even if the nearest white person was ten blocks away, and in his mind he always set about trying to weasel out of being mad. She regarded him thoughtfully for a moment. Then she pretended to shift the subject. "Didn't the old fellow ask you for nothing to eat?" she asked. "I thought he would be looking for you to bring him something." She had made herself sound quite casual. Now she moved to the door to the loft room, opened it, took the key from the outside, and fitted it into the lock from the inside.

"No use locking that door," Bert said, still in a whisper. "The old fellow says he's got to go to the toilet two or three times before morning, and he don't have any chamber."

Emmaline turned around slowly. "You sound right mad about things, Bert," she said with affected calm.

"What you mean 'mad'?" Bert said, clearing his throat.

He began to smile, but well before he smiled, Emmaline could see that he was no longer mad, that he really hadn't been mad since before they left the house, that his whispering was only a sort of left-over frog in his throat from his having been mad when she first told him.

He proceeded now to pull off his other shoe. He

arranged the two highly polished black shoes side by side and then, with the heel of his right foot, pushed them carefully under the bed. And now, since Bert was pigeon-toed, he sat there with the heels of his sock feet nearly a foot apart and his big toes almost touching. Before leaving the house, he had slipped on his white coat again, as protection against the mildly cool night air, because Bert was ever mindful of dangers to his health from the cold. He was perhaps even more mindful of dangers from uncleanliness. The socks on his feet, the sharply creased whipcord trousers, the starched shirt underneath the white coat, all bespoke a personal cleanliness that the symbolic whiteness of the butler's coat could never suggest. "Well, I'll tell you," he said presently, in his naturally loud and cheerful voice. "I *was* mad about it, Emmaline, but I'm not no more."

"*Was* mad about it?" she said, taking a step toward him. The emphasis of his "no more" was somehow irksome to her. "I tell you I *am* mad about it," she said. "And I aim to stay mad about it, Bert. I'm not going to have it."

"Why, no use being mad about it," Bert said. He dropped his eyes to his fcct and then looked up again. "No use my being mad about it and no use your getting that crazy-woman look in your eyes about it. Ever since you came over in the house for supper, Emmaline, you been acting your crazy-woman worst." He began laughing deep in his throat. Then he got up from the bed. In his sock feet, he began walking about the room. "Like this," he said. He trotted clownishly

213

about the room, bent forward at the waist, with his eyes sort of popped out. "You been walking around like this." He could nearly always make Emmaline laugh by mimicking her and saying she was a crazy woman. "You been walking around like 'Stracted Mag."

But Emmaline refused to laugh. "It's not so, Bert," she said. "You know it ain't." She didn't want to give in to his resolute cheerfulness. At a time like this, she found his cheerfulness a trial to her soul.

"Why, you been your 'Stracted Mag worst tonight," he said. He went up to her and pretended to jabber wildly in her face. The 'Stracted Mag to whom he referred had been a poor, demented old Negro woman wandering the streets of their home town when Bert and Emmaline were children, jabbering to everyone, understood by no one, but credited by all with a fierce hatred of the white race.

"Not me," Emmaline said very seriously, backing away from him. "You're the 'Stracted Mag here." It seemed downright perverse of him to be making jokes at such a time, but it was like him. Whenever he was put out of humor, whenever he quarreled with her—usually about her occasional failure to keep their rooms in order, or to keep his clothes in order and clean—or when he complained about some particularly dirty piece of work Miss Amy had set him to, he was always bound and compelled to get around at last to some happy, self-mollifying view of the matter. He could no more tolerate protracted gloom on any subject, from himself or from anyone else, than he could

214

go for more than an hour without washing his hands. Not, that is, except when he was awakened in the middle of the night. Then Bert wasn't himself. Right now, Emmaline could tell from the way he was acting that he either considered the situation too hopeless to be taken seriously or had already decided what was to be done. Anyhow, he had cooked up some way of looking at it cheerfully.

But Emmaline was not yet ready to accept a cheerful view. She pretended to resent his calling her 'Stracted Mag. "Who *you* to be calling anybody 'Stracted Mag. In *my* day she was giddy and foolish like you, not pop-eyed wild." Emmaline was nearly six years older than Bert and actually they had known each other only slightly in Thornton, their courtship and marriage having taken place after they had come here to work for the Tollivers. "In *my* day," Emmaline said, "she was simple foolish, not wild-eyed crazy."

"Naw! Naw!" Bert said in utter astonishment. "How can you say so?" Her contradiction of the picture he carried of that old Negro woman left Bert absurdly shaken. "How can you say so, Emmaline, when I seen her one time fighting a dog in the street?"

"Oh, I don't reckon you did, sure enough," Emmaline said in a tone she would have used with a child.

"You know I did!" Bert said. "Down on her all fours, in the horse manure, fighting and scrapping with that old spotted dog of Miss Patty Bean's. And it was just because she hated Miss Patty and all them Beans so."

"Well, not in my day," Emmaline insisted, stub-

215

bornly and purposefully. She stared straight into Bert's eyes. "In my day, she didn't mix with man nor dog. She muttered and mumbled and kept all to herself." Emmaline evidently knew the exact effect her contradiction was having upon Bert. Like the names of other characters in Thornton, 'Stracted Mag's name was on their lips almost daily and had ceased to be a mere proper noun for her and Bert. It had become a word whose meaning neither of them could have defined, though it was well-established between them—a meaning that no other words in their vocabulary could express.

Bert looked at Emmaline reproachfully. He could hardly believe that she would thus tamper with the meaning of a single one of their stock of Thornton words, or even pretend to do so. He felt as he would have felt if she had threatened to deprive him of his sight or hearing by some sort of magic. She could so easily snatch this word from his vocabulary and render him even less able than he was to express his feelings about things in the world. He saw that in order to stop her, he must tell her at once how easy it was going to be to get rid of the old man. Still sitting on the bed, he reached forth and took Emmaline by the arm, just above the wrist. "Come sit down on the bed," he said urgently. "I aim to tell you about the old fellow."

Emmaline took two steps and sat down beside him. With his hand still on her forearm, he felt the tension of her muscles. She *was* her 'Stracted Mag worst tonight! He often told her in a joking way that she was like that old Mag, but it was really no joke at all. He knew that many a time Emmaline would have left the Tollivers' service or said something out of the way to one of the old aunts if it had not been for him. Emmaline was a good, hard-working, smart sort of a woman —smarter than most anyone gave her credit for, but at a moment's notice she could get a look so bughouse-wild in her face that you felt you had to talk fast if you were going to keep her calm. Bert's mother had been that sort of woman, too. In fact, he felt that most of the women he had ever had much to do with had been that sort; he felt that he had spent no small part of his life keeping Negro women from blurting out their resentment at white people. Emmaline was more easily handled than some, but it was because, after all, she used more sense about what she expected to get out of life than most of her sort did. Like him, she had no illusions about someday leaving domestic service. She accepted as good enough for her the prospect of spending her life in the service of such a family as the Tollivers, provided she did not have to live in the leaking, lean-to kind of shack she had been brought up in, and provided that in her comfortable quarters she might at the same time be raising a family of her own. She and Bert saw eye to eye on that. Emmaline was smart and she was not an unhandsome woman. She was tall and, though she was a little stooped, her figure was slender and well formed, and the proportions of her head and her rather long neck were decidedly graceful. Yet when excited, as she had been tonight, her eyes seemed actually to swell from their sockets, her nostrils would spread until her nose seemed completely flat-

217

tened, and her heavy lower lip would protrude above her upper lip; at those times her shoulders appeared more stooped than usual, her arms longer, her brown skin darker.

"Look here," Bert was saying. "We going to get shed of that old man. You know that, don't you?"

"What you mean get shed of him?" she asked. There was contention in her voice, but already her eyes showed her satisfaction with what he said.

"I mean he can't stay here with us."

"Who says he can't, Bert?"

"You and me won't let him."

"What we got to do with it, Bert? All I know is we ain't going to stay if he does. Is that what you mean?"

"No!" Bert exclaimed—so loud that the baby stirred in her bed in the next room. "That ain't what I mean. You think we going to vacate here for *him?* Quit the best me or you either has ever had or is like to have?"

Emmaline said, "There's other people in this here very block we could work for—mighty good places, Bert."

"And bring Baby with us?" Because they had not given the baby a name, Bert used "Baby" as a name. "And you know it wouldn't be like working with folks from Thornton."

Emmaline's eyes seemed to swell again. She asked, almost begged, him to tell her. "What we going to do, Bert? He's nasty and ignorant, and living so close. I tell you this—just as sure as Mr. James is a Thornton white man, that old fellow is a Thornton sort of nigger. Maybe where one is there's got to be the other."

"We going to run him off!" Bert said. He had released her arm, but he took it again, and at the same time he began grinning at her. "We going to run him off." He said it with a carefree kind of enthusiasm, as though he were playing a game, said it in a loud voice, as though he were trying to wake the baby or trying to make the old man hear. "Why, we going to run him off just by telling him we don't want him. He'll know what we mean. He'll think we mean worser than we do, and he'll git. And nobody will care."

"Mr. James will care," Emmaline warned.

"Nobody will care enough to stop us. I studied it out while I was washing dishes," he said. "Mr. James has done done all he's about to do for that old man. He allows he's fixed things so we'll be afraid *not* to look after the old man and keep him. But Mr. James's not going to do no more than that. I can tell by the way you said he walked off across the floor of the loft room. Mr. James is through and done with the old fellow. He can say to hisself now that he done what he could. But both him and Miss Amy thinks heaps more of us and having us wait on them than to be letting us go because we run off such as him. Oh, Lord, we'll run him off all right."

Emmaline felt fully reassured, and her eyes seemed to have sunk back into their sockets. But she asked quietly, "How?" She could hear the old man snoring in his room and she could hear the baby beginning to whimper. But before she got up to go to the baby, she repeated, "How?"

Bert laughed under his breath. "We'll just tell him to git, and he'll git."

"When, Bert?"

"Well, tomorrow," Bert said thoughtfully. "And not the day after, either. We'll scare him off while we're new to him, and he'll think we're worser than we know how to be. He's lived hard, and with harder folks than you and me, Emmaline."

When Emmaline brought the baby in on her shoulder a few minutes later, her features were composed again, and Bert was humming softly to himself. He had removed his white coat and his shirt and had hung them on hangers in the big wardrobe beside the bed. At the sight of the baby, he commenced talking a baby talk that was incomprehensible even to Emmaline. But Emmaline beamed and let him snatch the baby from her in mock roughness. Uttering a steady stream of almost consonantless baby talk, he first threw the baby a few inches in the air, and then danced about the room with her—he in his sock feet, whipcord trousers, and gleaming-white undershirt. Finally, the baby's dark, screwed-up little face relaxed into the sweetest of smiles.

"Don't wake her up no more than need be, Bert," Emmaline protested feebly. "She ain't slept half her due all day."

Bert let himself fall across the bed on his back, holding the baby at arm's length above him. Now with his muscular brown arms he was bringing the baby down to his face and then raising her again like a weight. Each time her laughing little face touched his own,

220

Bert would say, "Timmy-wye-ea! Timmy-wye-ea!"
And the meaning of this Emmaline, for sufficient reason, did understand. It was Bert's baby talk for "Kiss
me right here."

Later on, after the baby had fed at Emmaline's
breast and had been sung to sleep on her shoulder,
she was put down in her own bed in the dark room.
Then Bert and Emmaline were not long in retiring.
After their light was out, they lay in bed talking for
a while, though not once mentioning the old man,
whose intermittent snoring they heard from the next
room. As they so often did, they went to sleep debating
what name they should give the baby. They could
never agree (probably the baby would be called Baby
all her life), but neither did they ever fully disagree
about the appropriateness of the various possible
names. They went off to sleep pronouncing softly to
one another some of the possibilities: Amy Amelia,
Shirley Elizabeth, Easter May, Rebecca Jane.

They were awakened by a terrible shrieking—a noise
wild enough to be inhuman, and yet unmistakably
human. Emmaline sprang from her bed and ran
through the darkness to the baby's crib. So swift and
unfaltering were her steps that as she reached her
hands into the crib, she imagined that Bert mightn't
yet be fully awake. She even muttered to herself, "I
pray God he ain't." Yet in the next awful moment,
when she would have caught up the baby—except that
she found no baby there—the thought that Bert might
be still asleep seemed the worst, last terror her heart

could ever know. Searching the empty crib with her hands, she screamed Bert's name. Her voice came so shrill and loud it caused a painful sensation in her own ears.

And Bert, who all the while stood in the darkness only a few inches from her, and with the baby in his arms, raged forth at her out of the darkness, "God, woman! God damn, woman! You want to make your baby deaf? You yell at me like that again, woman, and I'll knock you flat on the floor." It was Bert in his worst midnight temper.

His own movements had been swifter than Emmaline's. He had even had to open the door between the rooms, yet had arrived so far ahead of Emmaline that he was holding the baby in his arms by the time her hands began searching the crib. Perhaps he had awakened a moment before she had. It seemed to both of them that they were already awake when the baby cried out, and at first neither had believed it could be *their* baby making such a noise. The two of them had come, as on one impulse, simply to make sure about the baby. All of this, of course, they revealed to each other much later; at the moment they stood in the dark cursing each other.

"You'll knock *who* flat on the floor?" Emmaline cried in a voice only a trifle less shrill and less loud than that in which she had called Bert's name. "Give me that baby of mine!" she demanded. She felt about for the light switch. When she found it, she was asking, "You'll knock who flat on the floor, you bastardy, black son of Ham?" But when the light came on, her voice

222

and her words changed, and so, no doubt, did her whole face. She saw Bert, clad in his immaculately white pajamas, holding on his shoulder the tiny, wooly-headed baby, clad in its white cotton nightgown. Beads of sweat shone on the brown skin of Bert's forehead. His wide, brown hands held firmly to the little body that was squirming incessantly on his shoulder. And in the first moment of light, Emmaline saw Bert throwing his head back in order to look into the baby's face.

Emmaline moved toward Bert with outstretched arms. "Honey," she said in a new voice, "hand me m'baby. Let me have her, Bert."

Bert let her take the baby from him. He, too, seemed to have been changed by the light. "Something's wrong with her," he said. "She ain't made a sound since I picked her up." His eyes were now fixed on the little face. "Look at her eyes, Emmaline!" The baby's dark eyes were fairly bulging from her head, and she was gasping tearfully for breath. "I think your baby's dying, Emmaline," Bert said.

Emmaline seized the baby and began patting her gently up and down the spine. This soon restored the baby's breath somewhat and allowed her to begin shrieking again. Emmaline walked from one room to the other, and then back again. Back and forth she walked, talking quietly to the baby, patting her between the shoulder blades or sometimes gently stroking her little body. Meanwhile, Bert followed at Emmaline's heels, trying to peer over her shoulder into the baby's face. At last the baby left off shrieking, and began crying in a more normal way.

At this change, Bert went to the bathroom and washed his face and hands in cold water. When he returned, he said impatiently, "What's got in her?"

"She's sick somehow, Bert," Emmaline said. Though the baby had stopped shrieking, still she was crying passionately and with no hint of abatement.

"Maybe she's hungry," Bert suggested in a voice of growing impatience.

"I just tried her while you was in the bathroom and she wouldn't take it," Emmaline said. Then she said, "Oh, Lord," and by this she meant to say it was bad enough worrying over the baby without Bert's having one of his real fits of midnight anger. She thought of stories she had heard, as a girl, of men whipping their little babies when they cried at night, whipping them to death sometimes. "Let him try!" she said to herself, but it didn't quiet her fears. Also, she now thought she heard sounds coming from the old man's room. She had forgotten his presence there until now. What if he should take this time to go to the toilet? . . . Nate would kill him.

All at once she knew for a certainty that the old man *would* come in. Oh, Bert would kill him when he came! Or there would be such an awful fight somebody would hear them in the house and Mr. James would come out and maybe shoot Bert with that little pistol he kept on his closet shelf. All she could see before her eyes was blood. And all the time she was pacing the floor, from the baby's room, where the light was on, to hers and Bert's room, where there was no light except that which came through the open doorway.

"Someway you've got to stop her," Bert said, putting his hands over his ears. He nearly always woke when the baby cried at night, but the crying had never been like this before, had never begun so suddenly or with such piercing shrieks.

"I *is* trying to stop her, Bert, but I can't," Emmaline said excitedly. "You go on back to bed, Bert."

He sat down on the side of the bed and watched Emmaline walking and listened to the baby's crying. Once he got up and went to the dresser to peer at the face of the alarm clock. It was a quarter to one. "Aw, she's hungry and don't know it," he said after a while. "You *make* her take something. It's time she fed."

Emmaline sat down in the big wicker rocking chair in the baby's room, slipped off the strap of her nightgown, and tried to settle the baby to her breast. But the baby pushed away and commenced thrashing about, throwing her head back and rolling her eyes in a frightening way. Now Emmaline began to sob. "The baby's sick, Bert," she said. "She's afire with fever, she is."

"Let me walk her some," Bert said, coming into the lighted room.

"Oh, don't hurt her, Bert," Emmaline pleaded. "Don't hurt her."

"Why, I ain't going to hurt no little baby," Bert said, frowning. "I ain't going to hurt Baby. You know that, Emmaline." As he took the baby, his wife saw the look of concern in his eyes. He was no longer in his midnight temper—not for the time being at least. Or, anyway, he was out of the depths of it.

But Emmaline sat in the rocking chair sobbing while Bert walked with the baby from one room to the other. Finally, he stopped before her and said, "You cut out your crying—she ain't got much fever I can feel. Something's ailing her, and she's sick all right, but your carrying on don't help none."

In the far room Emmaline could hear the old man knocking about, as though he were in the dark. He was looking for the light, she thought. And she thought, Bert can hear him too. Suddenly she wailed, "If the baby's sick, Bert, then why ain't you gone to the house to get somebody to—"

"To get somebody?" Bert shouted back at her. "What in hell you mean?"

"To get some of them to call a doctor, Bert."

"Go wake Mr. James to call a doctor?" Now the baby began shrieking as at the outset, but Bert shouted above the shrieking. "On top of him sending that old fellow—"

"Then go out and find a doctor. Get dressed and go out and find us a doctor somewheres." She was on her feet and wresting the baby from Bert.

Bert stood nodding his head, almost smiling, in a sudden bewilderment. Then he went into the other room and took his shirt off the coat hanger. He was leaning over the dresser drawer to get out clean underwear when Emmaline heard the unmistakable sound of their door from the loft room opening. The sound came at a moment when the baby had completely lost her breath again. Emmaline commenced shaking the baby violently. "Oh, Lord! Oh, Lord God!" she cried

226

out. She was standing in the doorway between the two rooms. Bert looked over his shoulder. She thought at first he was looking at her, but then she saw he was looking at the shadowy figure in the other doorway.

Now the baby's gasping for breath claimed Emmaline's attention again. But even so, the shadow of a question fell across her mind: Did Bert keep his knife in the drawer with his underwear? It was a needless question she asked herself, however.

She could not see that Bert was smiling at the old man. Afterward, she did remember hearing him saying politely, "Our baby's sick." But at the moment the words meant nothing to her. There, in her arms, the baby seemed to be gagging. And then Emmaline felt her baby being jerked away from her. It happened so quickly that she could not even try to resist. She saw Bert springing to his feet. Then she beheld the dirty old man holding the baby upside down by her feet, as he would have held a chicken. Among the shadows of the room he was somehow like another shadow. Barefoot and shirtless, he gave the effect of being totally naked except for some rather new-looking galluses that held up his dark trousers. A naked-looking, gray figure, he stood holding the baby upside down and shaking her until her nightgown fell almost over her head, exposing her white diaper and her black, heaving little stomach.

Emmaline felt all the strength go out of her body, and it seemed to her that she was staggering blindly about, or falling. Indistinctly, as though from a great distance, she heard the voices of the two men. The old

227

man's voice was very deep and—she resisted such a thought—was a voice fraught with kindliness. Presently, Emmaline realized that Bert was standing by her with his arm about her waist, and the baby was crying softly in the old man's arms.

"But something *sure* must be ailing her," Bert was saying quietly. He was talking about the baby and didn't seem to realize that though Emmaline had remained on her feet, she had lost consciousness for a moment. "She don't yell like that, and she *woke up* yelling bloody murder," Bert said.

The old man smiled. He was gap-toothed, and the few teeth he had were yellow-brown. "Bad dreams," he said. "Bad dreams is all. I reckon he thought the boogyman after him."

Bert laughed good-naturedly. "I reckon so," he said, looking at Emmaline. He asked her if she was all right, and she nodded. "How come we didn't suppose it was bad dreams?" he asked, smiling. "It just didn't come to us, I reckon. But what could that little old baby have to dream about?" He laughed again, trying to imagine what the baby could have to dream about.

Emmaline stared at Bert. At some point, he had waked up all the way and had become himself as he was in the daytime. She had a feeling of terrible loss for a moment, and the next moment was one of fear.

What if Bert *had* straightened up and turned away from the dresser drawer with his knife in his hand? Yet it wasn't that question that frightened her. It was another. Why had she tried to start Bert on his way to get a doctor? She wasn't sure, and she knew she would never be sure, whether it was really to get a doctor, or to get him away before the old man came into the room, or to get him to that drawer where he kept his knife before the old man came in. Now, in a trembling voice, she said, "Let me have the baby."

The baby had stopped crying altogether. All signs of hysteria were gone. She sniffled now and then and caught her breath, but she had forgotten her nightmare and forgotten how frightened and quarrelsome her parents' voices had sounded a short while before. In the half-darkness of the room, her eyes were focused on the buckle of one of the old man's galluses.

Emmaline came forward and took the baby, who, though she seemed sorry to leave the old man, was now in such a happy frame of mind that she made not a whimper of objection. On Emmaline's shoulder, she even made soft little pigeon-like speeches.

It was during this time, while the baby cooed in her mother's arms, that Bert and Emmaline and the old man stood staring at one another in silence, all three of them plainly absorbed in thoughts of their own. It was only for a moment, for soon the old man asked to be allowed to hold the baby again. Emmaline felt that she could not refuse him. She told him that the baby was not a boy but a girl, that they had not yet named her, but that Bert usually just called her plain Baby; and then she let the baby go to the old man. Whatever other thoughts she and Bert were having, they both were so happy to have found the baby wasn't the least bit sick, after all, that they were content to stand there a while contemplating the good spirits the old man had put her in. The baby changed hands several times, being passed to Bert, then to Emmaline, and then back to the old man. Finally, she began to fret.

"Now she's hongry," the old man said with authority.

There could be no doubt that that was what this sort of fretting meant. Emmaline automatically stepped up and took the baby from him. She went into the lighted room where the crib was and closed the door. As she sat down in the wicker rocking chair and gave the baby her breast, she could hear the old fellow still talking to Bert in the next room. It occurred to her then that all the while they had stood there passing the baby back and forth and delighting in the baby's good spirits, the old man had been talking on and on, as though he didn't know how to stop once he had begun. Emmaline hadn't listened to him, but as she now heard his bass voice droning on beyond the closed door, she began to recollect the sort of thing he had been saying. Off his tongue had rolled all the obvious things, all the unnecessary things, all the dull things—every last thing that might have been left unsaid: He guessed he had a way with children; they flocked to him in any neighborhood where he lived and he looked after them and did for them. Along with the quality of kindliness in his voice was a quality that could finally make you forget kindliness, no matter how genuine. Why, he didn't mind doing for children when their folks wanted to go out and have a good time. Young folks ought to go out and have their good time of it before they got like him, "a decrepited and lonesome old

230

wreck on time's beach." What Bert and Emmaline needed was some of their old folks from Tennessee— or the likes of them—to show them something about raising children, so they wouldn't go scaring themselves to death and worrying where they needn't. Tears of pity came into Emmaline's eyes—pity for herself. It would be like that from now on. She heard the old man's voice going on and on in the next room even after she had heard Bert letting himself down on the bed. She even thought she heard the old man saying that if they didn't want him to stay, he would leave tomorrow. That's what he *would* say, anyhow. He would be saying it again and again for years and years because he knew that Bert would not have the heart, any more than she would, to run him off after tonight.

She got up and turned off the light, and then, with the baby in her arms, found her way back to the rocking chair. She continued to sit there rocking long after the old man had talked himself out for this time and had, without shutting the bathroom door, used the toilet and finally gone off to his own room. She went on rocking even long after she knew the baby was asleep and would be dead to the world until morning. During the time she and Bert and the old man had stood in the shadowy room in silence, each absorbed in his own thoughts, she had been remembering that the baby's shrieking had awakened her from a nightmare of her own. She had not been able to remember at the time what the nightmare was, but now she did. There wasn't much to the dream. She was on the Square in Thornton. Across the courthouse yard she spied old 'Stracted Mag coming toward her. The old woman had three or four cur dogs on leash, and she was walking between two Thornton white ladies whom Emmaline recognized. As the group drew near to Emmaline, she had the impulse to run forward and throw her arms about old Mag and tell her how she admired her serene and calm manner. But when she began to run she saw old Mag unleash the dogs, and the dogs rushed upon her growling and turning back their lips to show their yellow, tobacco-stained teeth. Emmaline tried to scream and could not. And then she did manage to scream. But it was the baby shrieking, of course, and she had waked from her nightmare.

As she rocked in the dark with her sleeping baby, she shook her head, trying to forget the dream she had just remembered. Life seemed bad enough without fool dreams to make it worse. She would think, instead, about the old man and how she would have to make him clean himself up and how she would have to train him to keep out of the way except when she wanted him to do for the baby when the baby got older. She even tried to think kindly of him and managed to recall moments of tenderness with her old granddaddy and her uncles in Thornton, but as she did so, tears of bitterness stung her eyes—bitterness that out of the past, as it seemed, this old fellow had come to disrupt and spoil her happy life in St. Louis.

In the next room, Bert, in his white pajamas, lay on their bed listening to the noise that the rocking chair made. It went "quat-plat, quat-plat," like any old country rocking chair. He knew that the baby must be asleep by now, but he didn't want Emmaline to come back to bed yet. For while he and Emmaline and the old man had stood together in the brief silence, Bert, too, had realized that the baby had awakened *him* from a nightmare. He had thought he was a little boy in school again, in the old one-room Negro grade school at Thornton. He was seated at the back of the room, far away from the stove, and he was cold. It seemed he had forgotten to go to the privy before he left home, as he so often used to forget, but he could not bring himself to raise his hand and ask to go now. On top of all this, the teacher was asking him to read, and he could not find the place on the page. This was a dream that Bert often had. It could take one of several endings—all of them equally terrible to him. Sometimes the teacher said, "Why can't you learn, boy?" and commenced beating him. Sometimes he ran past the teacher (who sometimes was a white man) to the door and found the door locked. Sometimes he got away and ran down to the school privy, to find indescribable horrors awaiting him there.

As he lay in bed tonight, he could not or would not remember how the dream had ended this time. And he would not let himself go back to sleep, for fear of having the dream again. There had been nights when he had had the dream over and over in all its variations. Why should he go back to sleep now and have that dreadful dream when he could stay awake and think of pleasant things?—of the pleasanter duties ahead of him tomorrow, of polishing the silver, of scouring the tile floor in the pantry, perhaps of washing Miss Amy's car if she didn't go out in the afternoon. He stayed awake for a long time, but without thinking of the old man at all, without even thinking of what could be keeping Emmaline in the next room.

And while Bert lay there carefully not thinking of his bad dream and not thinking of the old man, and while Emmaline thought of the old man and wept bitterly because of him, wasn't it likely that the old man himself was still awake—in the dark room with the three-legged chest of drawers, the unplastered walls, and the old harness hooks? If so, was it possible that he, too, had been awakened from a bad dream tonight? Who would ever know? Bert and Emmaline would tell each other in the morning about their dreams—their loneliness was only of the moment—and when Baby grew up, they would tell her about themselves and about their bad dreams. But who was there to know about *his?* Who is there that can imagine the things that such a dirty, ignorant, old tramp of a Negro thinks about when he is alone at night, or dreams about while he sleeps? Such pathetic old tramps seem, somehow, to have moved beyond the reach of human imagination. They are too unlike us, in their loneliness and ignorance and age and dirt, for us even to guess about them as people. It may be necessary for us, when we meet them in life or when we encounter them in a story, to treat them not as people but as symbols of something we like or dislike. Or is it possible to suppose, for instance, that their bad dreams, after all—to the very end of life, and in the most hopeless circumstances—are only like Bert's and Emmaline's. Is it pos-

234

sible that this old fellow had been awakened tonight from a miserable dream of his own childhood in some little town or on some farm in that vague region which the Tollivers called West Tennessee? Perhaps, when he returned from the toilet, he sat up in bed, knowing that at his age he wasn't likely to get back to sleep soon, and thought about a nightmare he had remembered while standing in that shadowy room with Bert and Emmaline. It might even be that the old fellow smiled to himself and took comfort from the thought that anyway there were not for him so many nightmares ahead as there were for Bert and for Emmaline, and certainly not so many as for their little woolyheaded baby who didn't yet have a name.

THE DARK WALK

1

It was a rather old-fashioned sort of place with no entertainment except expeditions to Pikes Peak to see the sunrise, horseback riding on Tuesday and Thursday, and a depressing dance ("For Young and Old") in the dining room every Saturday night. The first thing Sylvia Harrison's children said upon arriving was: "Why, there's not even a swimming pool!" To the two older children, Margaret and Wallace, it seemed an impossible place. They were aged fifteen and sixteen at the time, and they would have much preferred being back in the heat of Chicago. To them the depressing Saturday night dances in Mountain Springs were an anathema. Wallace said the notice on the bulletin board should read: "For the *very* young and the *very* old." Twelve-year-old girls, still wearing sashes and patent-leather pumps, danced with their grandfathers. Worse still, old ladies danced together and "broke" on each other. The music was unspeakable: a drum, a piano, and a saxophone. Margaret and

236

Wallace soon got in touch with school friends whose sensible parents were staying in Colorado Springs. The two of them were forever dashing over to the Antlers and the Broadmoor in a rented automobile; but even that was not much fun, because Sylvia always made them get back to Mountain Springs before midnight. And on Saturday night, for at least a few minutes, they had to appear at the Mountain Springs dance.

Those Saturday nights in Colorado were even more painful to Sylvia's two younger children, Charley and Nora. *They* had to stay at the dance until 10:30 and *they*, as well as their mother, had to dance time and again with old Miss Katty Moore, who owned and managed Mountain Springs Hotel. The three of them —Sylvia and the two younger children—took turns dancing with Miss Katty. When she approached their table they would whisper among themselves whose turn it was; and soon, off one of them would go in the arms of the muscular little old lady. It was a humiliating experience—the dancing was. But somehow it wasn't itself so bad as those awful moments when Miss Katty was approaching. It was that that the children dreaded all week long. The old lady would come toward them with a bouncing step, sometimes with her incredibly muscular arms outstretched as she snapped her fingers to the rhythm of the music. Her snow-white hair was bobbed, and shingled in the back. She wore a white satin evening dress, and, for dancing, a pair of low-quarter, white tennis shoes. As she stopped at their table she would roll her eyes back into her head until only the whites were showing. This was her facetious way of issuing an invitation to the dance. . . . An unbelievable sight the old woman was. And a dreadful reality she presently became for him or her whose turn it happened to be.

But why need this macabre invitation be accepted? Because old Miss Katty Moore was a native of Tennessee. Because she had taught gymnastics at Ward-Belmont School in Nashville when Sylvia was a student there and had taught Sylvia and all Sylvia's contemporaries there the art of swinging Indian clubs. It was, in fact, because of this old association that Sylvia took her family to Mountain Springs instead of to the Broadmoor that summer. She told herself it would be fun to see her old teacher again and she enjoyed thinking of the pleasure her old schoolmates would receive from the letters she would write them about Miss Katty. She pictured those old schoolmates— the half-dozen or so with whom she had kept up a regular correspondence through the years, pictured them opening her letters about Miss Katty as they stood on the front porches of their white clapboard houses in Tennessee. Four of them lived in the very town where Sylvia had grown up, and rarely did a month pass without her writing to and receiving a letter from one of them. Her life and theirs had followed such different courses in recent years that there was always something newsworthy to write. She knew how her "western trip" would interest them and could hear them exclaiming, "Good heavens! Miss Katty Moore in Colorado!"

But Sylvia Harrison would never have thought of going West at all except that Nate Harrison's business had taken him for several weeks to Denver and to Salt Lake City. She and the children had accompanied Nate to those places, and he had afterward gone with them through Yellowstone Park. After Yellowstone he had had to return to Chicago. Originally he had had his secretary make reservations for Sylvia and the children at the Broadmoor, and it was Sylvia herself, of course, who remembered about Miss Katty and changed the plans. Nate had laughed at her for it and had been especially *tickled* by the fact that she was going to keep in touch with her Tennessee friends during the summer and probably wouldn't write a line to anybody in Chicago. But he said it was all right if that was what she wanted and said there was no use in his trying to change her about such things. One thing he would never attempt, so he said, was to change Sylvia about such things as that. He, of course, never set eyes on Mountain Springs and never danced a step with Miss Katty Moore. During the summer Sylvia carried through her plan to write notes to her old schoolmates (all of whom replied with messages for Miss Katty) and when she was back in Chicago she wrote a long letter to be passed among them, in which she depicted the trip as "an awful failure" for the whole family. "The hotel was really a mess," she wrote. "The long train ride was ghastly. Miss Katty, despite her foxtrotting and two-stepping on Saturday nights, was the only bright spot for me."

✦

Afterward Sylvia would refer to that summer in Colorado whenever people tried to sympathize with her for having had to move about the country so many times. For more than ten years Nate's business had kept the family almost constantly on the move, but Sylvia said she would rather pack and move her possessions a hundred times than take one such trip as that. The children were always so keyed up on a vacation trip, and they were always so disappointed over the way things worked out. Whereas a move was a very different matter. It was like ordering the groceries. The only bad thing about a move, said Sylvia, was the respect in which it was like taking a trip—a certain inescapable human element. For instance, on moving day somebody in the family would burst into tears at the sight of some particular piece of furniture's being shouldered out of the house by the moving men. Or somebody would decide—"somebody" being always one of the children, of course—that he or she would never be as happy in another house or neighborhood as in the one they were leaving. It was nearly always Sylvia's lot to combat the bursts of tears, to remind someone that none of these houses was really home for them, to say again that home for them would always be Tennessee. Home was not Chicago or Detroit, or any of the other places they had lived. Home was the old Harrison place at Cedar Springs, or perhaps Sylvia's own family house at Thornton.

Yet there had been one occasion on which Sylvia herself had shed tears. It was in the year 1922, in the late spring of the year—toward the end of May. The

Harrisons were then setting out from Cedar Springs for Memphis, where Nate was going to act as a sort of "efficiency vice-president" of a concern that had been badly mismanaged. On the day of that first move the sycamores and the oak trees which shaded the streets of the country town still had the first greenness of spring, and so did the grass in the big yards about the houses and in the cow pastures that came up to the edge of town. In some of the ditches along the streets day lilies were already in bloom. Nate and Sylvia had planned to be up and on their way before sunrise while it was still cool and before the roads became dusty. But they didn't get away that early, of course. Even though they had only the two children then, it was all they could do to have everything and everybody ready to set out by 7:30. The moving vans from Memphis had waited there overnight to pack the last beds, and it was seven o'clock before even the vans could get under way.

At 7:30 on that spring morning the Harrisons drove west through the old town. All the family were in the new Nash touring car. Following them in the Ford sedan were the two servants and the family pets. As they drove the length of the one long block between their house and the town square they passed a number of their fellow townsmen hurrying along their way to work. It was the sight of one of these men waving good-by to them—a man whom Sylvia Harrison hardly knew—that made her forget herself that morning and look over her shoulder in the direction of the empty house they had left behind. And the one glance was fatal.

At the first little choking sound in her throat, Nate began to slow down the car and commenced speaking comforting words to her. But Sylvia only sobbed: "Go on. Go on, Nate. Don't stop the car. If only we could have left while it was still dark! I wouldn't have minded so much if we could have left before sunup. And why couldn't we have left before the spring was so far advanced? Oh, everything is at its peak, Nate!"

Nate tried to reason with her, saying that this was the normal time of year to move. He had to keep his eyes on the road but there was a smile of infinite tenderness on his face and he even reached out his right hand and pressed the back of it gently against her cheek.

But Sylvia continued as before: "We ought to have left last year, somehow. Or we ought to have left Cedar Springs before we ever had any children."

At this slight reference to themselves, the two children in the back seat also began to cry. Nate brought the car to an abrupt stop. Behind them, the brakes of the Ford sedan screeched. And Sylvia, turning just then to comfort the children, saw over the children's heads and through the isinglass rear window of the car the astonished faces of the Negro man and woman in the sedan. She saw the Negro woman, just after the sudden stop, trying to comfort the canary bird in the cage which she held on her lap, and saw the man reaching back with his long arm to pet Toto, the fox terrier, who was riding between the bundles in the back seat of the sedan. This picture of the servants and the pets seen over the heads of her weeping children immediately revived Sylvia's spirits. With tears still in her eyes she had begun smiling and even chuckling to herself; for here in these two cars were all the members of her household. A few miles ahead of them on the road to Memphis were the four vans of furniture— almost everything in the way of furniture that her family or Nate's had ever owned.

Never in all her years of moving would Sylvia Harrison allow her friends to assist her or to sympathize with her about her moving. Nate's rise in the business world of the Midsouth and Midwest was so continuous and so prodigious that it kept the family shuttling about the country for more than ten years. Yet Sylvia never complained and never willingly accepted sympathy. On the contrary, instead of ever permitting them to commiserate with her, the letters she wrote to her friends in Tennessee were likely to contain expressions of sympathy for them—not because life had kept them in Thornton and Cedar Springs or had taken them only as far as Nashville, but for a thousand disappointments and injustices they had suffered. The same kind of thing was true in her relationship with the new friends she made and with the old friends whose paths crossed hers at one time and another. And as long as Nate lived, not even he felt free to offer Sylvia advice on the subject of moving or even to lend a hand or express any sympathy when the time for packing arrived.

After Nate died in 1939 and when Sylvia was preparing to take her family from Chicago back to Tennesssee, those in her Chicago circle of friends dared not allude to the troublesomeness of moving. It had been that way, in some degree, when she left Cedar Springs, when she left Memphis, St. Louis, Detroit—everywhere. For a number of years she tried to conceal just how much furniture she did carry about the country with her, but someone—her husband, or one of the children, or even one of the servants—always let the cat out of the bag about the things she had to keep in the attic and the stuff she had to put in storage.

Wherever the Harrisons had lived they had gone out among society people, mostly among society people with a Southern background (of which they found no scarcity anywhere in the Midwest). They were admired everywhere for their geniality, their good breeding, and simply for their attractive appearances. Sylvia, even at the time of Nate's death when she was a woman of forty-four, was known in Chicago for her unusual prettiness, her charming manner, and for her very youthful figure. But she was also known—much to her distaste—as the poor, dear Southern woman who had had to move so often and who insisted on taking such a quantity of furniture everywhere. Such an attitude seemed uncalled-for and absurd to her. If there had ever been any scarcity of money, then it would have been a different matter. Her heart went out to people who had to move on a shoestring. The sight of an old rattletrap truck piled high with bare bedsprings and odd pieces of oak furniture could bring tears to her eyes. But in her case there had never been any risk or uncertainty about moving. There had always been more than enough money—both she and Nate had their own comfortable incomes from property back home—and there had always been the understanding that some day they would go back to Tennessee.

Most of the women with whom Sylvia had gone to boarding school in Nashville were women who had been, no less than she, well provided for. Their misfortunes were seldom of a money kind, although there *was* the case of Mildred Pettigru whose husband, after he had run through her small inheritance, deserted her in Shreveport, Louisiana, without even train fare back to her home at Gallatin. (Luckily, though, another schoolmate's husband who had done well in politics was able to procure the appointment of Gallatin postmistress for Mildred.) Except for Mildred's husband, however, and one other rascal, who actually ended in the penitentiary, the men whom Sylvia's friends married were responsible, energetic men who commanded the respect of everyone who knew them. Yet in the life of each of her friends there was some element or condition to touch Sylvia's loyal and compassionate heart. "I feel sorry for Letty Russell," she would say to Nate. "She and Harry have never had any children and while he's away on his contracting jobs she's stuck in the house with Harry's mother who's stone deaf and almost blind." Nate might shake his head sympathetically. Or another time he might point out to Sylvia that she was always looking for reasons to feel sorry for her friends, and then he would remind her that some people were inclined to pity *her* for all her labors in moving. *"That,"* Sylvia would reply, "is something I have imposed upon myself. It is of *my* choosing that we travel with so much furniture, Nate."

Needless to say, not all of Sylvia's girlhood friends remained in the section of the country where they were born, but it was with those who did that she corresponded most faithfully and it was the signs of unhappiness in *their* lives that disturbed her most deeply. At least once a year she went back to Tennessee for a visit, to see after her property there; and in that way she continually renewed her acquaintance with her friends' manner of life. She always visited in the home of one of them, making that her headquarters, and accepted invitations to meals in the houses of innumerable others within a radius of thirty miles of Thornton. She went to their bridge parties, their church guild meetings, their sit-down teas, their Coca-Cola luncheons. She sat with them individually on their porches and in their upstairs sitting rooms talking about old times and about present times. The fact that impressed itself upon her always was that in no household did she find the kind of harmonious relationship which she and Nate enjoyed. It wasn't that she found discord in the place of harmony. Rather, she found in place of either a vacuum. The husbands and fathers in these houses were not the tyrants of another day; they were instead . . . what *were* they instead? Sometimes, after such a visit, it seemed to Sylvia that the husbands had not been there at all.

And yet she observed that these same husbands exercised a kind of inhuman control over their families that their forebears had never done. The literal picture she carried in her mind of a typical, latter-day husband in Tennessee was one of a man in shirt sleeves, his tie removed, perhaps even his shoes off. He is seated in a canvas chair in the yard or in a wicker porch chair at the very end of the porch, reading *The Evening Tennessean* or the biweekly *Cameron County Democrat*. It is late afternoon and he is tired. At the other end of the porch is his wife with a group of friends. They are dressed fashionably, even elegantly. There has been an afternoon party here or at some other house on High Street or Church Street or College Street. But he, the husband, is a being who has retired from the social scene in Thornton. He is a working man—not a laborer but a lawyer or a dealer in electrical and plumbing fixtures or the manager of a chain store or even a doctor or a congressman. It doesn't matter. He insists on his right, his necessity to be like other men. But he insists also that his wife, Sylvia's girlhood friend, must continue to live as she always has, and he will insist upon sending his daughter to Ward-Belmont (this being before the Baptists finally took over Ward-Belmont). He is not to blame for things being the way they are, but probably he doesn't care that they are. It was he who said to his wife before she came to Chicago to visit Sylvia: "Buy yourself some really good clothes while you're there, but when you get back, for God's sake don't come near my place of business in them."

Nate, of course, said that Sylvia exaggerated this

247

whole matter. But she once pointed out to him that
even Isabel Sternberg, her old maid Jewish friend in
Cedar Springs, shared the experience. Isabel's old-bach-
elor brothers insisted that all the rituals of the table
be observed at their house, yet the brothers rarely ate
at home. They ate lunch and often dinner too at the
Cardinal Café, which was next to the bank, and left
Isabel to eat with the three old aunts and the little girl
she had adopted.

"The Jews," Nate had said, forgetting the real topic
under discussion, "are wonderful people. Especially
Southern Jews. Someone ought to write a history of
Southern Jews."

"It's no joke to be a Jew," Sylvia replied, thinking
affectionately and sympathetically of Isabel. "Not even
in the South."

During Nate's lifetime there were, on some occasions,
mild disagreements between Sylvia and him about the
necessity for moving from one house to another in the
same city. Sylvia complained that he never bothered
to get a sufficiently long lease on a house. Nate said
that the truth was it was not easy (especially during
the '20's) to get more than a year's lease on the kind
of house they required. Owners were always coming
back from Europe or deciding to sell the house. Sometimes Nate would shake his head and smile indulgently
at Sylvia, which was supposed to remind her of the
folly of carrying so much furniture about the country.
Sometimes he would flare up as though he were about
to lose his temper and threaten to buy a place, one

that would hold her furniture. Then Sylvia would give in. For that always seemed to her the most impractical idea of all. When Nate made that threat, she would go to the telephone and call the transfer company.

Any decision to move was Nate's, but the activity itself was all hers. After their first move from Cedar Springs, Sylvia took more and more responsibility until at last she would ask Nate to make-himself-scarce during the actual operation and not meddle in a woman's work.

There was hardly a picture or a piece of furniture for which she did not have some special provision in time of moving. She saved all her old faded and worn-out slipcovers to protect the upholstered chairs from the danger of snags and scars. Her mother's mahogany teacart and a certain little Chippendale night stand were always packed inside the cedar chest with the blankets and bed pillows. Somewhere she had obtained an old coffin crate into which the grandfather clock would just exactly fit. For her favorite Chinese-lacquer piece and for all the portraits and the painted tapestries there were special crates which she had had constructed before she ever left Cedar Springs. There were even a few things in the attic (or sometimes in a warehouse) which had been crated in Cedar Springs and had not been uncrated during all the years of moving.

One of the miracles of her moving technique was the way she could get the furniture set up and arranged in a new house so that any individuality in the house itself was completely obscured. If she had papering or painting done, it was in an effort to subdue obtrusive

249

architectural design. Long before it became fashionable, she was fond of painting doors, walls and all the wood trim in a room the same color—a dusty green, a flat gray, or an off white. By some means or other her furnishings were made to dominate whatever interior they were taken into. Within two days after the Harrisons had moved—whether into a modern suburban house or a Victorian city house—it was hard for any of them to realize how recently they had moved or actually that they had moved at all. Upstairs there would be the rosewood bed, six feet wide and nearly eight feet long, whose canopy had inevitably to be stored in the attic or in a warehouse. (Even the house on Ritchie Court in Chicago did not have ceilings high enough for the canopy.) Downstairs were the family portraits and the enormous painted tapestries representing scenes and characters from Tennessee history. (The pictures, like everything else in the house, seemed always to suggest a bigger house.) And downstairs, of course, were the heavy living-room and library pieces, and the innumerable china cabinets, chests, and sideboards overflowing from the dining room into the front and back halls. No matter if a house had all manner of built-in storage space Sylvia still preferred to keep her linens and china in the storage pieces that she brought along and to keep the family books in her own glass-fronted bookcases. This made it easier, so she said, to put her hands on things. It kept her from having to stop twenty times a day to think where she had put something the last time they moved.

✦

Despite Sylvia's express wishes to be left alone, her neighbors had been known to send over whole meals for her and her family on the day of a move. "It's as though one of us were dead," she said on one occasion. "The wonder is somebody doesn't send flowers."

One time she gave a dinner party only two days before she moved, just to prove to herself—and to everyone else, of course—that she could. It was an elaborate party, far more elaborate than she usually went in for. But in the rooms where she entertained her company all sorts of barrels and packing cases were in evidence. Guests had to talk to each other leaning over and around crates which were apparently packed and ready to be loaded. Sylvia, during most of the evening, refused to recognize the presence of the boxes and barrels. If anyone made reference to them she pretended either not to hear or to be offended by the reference.

Then, just as the party was breaking up, she called for everyone's attention, and she proceeded to go about opening barrels, crates, packing cases—revealing that all but one of them were empty and that she had not really even begun her packing. The one box that was not empty was filled with presents for the guests, presents prettily wrapped in tissue paper and tied with colored ribbons but which when opened turned out to be only absurd white elephants that Sylvia had not cared to move. . . . She had done this, of course, in a spirit of fun and gaiety. And whenever mention was made of it in later years, she would point out that it had happened in the Era of Practical Jokes, back in the '20's when she was young and energetic and full of

251

all kinds of foolishness. It had happened when she and Nate lived down in Memphis and at a time when they were only moving from one house to another, not from one city to another. Fifteen years later, after Nate was dead and when Sylvia was making the last of all her many moves, she could hardly consider that move from one Memphis address to another a move at all.

Nate always professed to be as baffled as everyone else by Sylvia's untroubled and independent spirit at moving time. He would tell about that party she gave in Memphis and how astonished and perplexed he had been by her behavior. Or he would tell about their first move from Cedar Springs to Memphis, not about Sylvia's crying that morning but about how well she had borne the hardships of that awful trip. When they left the town square they had two hundred and eight miles of bad roads between them and the city limits of Memphis. Here and there was a ten-mile stretch of blacktop, but most of the roads were gravel and there were frequent stretches of unimproved dirt roads. All day long they had pushed toward Memphis. But at sundown they were still forty miles northeast of the city. They had had every conceivable kind of delay. One part of the road was so rough that little Wallace became car sick, necessitating a long wait by the side of the road. Twice Nate took a wrong turn, and once when he got too far ahead of the other car the Negro man, whose name was Leander, took a wrong turn. . . . Once they had to travel for two miles over a new levee road that was still wet from a rain the previous night; and because Nate was afraid the car might slide off into the swamp water he made Sylvia and the children get out and walk for at least half the length of the levee, Leander's wife getting out with them to carry little Margaret who was only a toddler at the time. In addition to these delays they had, between the two cars, nine flat tires.

Nate said they would certainly have sought shelter at nightfall except that Sylvia wouldn't hear of it. She spent half the day leaning over the back of the front seat administering to the children who alternately fought each other, cried for something to eat, bumped their heads on the arm rest, and even vomited. Yet it was Sylvia who urged the party on. When they stopped for supper she insisted that she felt as fresh as she had at breakfast. And she reminded Nate that every piece of trouble had been made easier by the kindness of friendly people who happened along just at the right moment. . . . An old Negro farm woman had brought Wallace a glass of lemonade when he was car sick. When they waited at the fork of the roads for Leander to discover his mistake and rejoin them, the people from the nearest house came out and invited them into the house to rest themselves. Sylvia even caught a cat nap lying across the feather bed in one of the big downstairs rooms of that unpainted farmhouse; and Wallace joined in a game of kick-the-can which he had to be torn away from when Leander reappeared. Sylvia pointed out that during the entire day Nate and Leander had not changed a single tire or patched one inner tube without practical assistance from farmers—white

253

and colored—who left their work in the fields to help
them.

After supper in the hotel at Brownsville, Sylvia
would not hear to stopping for the night. "The way
people have treated us," she said, "I don't feel we've
really left home yet."

Ever afterward Nate described Sylvia as a real
trouper that day. He exaggerated the hardships of the
trip and pictured her as a sort of pioneer heroine. But
he always concluded by saying, with a broad smile on
his face, that Sylvia's courage and endurance had had
special inspiration on that occasion. Never until that
day, he said, had she imagined that human kindness
and friendliness might exist beyond a fifty-mile radius
of Middle Tennessee. And, besides, to urge her on she
had always before her the image of her precious furniture in the hands of those rough moving men from
Memphis.

Once in 1934 when they had been living in Chicago
for nearly a year Sylvia and Nate came home from a
party on a snowy winter evening and stayed downstairs
to talk for a while. They began by discussing the party
they had been to, but they ended, as they often did at
such times by talking about . . . the furniture.

Sylvia had actually started up the stairs. Nate had
put out all the lights except those in the chandelier that
hung above the stairs from the ceiling of the second
floor. On the third step Sylvia looked over her shoulder
and said, "Wasn't that Mr. Jackson witty tonight. And
weren't Nellie's stories about the Gold Coast charm-

ing? It was a delightful party. Everybody responded so well to everybody else's stories." By the time she had finished speaking she had turned all the way round on the steps. Nate, from the foot of the stairs, was offering her a cigarette. She wasn't a habitual smoker, but she accepted the cigarette, bringing one bare arm out from under her velvet cape to do so. Then, throwing back her dark cape, she reached for the banister rail with her other hand and let herself down onto the carpeted step. Nate lit her cigarette and his own. He stood with one foot on the first step and leaned against the heavy newel post. "People did listen to other people's stories more than usual tonight," he said. "It was a good evening."

They talked about the party for five minutes or so. They commented on how unchanged certain of their old friends from Tennessee, who had been at the party, were, how young the two Tennessee women looked— like young girls still, compared to Chicago women of the same age. Nate leaned against the newel post and blew cigarette smoke upward in the direction of the chandelier. In the bare, dim light from above, his blond wiry hair looked lighter than it usually did during this time of his life. The fullness of his tuxedo jacket concealed the paunch which he had acquired during just the last year or two. He leaned against the post in a casual, loose-jointed way that denied any of the stiffness of forty. Sylvia watched him from the third step. Her own hair was much lighter than his, though when they had married it had been a shade darker. When she threw back her cape, it fell over a wide area of the steps; and its white silk lining all about her was like an extension of her white evening dress. Her figure was not so slight as it had once been but that was, at least in part, because fashions no longer favored slightness. Her shoulders and her prettily rounded arms were bare and their skin could not have appeared softer or clearer. She was sitting now with her arms about her knees, her cigarette between the fingers of her right hand.

Presently she heard (and she saw in Nate's face that he heard) their oldest son, Wallace, calling out something in his sleep from his room upstairs. The two of them listened attentively for a moment. Then when they heard nothing more, Nate suddenly straightened and moved away from the post he had been leaning against. He went to a table in the hall, picked up a small metal ashtray and brought it back with him to the stairs, where he sat down on the bottom step. When he spoke again his voice sounded hoarse the way it did in the morning or at any time when he had not spoken for a long while.

"Wallace has always talked in his sleep," he said.

"Not always," Sylvia said, smiling a little. "Not during the time he wasn't sleeping in the sleigh bed. That sleigh bed is uncomfortable, but he likes it."

Nate was silent a moment. "Well, regardless of what he likes, if he doesn't get his rest . . . " He broke off there and was silent another moment. Finally he said: "I suddenly have a mental picture of all the stacks of beds we have, Sylvia, and bedsprings—in the attic, in the basement, and God knows-where."

"Well," Sylvia said, "this is where we always end when we stop down here to talk."

"I think of it as the way we *begin* to talk," Nate said. "When we get on the subject of your furniture I feel that I am mighty near to understanding the difference between the mind of man and woman. There's hardly anything I like better than hearing you chatter about your 'things.' "

Sylvia smiled affably, as she shrugged her shoulders. "I have little or nothing to say on the subject," she said softly. "Nothing you haven't already heard me say." She wanted to humor him in his mood, but the words would not come.

But Nate pursued the subject energetically, repeating things that she had said to him at one time or another in her own defense. She liked being able to put her hands on her things. She liked having the children grow up with the things she had grown up with. It wasn't important but she liked the idea of taking the furniture everywhere they went, since they could afford it, and of then some day taking it back to Tennessee with them. Why, he said to her, it would be as though she had never left Cedar Springs. Wasn't it that? he said, laughing. Wasn't it?

Sylvia nodded her head solemnly.

And now he began pointing out, with the same good nature, the tremendous expense which the moves had been to them. But he did this for the sole purpose of getting Sylvia to affirm that the moving, to her, had been worth every penny it had cost.

When at last they went upstairs Nate was still talking

to her about her "things." At the top of the steps he put his arm about her waist, and suddenly, as though at the sensation of having his arm about her, Sylvia remembered something he had said to her long ago when they were first engaged. They had been sitting out in the yard at her father's house after supper at night and Nate had been talking about the various avenues that might be open to him in business. As he talked there, hidden in the dense shadows of a huge willow-oak tree, she had been thinking how very boyish his voice sounded and once when he had leaned forward for a moment she saw the faint light from the porch outline his handsomely shaped head and for one instant catch in its faintly glimmering rays the cowlick on the back of his head. "What one has to remember," she recalled his saying finally, "is that everything changes so fast in our country that a smart person can't hold on to the past—not to any part of it if he wants to be a success. It's as though we lived in a country where the currency changed every week, and you had to go every Monday morning and convert your old money into new." When he said that in the dark that night it had given Sylvia a scare, had made her feel afraid of him. Recalling it now it only impressed upon her the gentle indulgence he had shown her during the years of their marriage, but that night it had meant to her, somehow, that she would never be able to think of Nate as a mere boy again, and never of herself as a girl. Presently her sense of fright and dismay had left her. But after Nate had taken the 10:30 train back to Cedar Springs and she had returned from the depot and gone upstairs to her room, she imagined that she could now see all her childhood and young ladyhood in a new perspective. She imagined that she was seeing it as she would see it when she was a woman of forty. How fine it would seem then to have grown up the way she had, in such pleasant, prosperous, pastoral surroundings, at just the time she had, and with just the friends she had had. How she would then cherish the bittersweet tone of things as they were in Middle Tennessee in 1915. For everyone said it would all be different in twenty years. There would be no Confederate veterans left then, no old ladies who had once danced with Jeff Davis, and none of the old-time Negroes. The white people and the colored people would be more alike and yet farther apart in their independence of each other. There would be none of the bitter memories of the Civil War to make anything that bespoke the past sound sweet to the ear. Life in a Tennessee country town then would be indistinguishable from that in any other place in the land. But in *her* time and in *her* town she had seen everything that was good in the noble past of her country meeting head on with everything that was exciting and marvelous about the twentieth century. *Her* generation, she was sure, had found growing up more exciting than any generation had in a thousand years. It seemed to her that the boys of her time were as different from their fathers as motorcars from oxcarts. And the girls . . . they were not so different from their mothers, not yet; but there was a feeling of exhilaration and anticipation in the air that made the joy of being young seem almost unendurable

259

to them and made it imperative, if they were to endure, that they bind themselves together in close friendships. Being young could not always have been like that, Sylvia told herself. Oh, surely not! And that night in her father's house, after she had put out the light in her room, she lay awake thinking of her friends and thinking of what it was like to have been young with them in that place and that time. She saw them in their summer dresses walking through the cemetery on their way to a picnic at the sand banks, saw them in the old clapboard grade school at Thornton writing Latin sentences on the huge blackboards, all of them wearing middy blouses and pleated skirts, and later a few of them at Ward-Belmont, in Nashville, swinging Indian clubs in Miss Katty Moore's gym class. She saw them dancing at the Christmas cotillion in Germania Hall, and dancing again at the old Thornton Wells Hotel on the Fourth of July, and saw them finally not as a group but each with the man she would marry walking down beside the river, under the shade of the giant trees there, following the half overgrown path known among them as the Dark Walk.

When this series of pictures had passed before her mind and she was about to drift off to sleep she found the same series beginning all over again. But this time the pictures were more in detail and in each there was a definite incident or character that revealed to her why her mind had photographed that scene. When they were picnicking at the sand banks that hot summer day they had climbed one high embankment and peered down into the next ravine to see a Negro couple there, copulating in the sand. The man was shirtless and his trousers had fallen down about his ankles. The sweat on the black skin on his buttocks and his back glistened in the blazing sunshine. The woman still wore most of her clothes. Her brown head lay back on the sand and her eyes were closed. The girls watched in silence for a few seconds, and then they hurried back to their picnic to talk, not of how the sweat had glistened on the man's skin, but of the rapturous expression they had all observed on the face of the woman. . . . Once as they sat at dusk on the porch at Thornton Wells an old woman from back in the hills had told fortunes with tea leaves all round. When the girls wearied of the fortunetelling, she proceeded to entertain them with more practical talk. She said that if they would notice how their true-loves held them when they danced that night they could judge what manner of men they were, what sort of husbands they'd make. "A man who don't hold you firm when he waltzes you," she warned them, "it's a poor bed partner he'll make." In the rooms which the girls shared in the hotel that night only Mildred Pettigru would not report what promise her true-love had shown. . . . Sylvia and Nate, strolling in the verdurous Dark Walk on a Sunday afternoon in May, had stopped near the ruins of an old lattice summerhouse, and there Nate had asked her to marry him. His face bending over her and his voice, suddenly gone a little hoarse, had seemed to fill the whole world.

✦

Nate Harrison died of a heart attack soon after his forty-eighth birthday, in January of 1939. By the standards of Chicago bankers and board chairmen he had still been a young man. At the time of his death he was president of the American Wire and Steel Mesh Corporation, a concern which he had been brought to Chicago to reorganize in the darkest days of the Depression. His death came entirely without warning. He had played handball at the Athletic Club in the early afternoon and returned to his office at three o'clock. He was found less than twenty minutes later lying on the floor beside his desk. Sylvia had to be summoned from an afternoon party at Indian Hills, up in Winnetka. She did not see him alive again.

Two months later she made her final decision about leaving Chicago. She decided that in June she would give up the big house they had been renting on Ritchie Court and move all her possessions, including her four near-grown children, back to Tennessee. Everyone told her that the move would be too great an ordeal for her just yet and that she ought to put it off another six months, but Sylvia wouldn't listen. "Moving has practically been my life's work," she said to them. "It doesn't upset me the way it does other women."

2

There was an interval of nearly three months between the time that Sylvia announced her decision to leave Chicago and the day of the actual move from Ritchie Court. Sometime during the first weeks of this interval she began speaking of herself, to her children and to all her acquaintances, as "one of the newly poor." No one—probably not even she—could remember when she first used the phrase, but everyone was soon aware of how much she seemed to enjoy thinking of herself as a widow in straitened circumstances. Her friends in Chicago accused her of taking pleasure in the role, and so did her children. Sometimes she would admit that there was some truth in their charge and would even laughingly suggest that it was a play for sympathy on her part. But she always returned to the position that Nate's death had left the family in "straitened circumstances" which necessitated the move back to Tennessee.

From time to time she practiced little household economies, like shutting off the heat in rooms that were seldom used. She bought an electric sewing machine and attended the free classes in tailoring to which the purchase entitled her. The economy of which she tried to make the most was the dismissal of her part-time chauffeur and yard man. But even this did not represent any appreciable saving or the loss of great services. The Negro man who had done that work was the same Leander who had set out from Cedar Springs with the Harrisons seventeen years before. For several years now he had been employed by them only on a part-time basis, and had found other employment with another family in the neighborhood. Sylvia's economy in that quarter was as negligible as in any other.

✦

Everybody recognized her pretensions to poverty as mere pretensions. Her daughter Margaret, who had had a course in psychology at her finishing school in New York that very year, suggested that she was "suffering from certain deep psychic disturbances." Fortunately, however, neither Margaret nor anyone else made the mistake of thinking Sylvia was subject to any real delusions. After Nate's death in January, Margaret had remained at home with her mother, instead of returning to school. Wallace, who was a student at the University of Virginia, had, of course, returned to Charlottesville after the funeral. By the time he came home for a few days at Easter, Sylvia had made her plans to move the family back to Cedar Springs and had invented the fiction of their financial reverses.

Wallace lost no time in expounding his theory about this fiction of his mother's. She had made it up, he said (at the dinner table on Easter day), to prevent the usual brand of sympathy she received whenever she moved. Whether or not he really believed this to be Sylvia's motive he insisted upon it in a teasing, good-humored way throughout his Easter visit and even afterward in letters he wrote home. The other children followed his lead, and as far as they were concerned there was never any further effort to interpret Sylvia's talk of financial reverses. No doubt they all knew that their father's life insurance did not entirely countervail the income from his business activities and knew that the family's income from investments and from the Tennessee property had diminished during the Depression; but they knew also that their losses were not commensurate with

Sylvia's representations of them. They humored their mother in her economizing, teased her about it sometimes, and on the whole gave about as much thought to it as they might have to any other irksome little habit she might have had. Certainly it never occurred to them once that their mother was concerned, consciously or unconsciously, with justifying in their eyes her plans to return to Tennessee.

There were two people in Sylvia's acquaintance, however, to whom this possibility may have occurred. One was a man who, by Sylvia's standards, had had no vital connection with the Harrison family. His name was Mr. Peter Paul Canada and he was the owner of the house on Ritchie Court. He was a very kind and very rich old widower, and he had held on to this house, instead of selling it, because it was here that his wife had spent her happiest years. . . . The other person was Sylvia's former chauffeur, Leander Thompson.

Soon after Easter, Sylvia had gone by appointment to Mr. Canada's office in the Loop district. To him she had described herself as a widow in straitened circumstances and had made known her intention of giving up the house. Mr. Canada at once said that he would not hear of such a thing. He insisted that she and the children must continue to occupy the house without paying rent. There would be the greatest difficulty, he insisted, in finding a renter for a big house like that in these times, and it would be enormously to his advantage to have it occupied. Sylvia, as though she had not heard him, then repeated that she and the children were returning to Tennessee because there would be no problem of a place to live there. Presently, however, she seemed to realize what *he* and what *she* had said, and she smiled self-consciously. "It isn't really just a matter of rent or a place to live," she said with a worried expression about her eyes which indicated that for the moment she could not remember what it *was* a matter of. "It is a matter also," she said uncertainly and after a pause, "of other property we have in Tennessee. There is a good deal of farm land and some downtown real estate in Nashville to be looked after. And then, too, I still have my own family place at Thornton, which is a little town not too far from Cedar Springs."

Now she smiled self-consciously again and blushed a deep red. She had not only divulged the considerable extent of her property but had possibly made it, by her rambling speech, seem larger than it was. She did not try to correct this impression; the person to whom she was speaking was, after all, only her landlord. She sat blinking her eyes while Mr. Canada said: "What about your children, Mrs. Harrison? They have so many educational and social advantages in a place the size of Chicago, I should think."

"Oh, it's just the children I am thinking of," Sylvia said with enthusiasm, reminded at last of what the matter was. "It is very much to the interest of the children to go back to Tennessee where their property is and where . . . where their name will mean something to them."

"I see," said Mr. Canada, putting a freckled, wrinkled old hand up to his forehead and rubbing his brow. On one freckled finger was a wide, gold band

and on his starched white cuff shone a monogrammed gold cuff link. "I had thought probably," he said sweetly, "that your children, having—to some extent—grown up here in Chicago considered themselves real Chicagoans."

Lowering his hand from his forehead Mr. Canada now turned his face away from Sylvia and toward a window that opened above the tops of other office buildings. Under different circumstances Sylvia might have attached significance to what Mr. Canada said and to his glance out his office window. But as things were —that is, he being only her landloard, she accepted the old gentleman's words that day as mere gestures, as marks of half-absentminded civility, and she replied by drawing from her purse a list of articles of furniture that had been in the house when she moved there. It was really to present this list and to have it verified that she had called in person instead of giving notice to Mr. Canada by telephone or mail. Mr. Canada looked over the list hastily and said that so far as he could recall the list seemed complete.

Only a few days after this interview with Mr. Canada, Sylvia's former chauffeur came to her house. He arrived shortly before dinnertime, and when he and Sylvia had dealt with the matter that had brought him there, Leander asked to be allowed to stay and serve the evening meal. But Sylvia very politely refused his request. Having always preferred women servants in the house, she had never let Leander serve meals unless they had just moved and hadn't yet found a downstairs maid. As chauffeur and sometimes as gardener he had served the family long and well and had been a willing worker when called upon to lend a hand in spring cleaning or at moving time. Nate had been genuinely attached to Leander, and so indeed had Sylvia. But for several years now—since the children had begun to drive—the family had required little chauffeuring. Leander had, with the consent of all, taken another job in the neighborhood but had continued, in his spare time, to care for the minuscule bit of lawn between the house and the sidewalk and to come once or twice a week to wash the cars or perhaps to drive Sylvia or one of the girls to a party. The little work he had done for them before Sylvia dismissed him altogether could hardly have been worth his while, and no doubt he had continued to do it only out of old-fashioned attachment for the family.

The purpose of his coming to see Sylvia that day had been to request that she take him back to Tennessee with her and the children. Sylvia had tried to deal with the matter as quickly as possible. "Ah, no, Leander," she said, "times are not what they were with us. It's out of the question. But you're looking well, Leander."

"No'm," said Leander, "times aren't what they was. That's why I'd be thankful to go back to Cedar Springs with you." They were standing in the servants' dining room, behind the kitchen. In the kitchen, dinner was being prepared, but as soon as Leander and Sylvia began to speak there were no more sounds of running water from that quarter and no conversation between the cook and the maid. The awareness of an audience seemed to inspire Sylvia.

"Listen here, Leander," she said, raising her voice, "the good Lord hath dealt heavily with us Harrisons. We're having to leave all this opulence behind us. There's not the remotest possibility of my taking on the services of a chauffeur at a time when I'm having to drag my family back to the country in order to make ends meet."

As Sylvia spoke Leander stood nodding his head understandingly. He was a tall man with skin the color of wet sand, and he wore a small mustache. In his two hands he held his chauffeur's cap and as he nodded his head or when he spoke he would occasionally lean forward as though under his cap his hands were resting on a walking cane. "Times *are* bad, Miss Sylvia," he said, "and there's no place like the country when hard times come."

"No place on earth, Leander," Sylvia said, despite herself.

Leander nodded and raised one hand to stroke his chin. "But I suppose you'd go back anyway, wouldn't you, Miss Sylvia?" he asked. "Or maybe would you think the children wouldn't like it there? As for me, I don't think that's so." Sylvia looked at him blankly, as though she had heard a noise somewhere off in the house that had distracted her. "They say there's nothing so green as a city boy in the country," Leander continued, "but Wallace and them will take to it after a while. That's sure, and I wouldn't give it a thought if I was you. And for folks like you and me there's no

269

place like the place we was born. It's only the ride back I'm asking, Miss Sylvia."

Sylvia suddenly sat down in one of the straight chairs by the table, as if thereby to express her dismay. "I don't know why you're bothering to say all this, Leander. If Mr. Nate felt times were so hard that he could only keep you part time two years before he died, how do you imagine I can re-hire you now?"

"I don't reckon you understood me," Leander began.

But Sylvia interrupted: "Yes, I did, Leander. But with all the luggage the children will have there won't be a spare inch of room in either car."

Leander bit his lower lip, thoughtfully, and nodded his head again. A few minutes later, after Sylvia had declined his offer to serve dinner, he took his leave for that day.

The children had laughed openly at Sylvia's efforts at economy. Charley, who had a head for figures, made an estimate of how much more it had cost her getting the cars washed at the service station and taking taxis in bad weather than it would have cost had she kept Leander on. His mother took such teasing in good spirits. But once when Margaret implied that having a chauffeur had always been an extravagance for them and that through the years Leander had made a good thing of them, Sylvia declared that not one of her children had an ounce of practical sense. Presently she rose and left the family circle, remarking as she did so that it was just as well Margaret had stayed home from

"that finishing school" where they filled her with nothing but nonsense. A day or two later Margaret tried to
apologize for whatever her offense had been, but Sylvia
only fixed her with an icy stare and forbade any further
talk on the subject.

This incident with Margaret was the last, not the
first, of its kind. Others like it had occurred earlier,
during the two months just after Nate's death. The
children had, at that time, found Sylvia particularly
sensitive to any criticism of any aspect of the life she
and Nate had made. They found she could not tolerate
their accustomed jokes about her furniture, about her
long, unbroken correspondence with relatives and girlhood friends in Tennessee, about her clinging to every
Southerner she met in Chicago, or about the annual
trips back home to see after the two family houses.
None of her efforts to maintain a continuity with the
world she had grown up in was a permissible subject
for their levity. Much less could she countenance any
levity about the number of times the family had
moved, for this she interpreted as a reflection upon
Nate's career. A casual remark about the steel mesh industry could be the cue for a lecture to the children on
Nate's capabilities and attainments. She talked about
his great "drive" and his "genius for efficiency" and
how these qualities had destined him to a place of lead-
ership in the business world. She told them that when
he was a boy in Cedar Springs everyone had supposed
he would take over management of the Harrison farm
land and become a member of his father's law firm,
but that almost from boyhood he had had an insatiable

curiosity about the "theory and management" of the nation's big business and industry. "Nate never felt any attraction toward a country law practice," she would say, "or toward managing and developing the land he and I inherited. He felt drawn toward things that were in a sense foreign to our Southern, country sort of up-bringing. And with his energetic mind it was inevitable that he should find his opportunities and make good in them."

Sometimes during this period, Nate's business associates would drop by. She would talk to them, in the presence of the children, about Nate's business career. In these accounts she seldom made any reference to herself, and those she did make were only parenthetical. She would say: "After Nate finished college in Nashville (where he and I met and first went-together) he took a master's degree in economics at Yale." Or another time: "Probably a man of Nate's abilities could not have hidden himself so far in the country that the world would not have found him. After his year at Yale (when he and I had married and settled at Cedar Springs) it did seem for a while that his interest in finance and industry might turn out to be just a hobby, like his father's concern with Roman history; but actually Nate was only waiting for the right opportunity. He had turned down other things, but when the right thing came along he didn't hesitate. Part of his success, I guess, was his being able to make the right decisions."

She would talk of Nate's having gone first to Memphis, then for a short time to Cincinnati, then to Detroit, and so on. But in this connection she never referred to the actual moves which Nate's career had entailed for her. It was as though Nate had gone to all those places alone.

The Harrison children tried very hard not to say things that their mother could construe as criticism. They were ever gentle and considerate with her during this time and wanted to be whatever help and comfort to her they could. With their father all four of them had had a happy and affectionate relationship, and his death was a shock and grief to them individually. Yet being—each of them—of a normally happy and adjustable temperament they soon became absorbed again in the interests and excitements of their daily lives. Wallace returned to college in Virginia. The two younger children missed less than a week of school. Margaret did not go back to New York, but she began seeing her friends quietly and played in a tennis tournament at the Saddle and Cycle that spring. Their years of moving from city to city had not had the effect upon them that one might have supposed it would. Instead of giving them a sense of not belonging it had defined for them, to a degree beyond that enjoyed by most children, the kind of world they felt they did belong in. Wherever they had lived they had attended private schools, had gone to fortnightly dancing classes, had spent their leisure hours at the Country Club or in other houses like their own. Though they sometimes had shed tears at leaving a neighborhood or a city, they were never in much doubt about what life would be

273

like in the next place. Unlike many of their friends they had no illusions about their school or their club's being the only one of its kind in the world. And somehow, as a result, they had in common among them an appreciation and enjoyment of life as they knew it which was more binding than any mere bond of kinship.

It was just exactly a week after Sylvia had gone to her landlord's office that she received a telephone call from him. At the time of her visit to him he had hardly been willing even to glance over the list of articles that had been in the house when Sylvia came there. But now he wished to come to the house and have a look at a few of his things. He had decided that since she was moving he should take the opportunity of disposing of the odds and ends of furniture he had left there. He wondered would it be convenient for him to come by that very afternoon. Sylvia, after a moment's hesitation, said, yes, she supposed it would be.

In order to make sure that Mr. Canada found his things Sylvia stayed home from a piano recital in which her younger daughter, Nora, was playing that afternoon. It was half past three when Mr. Canada arrived. She was waiting with the list in her hand when her maid showed the old gentleman through the broad doorway at the end of the living room. She was standing by the fireplace at the other end of the long room and she began at once to walk toward him. She greeted him in a polite, businesslike manner but without asking him to sit down. Her thought was that they would begin their inspection at once.

"The first thing," she said, "is the great console table in the hall. We left it where it was and have used it mainly because it was too heavy to move."

But before she had finished speaking she recognized an expression of confusion on Mr. Canada's face. Presently he said, "The console table? Yes. Oh, yes." Sylvia was a moment trying to account for his sudden confusion and abstraction. Then she did—to her own satisfaction at least—account for it. He had been suddenly moved, she reasoned, by the sight of this room where he once had been so happy but which he had not entered for several years now.

"Oh, won't you sit down, Mr. Canada," she said quickly, with apology in her voice. He was only her landlord, but his age and the circumstances, she reflected, did entitle him to more than mere civility from her. "My mind was so on this list," she began, "that I . . ."

He interrupted, saying, "It's more than kind of you to have let me come at all. I sincerely hope I didn't interfere with any plans."

"Indeed not," she said. "I seldom go anywhere these days."

Together they walked out of the living room and into the main hall of the house. As they entered the hall they faced a wall which was covered by three of Sylvia's painted tapestries. Sylvia guided Mr. Canada directly toward that wall. Two of the tapestries were impressive for their great size and height if for nothing

more. Within their narrow, gilded frames were represented human figures of considerably more than life
size and with a distinctly allegorical look (despite their
nineteenth-century dress). Hung between these two
was a horizontal pastoral picture, and below it stood
Mr. Canada's table—a heavy Jacobean oak reproduc-
tion.

Sylvia and Mr. Canada stopped a few feet from the
wall and stood there in silence for a moment, like two
people before an altar. At last Mr. Canada said in a
voice full of mystification: "They were here, you say,
when you came? They're larger than I remember them,
certainly."

Sylvia drew away from him a little and looked directly up into his eyes. "The pictures, Mr. Canada?
Why, they're ours, I assure you—*mine,* that is!" Her
eyes shone and her lips had already parted to pro-
nounce the absurdity of his claim when he suddenly
burst into hearty laughter.

"I'm so sorry," he said. "I thought you were pointing
them out as something that was mine." He continued
to laugh, and it was not too hard to see that he was
laughing partly at his mistake but partly too at Sylvia's
show of temper.

Sylvia didn't share his amusement. "It is the table
that is yours," she said.

"Well, now," he said, checking his laughter and
leaning forward to put his hand on the dark surface of
the table top, "so this is a console table. To tell the
truth, Mrs. Harrison, I haven't the slightest recollection of it, though I suppose it does belong to me."

"It's all yours, Mr. Canada," Sylvia said sulkily, employing the slangy phrase of her children to express both disparagement of the table and resentment against its owner for taking up her afternoon this way.

But Mr. Canada, instead of taking notice of Sylvia's tone of voice, commenced praising the tapestries, insisting that he did really have some vague recollection of pictures like them—not among his wife's possessions but in his father's old house over in the Western Reserve.

Sylvia assured him that she didn't think the pictures were works of art but said that they were of historical interest to people from Tennessee. One of them pictured Davy Crockett making his way through the wilds of West Tennessee wearing a swallow-tail coat, a black shoestring tie, and on his head a coonskin cap. Its companion picture represented Bonnie Kate Sherrill, the heroine of East Tennessee, holding hands with gallant young John Sevier, presumably just after he had rescued her from the Indians at Fort Loudon. Sylvia identified these figures and prolonged the incident further by pointing out the quaint anachronisms in their dress and by telling how her father had commissioned the painting of the pictures by a small-town house painter who, though totally illiterate, was steeped in the legends of pioneer days.

But it was not vanity that had set her to talking about the tapestries. Mr. Canada's refusal to notice her rudeness and his giving himself so to praise of her pictures had finally made her see that it was not to look at his possessions he had come there today. She understood that the sooner she ceased to treat him like an ordinary tradesman the sooner she would learn his real motive.

From the hall she led him to the far corners of the house, checking off the articles in the order in which they appeared on her list. In less than half an hour she and Mr. Canada had returned to the living room where Sylvia had invited him to join her for tea or for a Coca-Cola. In the course of their inspection her manner toward him grew more courteous, but by the time they came to the living room she was beginning to despair of discovering an ulterior motive. They sat down in two chairs about midway in the long room, and she spoke again in her business voice: "I presume it will be all right if we don't move exactly on the first of the month, Mr. Canada. My younger children's schools don't let out until the fourth or fifth of June."

Mr. Canada suddenly blossomed with smiles. He was a man whose general manner and appearance attested to his seventy years. But at a moment like this one the years seemed to fall away from him. The color rose in his face, and in his eyes shone an ardor and a naïveté that were youthfulness itself. "Your question hardly needs an answer from me," he said. "The longer you stay, the more it is to my advantage. And by the way," he said, the words now spilling out, "speaking of your children, I happened to lunch recently with Louis Norris, who is principal of your younger boy's school. He says your boy's a good student and that a scholarship could be arranged for him

278

if you decided not to leave. He said it would be a shame . . ."

But here Sylvia interrupted. And now it was she who burst into laughter. "Mr. Canada," she said, "how very kind of you. And how transparent!"

"I don't quite follow you," he said with dignity and without appreciation of her humor.

"Let's not speak of it again," said Sylvia, suddenly looking very serious.

"I didn't mean to offend you," he said.

Sylvia didn't answer. She was content now to let him think her offended. That was the easiest way of changing the subject. Presently she began to talk to him about things that she would have talked to any other visitor about. How changeable the weather had been lately—"summer one day and winter the next." What a dreadful train wreck that was down in Englewood yesterday! . . . But as they talked and drank their Coca-Colas Sylvia kept thinking of how long Mr. Canada had waited for her to mention the children and how, after all that waiting, he had given himself away by pouncing so upon his opportunity. Like Nate, she reflected, casually, this old gentleman seemed incapable of using his intelligence for anything outside the sphere of business.

Just when Mr. Canada was leaving the house that afternoon Sylvia's daughter Nora returned from her piano recital. At the front door Sylvia introduced them to each other and then detained Nora to ask how the recital had gone. "You didn't miss a thing, Mother," Nora said. "You should be glad something came up to

279

keep you away." She said this in Mr. Canada's presence, and when he had gone Sylvia reprimanded Nora for the rudeness. "Why do you care?" Nora asked, taking off her jacket. "Is he trying to court you, Mother?"

"Nora!" Sylvia said, with exasperation. "How absurdly you are behaving. The man is old enough to be my father."

"Oh, is he?" said Nora. "Well, it's not easy to tell the ages of grown people."

Before the day of the move from Ritchie Court arrived, Sylvia had had other visits from Mr. Canada. Usually he made some pretense of business, but of his half-dozen visits there were at least two occasions when he forgot to mention any reason for coming. After the first day Sylvia always received him hospitably and chatted with him in the living room during the hour or more that he stayed. Her children could not understand why she tolerated his attentions, and Sylvia was not at all clear about it in her own mind. She resented his clumsy gestures about the house rent and the scholarship for Charley, and she was embarrassed before her children to have to acknowledge his obvious aspirations as a suitor. But to the children she laughed both about his gestures and about his aspirations, and she continued to let him come to the house. She continued even after the children's amusement at the situation turned to disapproval and their good-natured teasing to accusing silence. Yet to the very end there was no change in hers and Mr. Canada's relationship and she was ever looking forward to the time when she would see him no more.

She looked forward to that time, she soon found, with just the same pleasure that she looked forward to the day when she would not see Leander Thompson again. For Leander, like Mr. Canada, didn't come to see Sylvia just the one time. Actually, he turned up again on the very morning after Mr. Canada's first call at the house, and he stayed even longer than Mr. Canada had done.

Sylvia was still at the breakfast table when he arrived, and she waited until she and Margaret had had their second cups of coffee before telling the maid to let him come into the dining room.

Leander began speaking before he was well into the room. "Miss Sylvia, I've been let go," he said. "Those people have accused me of taking things—over there!" As he spoke he had come forward, and he stopped within a few feet of Sylvia's chair at the table. As he said "over there" he gestured with his cap in the general direction of the house where he had been working since he left the Harrisons' service. "Miss Sylvia, you know—and you know, Miss Margaret—that I wouldn't take nothing that didn't belong to me. They say I took two pocket watches and a bottle of their whisky, and you all know how sparing I am of whisky."

He was in such an obvious state of excitement that Sylvia asked him to sit down in one of the straight chairs that were lined against the wall. At first he refused, but Sylvia said that she would not talk to him until he had sat down and calmed himself. Once he

281

was seated, Sylvia asked, "When did all this happen, Leander?"

"It happened just this morning when I came in to work. They—he, Mr. Warren—said they found the pocket watches and half bottle of whisky on my shelf in their garage where I generally keep my things. But, before God, somebody else had put them there." He spoke hurriedly, running his words together in a way totally unlike his usual, deliberate manner of speech. Presently he slumped in the chair and stared at the floor, all the while shaking his head. "What would I do with their watches or their sort of whisky?"

A rather dazed expression came over Sylvia's face, and it was Margaret, having observed her mother's expression, who spoke next. "Leander, we believe you," she said impatiently. "But you ought not to take on this way!" Margaret had never seen Leander cast aside his cheerfulness or his dignity before—not to this extent. And when he raised a beseeching gaze to her, she quickly dropped her eyes to her empty coffee cup.

Sylvia glanced at Margaret and for a moment watched the peculiar expression which had settled about her mouth. Then she said, "Leander, how long has it been since this happened? What time was it?"

"I've just come from over there, Miss Sylvia."

"You didn't wait long. Didn't you try to explain?"

"Not over much."

"Did Mr. Warren threaten to have you arrested?"

"No'm. He offered to pay me a month's wages, but I said, 'No, sir—nothing!'" Until now Leander had continued to look at Margaret, and now it was only out of the corner of his eye that he glanced at Sylvia. "I'm not making this up, Miss Sylvia," he said.

"I thought possibly you were," she said.

"No'm," Leander said, "it's something that happened."

"I might be able to persuade them to forget it," Sylvia said, rising from her chair.

"I don't want you to do that, Miss Sylvia," Leander said, also rising. "I'm through over there." On his feet again, he seemed more himself. But Sylvia looked into his face and was aware that there was still something different about him. She told him to go out and see if their cars didn't need a washing and to come back and talk to her again after that.

When he had gone and she and Margaret had passed from the dining room into the living room, Sylvia said: "You certainly behaved in a queer fashion, curling your lip at poor Leander."

"I couldn't help it, Mother," Margaret protested. "I honestly couldn't. I was suddenly filled with revulsion and loathing for him. He's so obviously schizophrenic! He stole those things just so he *would* be caught. You must have felt the same way I did. He's pathetic, but any real psychopath is repulsive to a normal person."

"You're mistaken, Margaret," Sylvia said with emphasis.

"You don't think he took those watches and that whisky?"

"Of course he did. But he's not crazy. He's only hell-bent upon going back to Tennessee with us."

"So hell-bent that it's made him lose contact with reality."

"Leander's not crazy, Margaret; he's only willful. I'm not a bit surprised he's done this. When we left Cedar Springs, Margaret, I let it be known among the Negroes that I wanted a married couple to take with me. Leander wasn't married, but he got married on two days' notice! You've heard me tell that. And he married the stupidest girl he could find just so he could be sure we'd send her back home pretty soon . . . *as*, of course, we had to do."

Margaret, who knew this story of Leander's marriage quite well, hardly listened to her mother now. Evidently Sylvia had convinced her of Leander's sanity, and by so doing had robbed the incident of all psychological interest. Her thoughts returned to something more substantial—that is, to the impression which Leander's physical appearance had made on her. "When he looked up at me with that dopey look in his eyes it was all I could do to keep from shuddering," she said. "And he looks like a different person with that mustache shaved off."

"Oh, *that's* what's different," Sylvia said. "His mustache is gone."

"He looked silly with it," Margaret said thoughtfully, "but even worse without it, after all." Leander had grown his mustache only since he left the Harrisons' full-time employ, and when it first appeared there had been a good deal of fun made of it by the Harrison children. He had told one of them at the time that "somehow" he always got so he looked like whomever he worked for, and his new employer wore a small black mustache.

"He looks naked without it," Margaret said with finality. "That's it—naked and perfectly ghastly."

"One thing is certain," Sylvia said with a faint smile. "He didn't stop to shave his mustache after they accused him of stealing this morning."

When Leander returned from washing the cars he gave Sylvia a second, slightly more detailed account of his dismissal. Sylvia showed little interest. She heard him out, but when he had finished she made no comment. And from that moment both she and Leander were satisfied to make no further reference to the incident. They talked together for nearly an hour that morning, and on each of Leander's subsequent visits to the house they talked for as long a time. The scene of their talks was usually the plain, square little servants' dining room behind the kitchen. They sat on opposite sides of the room, facing one another across the brown oak table, each in a straight chair against the buff-colored wall. The avowed topic of their conversations was always the problem of finding Leander another suitable job, but Leander's many digressions and parentheses—the latest news he had had from Cedar Springs or some anecdote he remembered from his years with the Harrisons—were so frequent and lengthy that only Sylvia's persistence kept the purpose of their talks before them.

The many calls which Leander and Mr. Canada paid could hardly have escaped comment from Sylvia's children. The very number of times the two men came was enough to draw comment, but it was the regularity with which the visits of the two men were alternated that inspired the children's real efforts at wit. Wallace was off in Virginia, but even his letters were filled with references to his mother's "two suitors," about whom his younger brother had kept him posted.

Margaret and Nora called Sylvia a "wicked two-timer" and warned her that sooner or later she would get her dates mixed. Sylvia entered into the fun and occasionally referred to her callers as the Black Knight and the White Knight. Yet despite all the fun and teasing, Sylvia could, almost from the beginning, detect a growing dislike on the part of the children for the two men as individuals and could detect their increasing disapproval of her continuing to let them come to the house. And their dislike and disapproval, strangely enough, seemed to increase her own unwillingness, or inability, to put an end to the visits.

Each time Leander came he appeared a little more unkempt than the time before. Patches even appeared on his coat sleeves and trousers, and he gave up his chauffeur's cap in favor of a floppy old fedora. Sylvia's two daughters said they "lived in dread" of meeting him when coming or going and of having to explain him to their friends. What difference did it make that it was only a pose and that he had a closet full of clothes wherever he lived? He looked and behaved like a tramp or something out of a book, bowing and scraping before them as he had never done in the past. And they were completely disgusted when they learned that though their mother had found him several jobs he refused them all because the employers were not up to his standards. "It's plain that he's not going to take another job," Margaret said, "and it's plain that you're going to continue to feel responsible for him, Mother. So why not just give in and agree to take him back to Tennessee with us?" In reply Sylvia had opened her mouth to make one of her hard-times speeches, but they all broke into laughter. And she only laughed with them.

Mr. Canada's presence they found harder still to explain to their friends. What could they say upon coming into the house with some friend and finding their mother, who still wore black whenever she went out, entertaining a strange old man in the living room. It would not have been so bad if he had been someone she had always known or someone that they or she knew something about. In that case they could have at least pretended he was there to express sympathy or to offer advice.

It was a busy season for the three Harrison children who were at home. It seemed to Sylvia that they were enjoying their friends more than ever before, were more than ever absorbed in the life from which she was about to take them. With her they were affectionate and considerate, as they had always been. Their criticism of her tolerance for Mr. Canada and Leander did not carry over into other things. It was clear that they felt no resentment of the move they were about to make, and she understood why they did not. They had been brought up always in the expectation of the family's some day returning to Tennessee. The possibility of not returning had hardly occurred to them. Being young, they were excited by the prospect of any change, and they had no real conception of just how great a change this would be. And, in the last weeks before the move from Ritchie Court, Sylvia became aware that she was herself no longer so sensitive to remarks the children made about her and Nate and their family background. One Saturday morning she overheard Charley and one of his fourteen-year-old friends in the living room talking about the family portraits which hung there. The friend was one of a set of new friends whom Charley had just recently begun bringing to the house, and he was seeing the portraits for the first time. From the next room Sylvia could tell that the two boys were stopping before each of the four pictures in there. The first three they came to were portraits of men, dark pictures in which only the faces and white shirt fronts were immediately distinguishable. Two of these were by a "famous" itinerant painter of the 1830's—as was also the fourth picture—and were thought remarkable for the family resemblance between the subjects. The fourth picture was much the largest and the only colorful picture of the group. It was a full-length, life-size portrait of a great-grandmother of Sylvia's, a raving beauty according to the painter's brush, standing in white voile and silk with her little twin daughters—not a day over three —on either side at her feet. One of the little girls was standing, holding a bouquet of flowers in her arms.

288

The other was seated and held a bowl of fruit in her lap. Both of them were barefoot, yet they wore grownup-looking pastel dresses, décolleté like their mother's; and their facial expressions suggested that they were making a conscious effort to look as dour and disenchanted as all their elders in the other portraits.

The portraits of the men had brought only the briefest comment from Charley's friend. About one he said: "That old gentleman looks like he has the sour belches." About another he asked, "What is that supposed to be in his hand?" But when he came to the portrait of the great-grandmother he responded at once with warm feeling. It was the prettiest portrait he had ever seen! It looked exactly like something out of *Gone with the Wind!* That was his first reaction. A moment later, however, with astonishing abruptness he changed his tone completely. "No," he said, "I don't think I like it so much after all. Those two little girls give me the creeps!"

Charley laughed when he said this. And presently his friend laughed and said: "They *are* funny, aren't they? They are like two little dwarfs, not like real children."

"I had never thought of it, but that's so," said Charley.

"Children aren't just little grownups," his friend continued. "They're made differently. I've noticed that myself and I'm not even an artist. Why, those two little girls look like something out of the funny paper." Then for several minutes he and Charley stood before the pictures giggling.

Sylvia, in the dining room, only smiled a little and quietly continued with the inventory she was taking of her china.

3

Even if Sylvia had wanted them there the Harrison children could hardly have been kept at home on the day of the move. Nora stayed until noon, but she was there because most of her friends lived in the neighborhood. Even she was in-and-out during the morning, and at noon she was to dress herself in her most grown-up clothes and set out for a luncheon being given for her in the next block. The other children had left the house soon after breakfast on their last rounds of visits with friends. Wallace, just back from Virginia, had an all-day date with "a certain Hollins College girl who lived up in Evanston." She and he would make his rounds together. And the two other children—Margaret and Charley—each had a variety of appointments to keep.

Not one of them had left the house without apologizing for not staying to help, but Sylvia had laughed at them and said having them out of the way was good riddance. She required only that they get in touch with her in the early afternoon, by which time she expected to be able to gauge the hour the vans would be loaded. "Before nightfall," she had told them at breakfast, "we'll be on our way to Tennessee." They would spend the night somewhere along the way in Illinois. They would set out, as she and Nate and their whole tribe had set out from Cedar Springs so many years before, in two cars. But this time there would be no servants and no pets, and probably there would not be so many flat tires along the way. Wallace would be driving the Packard limousine, and she and Margaret would take turns at the wheel of the roadster.

At about ten o'clock that morning Sylvia happened to be in the sewing room, which was one of the little rooms that opened off the back hall upstairs. She had, at the last minute, discovered a tear in one of the old summer slipcovers that she always put on the living-room furniture when she moved; and now, though the movers were already putting some of the heavier pieces in the vans, she was taking time out to mend that tear.

She had just finished this job of mending and was closing the sewing machine when she heard a hurried tiptoeing on the back stairs. She knew at once it must be Nora, since all the other children were already gone. Presently Nora stood in the sewing-room doorway, all out of breath. After a moment she said, "Mother, Le-ander's downstairs and says he still wants to go with us. . . . And so is Mr. Canada."

"Well, Leander can't," Sylvia said almost before Nora had stopped speaking. "And I don't dream Mr. Canada wants to!"

"I didn't mean Mr. Canada did," Nora said in a whisper. "He has some sort of flower in his buttonhole, and he's brought you a dozen roses, I think."

Sylvia was gathering up the bulky slipcover that she had mended, not looking at Nora. "Mr. Canada is a very nice old man," she said.

Nora said nothing for a moment. Then she whispered, "But what shall I say to Leander? I think he's been drinking." Nora was now a girl of fifteen. She looked quite grown up and was already allowed to go to parties with boys sometimes. But her whispering and this carrying of messages between adults were things she still seemed to take a childish pleasure in.

"Why, my child," her mother answered, stuffing the electric cord into the machine and looking squarely at Nora for the first time, "say to Leander that he can't. I don't want to see him. He knows I haven't time to fool with any of his foolishness today. Tell him to go off somewhere else and sober up. It is our prerogative as one of the newly poor not to have to fool with the likes of Leander."

So saying, Sylvia gathered the slipcover under one arm, asked Nora in which room Mr. Canada was waiting, then, slipping past Nora, she walked toward the head of the staircase. Her step was light and quick. As she passed a wooden packing case in the center of the hall she stretched out her free hand and ran her fingers lightly along one side of it, barely touching its rough surface with her fingertips. It was a graceful, youthful gesture, plainly inadvertent, and plainly indicative of how absorbed she was in her thoughts of the moment. There was nothing about the way she walked or about any of her movements now to suggest the precise, deliberate, middle-aged manner in which she had dealt with her sewing machine and with her daughter. Even the matronly styled housedress she had put on this morning did not altogether conceal the still youthful lines of her figure. And suddenly, as she reached the head of the back stairway, the serious, staid expression on her face gave way to one of amusement. Waiting downstairs to see her were two persons whom she had been fully expecting to arrive at the house sometime during this day. What amused her, suddenly, was the thought of their arriving at the same moment. Each had come, she knew, because in the goodness of his heart he wanted to be of help to her in the move. They honestly imagined—it seemed incredibly funny to Sylvia—that she needed the help of a man at such a time . . . *she* to whom moving had been a life's work.

Sylvia started downstairs that morning with the intention of dismissing her two callers immediately. But, by the time she was halfway down the straight flight into the back hall, she had witnessed—in the hall below— a spectacle that would change her plans for that day and for many another after it. What she saw was actually only a little scene between Leander and Mr. Canada, but she recognized it at once as a scene from which enormous meaning for herself might be drawn. At first glance she observed only that the two men were standing in conversation with one another at the far end of the hall. Yet even that was enough to arrest her momentarily on the stairs. Somehow, even that filled her with sudden alarm—an emotion to which she was almost a total stranger. When she saw, a moment later, that their conversation was by no means a civil one, that both were talking at once and shaking their heads (if not quite their fists) at one another, the sight filled her with such consternation that she dropped the heavy slipcover on the steps.

As she stooped to gather the slipcover into her arms again, it occurred to her first to turn back up the steps. Deciding against that, her next impulse was to call out to Nora to stay upstairs out of harm's way. She did neither, however. When she presently realized that Nora had, of her own accord, lingered above, she proceeded very slowly down the steps with her eyes fixed on the two men. They were standing near the doorway that led into the front part of the house. Apparently neither of them realized that it was she who was approaching. If aware of anyone's presence they probably thought it was Nora returning with messages for them. Only when she was almost at the foot of the stairs, Sylvia saw Mr. Canada glance at her for the first time. Seeing her, he dropped his eyes to the floor and commenced backing through the doorway and into the dark center hall beyond. His face, already flushed with anger, grew even redder, and Sylvia knew that he would be overcome with embarrassment at having seemed to invade her domestic privacy. Leander, on his part, appeared to understand what Mr. Canada's withdrawal meant. Without looking at Sylvia he turned and walked directly into the kitchen, his head literally bowed down.

At the foot of the stairs Sylvia stopped again. She knew now that she was still not ready to order either Leander Thompson or Mr. Canada away from the house, even knew that she would need them there that day until the very last piece of furniture was loaded on the last van. That neither of them would be of any assistance whatsoever in the business of packing and loading she knew also, and knew, in fact, how much they would be in the way. She might even have predicted—so clear was she, in a sense, about the turn events were going to take—how Leander in the course of the day would manage to break out a window light in the library (when trying to get out of the way of the movers) and would upset a huge bottle of cleaning fluid on the parqueted floor of the hall. Or how Mr. Canada would have to be asked, time and again, to get up from a comfortable couch or chair that the movers were ready to load. But any hindrance or inconvenience which their presence would be to actual moving seemed unimportant. The important thing was the fact that Leander's and Mr. Canada's quarreling there in the doorway had filled her with consternation and alarm.

Until now Sylvia had supposed that the two men represented for her the two sides of a rather simple question, the question of whether or not it was wise of her to be taking her family back to Tennessee. On one side Mr. Canada seemed to represent everything that was against her doing so. Not since the first time he came to see her had he made any direct reference to the subject, but his talk had always been about things pertaining to Chicago. Sometimes it was about the business world in which Nate had lived, sometimes about the civic enterprises to which he nowadays devoted much of his time, sometimes about his own career and the opportunities which Chicago offered "a young man with good connections and a head for business." For a while after each of his visits Sylvia had been able to think of almost nothing but her own selfishness.

In her selfishness she had never made any effort to understand Nate's business career and thereby to share his greatest interest in life. In her selfishness she had insisted always upon the temporariness of their life away from Tennessee, had lived as though the great facts of their life were that they had come from Cedar Springs and that they would someday return there. And now in her selfishness she was about to take her children away from a place which perhaps meant the same to them that Tennessee did to her. . . . On the other side, Leander seemed to represent everything that favored the move. Although he refused any job she found for him, still he didn't go on trying to persuade her to take him with her to Cedar Springs. Instead, he talked to her about other moves he had made with the family. He recalled the number of flat tires they had had the day they left Cedar Springs and drove to Memphis, and how helpful the country people had been along the way. He recalled times when one or another of the children had cried over leaving some house and how Sylvia would always say, "I have no feeling about this house. This house isn't home to *us*." But he talked even more about Cedar Springs itself, about the colored people and the white people there. He spoke of having written his sister-in-law that the Harrisons were coming home and of her having replied that "every colored person in Logan County" was hoping to work for them. He reminisced about members of Nate's family in Cedar Springs, asking her which of them were still alive. And he asked about her own brother in Thornton and her brother in Nashville. He said he supposed they would look after her land and money for her and that that was probably her big reason for going back. He said it was good to have kinfolk to fall back on. He said it was good to live in a place where they knew who you really were. There wasn't anything in the world like living in a place where there were no questions you didn't know the answers to.

But after Leander's visits it had been just the same as after Mr. Canada's. Sylvia could think of nothing but her own selfishness. She had judged herself, she had condemned herself, yet she had never considered giving up the move. She could no more have thought of that than she could have thought of trying to change the sequence of the seasons. It sometimes seemed queer to her that after hearing both sides of the argument, so to speak, she experienced exactly the same sensations. And she wondered exactly what position Leander represented in the argument. That is, it was easy for her to associate Mr. Canada with Nate and thus make him represent one side. But was it possible to make Leander the symbol for what might be called her side of the argument? While she was still paused at the foot of the back stairs she realized that this had indeed *not* been possible by any ridiculous stretch of the imagination. And now the cause for her alarm and consternation became clear to her.

297

She had no side, no voice in the argument, and had never had one. The two voices she had been listening to for weeks past had both been Nate's voice. They were voices she had heard for years and years. The two men, quarreling in her back hall, seemed to represent the two sides of Nate. He had, through all the years, *wanted* her to *want* to go back to Tennessee. That was what his tolerance had meant. Her own wishes had never entered into it. That was what Nate's tolerance had meant. It had meant his freedom from a part of himself, a part of himself that would have bound him to a place and to a past time otherwise inescapable. He had *wanted* her to insist upon taking all that furniture everywhere they went. That was what his tolerance had meant. She felt now an immense weariness, felt as though she had been carrying all that absurd furniture on her back these twenty years. And for what purpose? Why, so that Nate might be free to live that part of life in which there somehow must be no furniture. His selfishness, for the moment, seemed so monstrous to her that she almost smiled at the judgments she had passed upon herself.

It was not then, however, that Sylvia made her decision which so baffled everyone. Perhaps there was no actual moment of decision. But as she went about the duties which that moving day held for her she found herself imagining a life totally different from any that she would have before been capable of imagining. She envisioned herself not as a widow living alone in the City of Chicago, not even as a woman living in an

American city, but merely as a Person alive in an Un-named City. The nameless streets of the Unnamed City were populated with other Persons who were all sex-less, ageless, nameless; and in some unaccountable way she seemed to excel everyone there in their very sex-lessness and agelessness and namelessness. This vision kept returning to her all day long, interrupting her efforts to concentrate on the tasks she had set herself, sometimes so disconcerting her that she could not an-swer the questions of the moving men. Yet whenever it faded from her mind's eye her one thought was that she must recapture it. And nothing helped so to keep it before her as the presence of Leander and Mr. Canada.

Their presence was so indispensable to her that there was no promise she would not have made to keep them there that day. As for the trouble between them in the hall, she had guessed its cause before she had ex-changed a word with either of them. While waiting for her they had met, and each had regarded the other as an intruder. They had met, as it turned out, in the so-called center hall, by the telephone. Mr. Canada, wish-ing to call his office, had had to wait several minutes while Leander finished a casual conversation with someone whom he addressed in terms of endearment. In the closeness of that little passage where the tele-phone was situated (actually a windowless area under the broad landing of the front stairs) the smell of whisky on Leander's breath was unmistakable to Mr. Canada. And so, in Sylvia's interest, Mr. Canada felt obliged to ask him the nature of his business in the

house today. Leander, resentful of being questioned
by a stranger in the Harrison house, replied that he
would like to know the same of Mr. Canada. Then,
by mutual consent, they had stepped into the back hall
to settle the matter.

The details of the incident were revealed to Sylvia
in the course of the day; but the details interested her
little, and neither did the whole incident itself once
she had guessed its cause. The behavior of the two
men became more and more clownlike as the day pro-
gressed. Mr. Canada's manner with the movers became
more imperious each time he was asked to rise from
a comfortable chair, and there were moments when
Sylvia feared that one of those big, burly men, sweat-
ing through their khaki coveralls, might lay hand on
the old gentleman.

With the moving men Leander was humility itself,
particularly with those of his own race. Yet he impeded
the general progress by forever getting in the way and
by the more insidious means of sharing his whisky
with some of the movers themselves. After Sylvia explained Leander's history to Mr. Canada and explained
how his rags and even his drinking were supposed to
draw her sympathy, and after she assured Leander that
Mr. Canada was not there in the role of the landlord
evicting a tenant, each of them became reconciled to
spending that day under the same roof with the other.

Toward the end of the afternoon, only a short while
before her scattered children began to gather in, Sylvia
stood just inside the front door of the house watching
the last of her furniture being loaded on the last van.

Behind her in the big entrance hall were her former chauffeur and her former landlord. Mr. Canada was leaning against the oak console table, which was the only piece of furniture left in the hall and on which the dozen roses he had brought Sylvia had been placed in a large watering can. At the rear of the hall Leander sat on the bottom step of the stairway, his elbows resting on his knees, his face buried in his hands. Though neither of the men had been allowed to lift a hand in the moving, both were in shirt sleeves and both appeared to be in a state of near-exhaustion.

Sylvia watched her furniture disappearing into the dark mouth of the van. As she did so there came to her again the vision of that strange, vague life in that strange, vague city—a city and a life which, being without names or attributes of any kind, could exist only as opposites of something else. And now, at the end of the day, that something else was somehow revealed to her. It was a particular moment in time, a situation, a thing she had experienced, a place. She thought at first it must be something that had happened at Cedar Springs, but almost at once she saw that it wasn't the town where she had gone to live as a bride but was that neighboring town where she had lived as a girl. It was Thornton, the old, dying town on the bluffs above the Tennessee River. It was there that she had known the name and quality of everything. It was there, more than anywhere else, that everything had had a name. Not only the streets and alleys there had had names; there had been names for the intersections of streets: Wifeworking Corner, the Blocks, the Step-down. Not only the great houses and small houses had names; on the outskirts of the town were two abandoned barns known as the Hunchback's Barn and General Forrest's Stable. Usually the houses bore the names of the families that had lived in them longest or lived in them first. But some of the houses had names like Heart's Ease and Robin's Roost and New Scuppernong, and some had more than one name; there were cases where two families in town obstinately called the same house by different names because each family had once owned and given a name to it. For every little lane or path or right-of-way through the fields surrounding the town there was a name, and down along the river underneath the giant sycamores and willow oaks and poplars, just below the bluffs on which the town stood, there was that path which had been known since Indian times as the Dark Walk. On Sunday afternoons in the early spring, and in the fall after the mosquitoes were gone, courting couples from the town strolled there. In Sylvia's grandmother's day it had been the custom for the town's best families to stroll there, dressed in their Sunday finery, after church. In those distant days the Dark Walk had been kept as a sort of town common or park, with the grass trimmed right down to the water's edge. But to Sylvia's generation it had a very different character. Vines of muscadine and fox grape reached from tree to tree, often obscuring any view of the river, and an undergrowth of pines and dogwood and Judas tree had sprung up between the walk and the steep escarpment. For the young people of that latter day there was an element of mystery and danger in the walk. It had not yet become the illicit kind of lover's lane which it was surely destined to be in another, still later time. It was protected from that fate by the townspeople's memory of what it had once been, and it was in a sense still considered the private property of the genteel and the well-to-do. Sylvia and her contemporaries went there with the consent—even the blessing—of their elders, and the danger and mystery of which they were aware existed only in the bright colored spiders which sometimes spun their webs across the path or in the fat water moccasins hurrying innocently across the path into the rank growth of creeper and poison ivy. Sylvia had gone there with Nate, and he had brushed aside glistening spiderwebs, had tossed a rock in the direction in which she had thought she saw a moccasin, and had asked her to marry him. To her on that day so long ago it had seemed an additional happiness that he had asked her while they strolled in that traditional spot. Then and during the many years since, she had cherished the image of herself as a young girl in white dimity repeating and sharing the experience of all the other girls to whom life had seemed to begin anew as they lingered by the ruins of an old lattice summerhouse or at the point where Thornton Creek joined the river.

She had cherished the image. And then the last afternoon in Ritchie Court, while she stood in the doorway of the house she was about to leave, she called up the image, and she found it had changed. She and the other young girls no longer seemed to be beginning life anew in the Dark Walk. They were all dressed in black, and it seemed that the experience they had shared there was really the beginning of widowhood. From the moment they pledged their love they were all, somehow, widows; and she herself had become a widow not the day Nate was found dead in his office but the day he asked her to marry him, in the Dark Walk. It seemed to her that in some way or other all the men of that generation in that town had been killed in the old war of her grandfather's day. Or they had been set free by it. Or their lives had been changed in a way that the women's lives were not changed. The men of Nate's time had crossed over a border, had pushed into a new country, or fled into a new country. And their brides lived as widows clinging to things the men would never come back to and from which they could not free themselves. Nate had gone literally to a new country, but Sylvia knew in her heart that it would have been the same if they had never left Cedar Springs. She could not blame him, but she could no longer blame herself either.

When the movers began tying up the gate of the last van Sylvia turned and stepped back into the hall. Without looking at him she called Leander's name. Leander lunged forward from his place on the steps. He staggered the length of the hall, dragging his coat and tie after him, and stopped directly before Sylvia, his eyes downcast, the very flesh of his face seeming to hang half molten from the bones. Is this Leander? Sylvia asked herself. And then: Is he really as drunk as this? Aloud she was saying to him: "I am going to arrange with the moving men for you to ride back home in the van." There was not kindness but disdain for him in her voice, and Leander did not lift his eyes. "The children and I are not going, after all," she said. Leander's face registered nothing. To Sylvia this seemed to mean that he had known before she had that she would make this outrageously sudden and irrational decision.

Watching his face closely, though without hope of understanding what was going on in his mind, she continued, "We're not going, but the furniture is going, as planned, and there'll be a place for you." As she spoke, it came over her that whether he was now drunk or not, the character of this man had suffered real degradation of some kind during the time since he first came begging her to take him back to Tennessee. Instead of the disdain and the contempt which his abject, groveling manner inspired in her she wanted to pity him and blame herself for his pathetic condition. Tears did come to her eyes momentarily, but they were not for Leander, and she hadn't the illusion that they were. When at last Leander looked up he seemed in no wise moved by her tears. Their eyes met for one meaningless moment and then each turned away, he in the direction of the van outside the door, she, her eyes dry again, toward Mr. Canada, who was still leaning against the console table and staring at her. "Would you happen to know of a place," she said to Mr. Canada in a tone of utmost indifference, "a temporary place . . ." Mr. Canada moved toward her mechanically. She read in his face that he was trying to decide something—some such question as whether he should exercise his authority in an apartment building that he owned or perhaps use his influence elsewhere to find a suitable place for her and the children. A certain brightness came into his eyes, as it had that day when he mentioned the scholarship for little Charley, but not the same brightness exactly. This and a sudden color in his face and a quickness in his step made him seem less an old man than she usually thought of him as being. But instead of an effect of youthful ardor and naïveté there was one of shrewdness and of a relish for this opportunity to show his powers and resources for their own sake. His eyes shone, Sylvia observed, but not with love for her.

In only a minute or two he was leaving to arrange for a place for her to take her family that night. "Anything but a hotel," she said as he turned away.

"I think I know what you want," he said, not looking back. His phrasing and the tone of his voice were precisely those she had heard from the mouths of a hundred real-estate agents, and as he went down the cement steps to the street Sylvia found herself watching him with just such indifference as she would have watched one of those agents. Yet, somehow, the way he slipped into his jacket going down the steps, his agedness, his obvious loneliness, even the very fact of his considerable wealth all seemed to Sylvia deserving of her pity—of that at least. And she was, at this moment, conscious of her guilt for having permitted him to continue coming to see her. She would no more have been capable of shedding tears for Mr. Canada, however, than she had been for Leander. And possibly nothing in the whole world except the sight which awaited her when she turned back into the hall could have evoked from her the torrent of tears, the violent, uncontrollable sobs which then, for minutes that seemed hours, wrenched and shook her physical being. . . . She had turned back from the doorway and had caught, in a mirrored panel on the opposite wall, one miserable glimpse of her own image.

As she wept, she hardly knew why she did so. Yet she did comprehend now that it was because she was too full of sympathy for herself that she had not felt sympathy for Leander or Mr. Canada. She kept thinking of the hurt she had done them both and it occurred to her that she might be about to hurt her children by remaining in Chicago, where, for them, there might conceivably be the same obstacles for understanding that there had been for her in Tennessee. But how could she *know?* One knew too pitiably little about what one did to one's self, without trying to know what one had done to others. She didn't at all understand the full meaning of the decision she had made this afternoon. But she believed that in time an understanding of it would come to her. It would come without her knowing it, perhaps while she slept. She knew, at least, that in the future she would regard the people she loved very differently from the way she had in the past. And it wasn't that she would love them less; it was that she would in some sense or other learn to love herself more.

When the children came in, one by one, and Sylvia told them of her decision that the furniture should go on but that they should stay in Chicago and move into new quarters, each of them seemed more stunned and at the same time more overjoyed than the one before. Even the knowledge that their new quarters would be in an apartment house which Mr. Canada owned did not dampen their enthusiasm. And when finally the vans pulled away from the house, they all stood in the street laughing at the sight of Leander's feet which were all that could be seen of him as he lay, already asleep, amid the furniture.

Her family slept that night in an apartment whose windows overlooked Lake Michigan. There were seven large rooms, all without furnishings of any kind except the beds which Mr. Canada had had sent up from the basement of the building. Next morning the four children woke early, and they were all still excited by the unexpected change of plans. Sylvia did not wake early, however. She slept until almost midday, and the children, knowing how exhausted she would be from the strain of yesterday, went tiptoeing and whispering about the bright, empty rooms, careful not to wake her from her sound sleep. They took their turns going out to breakfast so as not to leave her to awake alone in a strange place.

When Sylvia woke at last it was after 11:30. The door to the room where she slept was closed. Beyond it she could hear the lowered voices of the children. Upon waking there was no moment of confusion for her, as there probably had been for each of them that morning. She knew at once where she was. And she did not immediately let them know that she was awake. She got out of bed and walked barefoot to the window that opened on the Lake and for some time stood gazing upon the scene outside. She knew that the day and the hour had come when she must think of herself not as one bereaved but as a being who had been set free. Presently she would face her children in the empty rooms of this strange apartment and they would see her still as the widow of Nate Harrison, but Sylvia knew that that did not describe who she was today or who she would be in days ahead. Barefoot and clad only in her silk nightgown, her figure in the window could almost have been mistaken for that of a little girl. She looked diminutive and fragile and defenseless. And as she stared out over the treetops along Sheridan Road and at the vast green waters of Lake Michigan, she didn't fail to be aware of her own smallness. But she was aware too that the discovery and the decision she had made about her life in the past twenty-four hours constituted the one important discovery and the one important decision that anyone, regardless of sex or age or physical size, could make. Nothing could alter that certainty. It had no relation to one's sex or to the times in which one lived or to one's being a woman from a country town in Tennessee or to one's being the mother of four grown children established in an apartment on Lake Shore Drive. It was not diminished, either, by any thought of the boundless and depthless waters of the lake or the endless stretches of the city.

Finally Sylvia turned back to her new room and to the sound of her children's adult voices. As she walked toward the door leading to the other rooms she began thinking of the immediate need to furnish the apartment. She would go shopping today—this very afternoon. She would bring into her new quarters only what was new and useful and pleasing to the eye. She thought with new pleasure of being surrounded only by what she herself had selected. Everything would be according to her own tastes, and even of that there would be only enough to serve the real needs and comforts of the family. There must be nothing anywhere in the apartment to diminish the effect of newness and brightness or to remind her of the necessity there had been to dispense with all that was old and useless and inherited.

$\mathcal{V}$OICES OF THE $\mathcal{S}$OUTH

Fred Chappell, *The Gaudy Place*

Ellen Douglas, *The Rock Cried Out*

George Garrett, *Do, Lord, Remember Me*

Lee Smith, *The Last Day the Dogbushes Bloomed*

Elizabeth Spencer, *The Voice at the Back Door*

Peter Taylor, *The Widows of Thornton*